THEY COULDN'T HAVE KNOWN

SANDEN GREVELLE

© Sanden Grevelle 2015

Published by Highfields Publishing

www.highfieldspublishing.com

All rights reserved. No part of this book may be reproduced, adapted, stored in a retrieval system or transmitted by any means, electronic, mechanical, photocopying, or otherwise without the prior written permission of the author.

The rights of Sanden Grevelle to be identified as the author of this work have been asserted in accordance with the Copyright, Designs and Patents Act 1988.

This is a work of fiction. Names, characters, businesses, places, events and incidents are either the products of the author's imagination or used in a fictitious manner. Any resemblance to actual persons, living or dead, or actual events is purely coincidental.

A CIP catalogue record for this book is available from the British Library.

ISBN: 978-1-904728-98-6

Book editor and agent: Joy Tibbs (joyofediting.co.uk)

Book layout by Ebooks by Design

CONTENTS

PART ONE 1
CHAPTER ONE...3
CHAPTER TWO 47
CHAPTER THREE.. 89

PART TWO 139
CHAPTER ONE... 141
CHAPTER TWO 173
CHAPTER THREE... 207

PART THREE 237
CHAPTER ONE... 239
CHAPTER TWO 249
CHAPTER THREE... 271

PART ONE

CHAPTER ONE

I

Stunned by the impact, Gill lay on the damp grass looking at the stars in the void. She ran her tongue over her teeth to check for damage. As she spat out bits of grass, she realised she was also trying to spit out the taste of Allen's clumsy kiss. She felt she might never stop spitting.

Gill had been fleeing across the fields in the dark from Allen's shocking approaches when she had run full tilt into the side of a black cow standing at the edge of the new concrete runway. As she lifted her head she heard a ringing in her ears, which, though fading, set her heart pounding anew. *Was she hearing the bluebells ring, a sound that summons the fairies and bodes ill for human ears?*

Breathing deeply, Gill struggled with her thoughts. There were bluebells in the woods nearby, but she knew they were yet to flower in their heady scented profusion. She also knew that they weren't all bluebells – despite their similar appearance – and therefore not all headily scented, nor so empowered.

She tried to clear her head. *What was she thinking? Had she heard the bluebells ring? Nor so empowered?*

Gill was reassured by the fact that, as she was aware of

the madness of these thoughts, she must be coming to her senses. She rolled over and tried to focus on the ground, but was disorientated as she could still see stars from the impact. She recalled the Royal Air Force crews stationed at the airport telling how, when flying home on starlit nights during the wartime blackouts, they became disorientated when the towns below twinkled as cats were put out for the night.

As Gill lay there she could hear the cow, unperturbed by the collision, calmly munching the sweet-smelling grasses and herbs, about which Allen had been trying to teach her for as long as she could remember.

She tried to get up, but the excruciating pain in her foot made her gasp and she sank back to the ground. She looked around in desperation for help, but there was little hope anyone would pass by the runways in the dark. From her perspective on the ground she could just make out the low silhouette of a wall in the distance and slowly began to drag herself over the grass towards it. She cried out as she snagged her damaged foot on the rough ground, but there was no one to hear.

After what seemed like an age, she reached the ruins of an old greenhouse that the bulldozers had not completely flattened in their southward pincer movement, leaving the low brick wall standing amongst the collapsed superstructure and shattered glass. However, even in the short time since its destruction these remains were becoming engulfed in a scramble of wild plants and abandoned crops, especially the now half-wild tomatoes.

It had been a cold April up until then, with unseasonal snow and sleet, but despite the deepening cold under the clear sky, Gill broke out in a sweat from the pain and the effort. As the sweat cooled on her body she shivered and realised she was at risk of exposure. At that point, as if by divine intervention, she found a large hotbed of still-fermenting, sweet compost at one end of the wall. Gently collapsing onto the warm, soft pile, she fell into a deep sleep.

II

Gill awoke with a start and was transfixed. The dark shape of a man surrounded by a rainbow-coloured aurora loomed on the early morning mist in front of her, shimmering like a vision. She had heard locals talk of the phenomenon, which, in their usual mystical way they had called a spectre, attributing great significance to it. An omen.

'What on earth are you doing out here on your own at this time in the morning?' a man's voice from behind her asked.

Further startled, she turned her head to see a tall, lean, young man standing behind her with a bemused smile on his face. He was handsome with symmetrical features, high cheekbones, a square head and thick, wiry, dark hair combed straight back.

'Thank goodness you're not wearing a suit and bowler hat, and carrying a briefcase and rolled umbrella!' she said before she could stop herself.

'Why on earth should I be?' he replied, puzzled.

'No reason,' said Gill, just stopping herself from explaining the locals' unlikely belief in such a figure haunting the scenes of fatal crash landings.

As the young man moved in front of her, the spectre disappeared and she realised that the rising sun had cast his shadow, surrounded by a rainbow-coloured aurora, onto the dense mist in front of her. It had been no spectre, but she felt that it could still be an omen; of what she did not know.

Her first reaction was to ensure that her hair was covering her ears, and her second was a feeling of relief that she was wearing baggy Women's Land Army, trousers rather than a dress or skirt. Puzzled by the increasing interest she was arousing in men, she always tried to dress down so as not to attract attention, despite the ending of clothes rationing. Although not one herself, Gill had known the Land Army girls well during the war. They had spoiled her a treat. If they hadn't been so watchful when she was around, she might have learnt something about sex, which had been their main topic of conversation.

Gill also went to huge lengths to avoid going anywhere near the two temporary camps near the new airport, where the men working on the runways, mainly Irish, were housed in the wooden huts of 'Timber town' and the modified corrugated iron Nissen huts of 'Tin town'.

'Well, what on earth are you doing out here on your own at this time in the morning?' the man repeated.

'What on earth are you doing out here on *your* own at this time in the morning?' retorted Gill warily.

The stranger grinned. 'I'm at work. Are you all right?'

'I think I may have broken my foot last night. And I only just managed to crawl over here,' continued Gill, reassured by his reaction.

'You were lucky you found this compost heap. You might not have survived the night otherwise.'

'Yes I know. But it's a hotbed not a compost heap. By the way, did you hear the bluebells ring?' Gill asked, despite herself.

'What?'

'Sorry, nothing. I must still be a bit dazed.'

'Let's have a look. My name's Piotr, by the way. What's

yours?'

'Gill. Yours is unusual. Where are you from?'

'Poland originally. I reckon I only got my job so people could make jokes about it.'

'Why? What do you do?'

'Basically, I hold a pole up vertically all day and people say: "Don't they make a lovely couple" or something like that, which gets annoying after a while.'

'I'm sure it does,' said Gill, not wanting to be annoying in turn by asking what sort of job involved holding a pole up vertically all day.

Piotr bent down and gently examined Gill's foot and ankle. She was surprised and somewhat ashamed by her reaction to his gentle touch, and felt even more relieved that she wasn't wearing a dress or skirt of any description.

Piotr also trembled slightly as he tentatively touched her ankle. It was the first time as a young man that he had ever touched a young woman and he desperately wished she had been wearing a dress or skirt of some description.

Gill's foot and ankle were tightly swollen – an angry, florid mixture of scarlet and blue – and the initial pleasure of his touch was lost in the pain. She fell back, exhausted.

'Where do you live?' Piotr asked, trying not to notice the sensuous curves of her body as she lay on the hot bed.

'About a mile away, in the last old farmhouse.'

'I know it,' replied Piotr, flushing slightly and shifting awkwardly on his feet; signs of vulnerability that puzzled but reassured Gill.

'I'll try to get you home,' he said, lifting her from the ground.

'Careful! You're shaking. Put me down if I'm too heavy.'

'No, it's OK.'

They were both equally embarrassed by the intimacy of the situation, as it was the first time either had been so physically close to a member of the opposite sex since adolescence. Piotr was becoming aroused as he smelt her hair, felt her arms around his neck, found his left hand perilously close to her left breast and felt her firm thighs on his right arm.

In the temporary air traffic control tower on the north side of the new airport, an air traffic controller – an RAF man, like most of the flight staff posted to the new airport – was surveying the scene. As the silhouette of Piotr carrying Gill rose through the low morning mist, he imagined he was seeing a man rescuing a woman from drowning in a silvery sea; the illusion reinforced by the antlers of a young buck appearing to float like driftwood before disappearing beneath the waves when it lowered its head to graze.

Taking many stops along the way, Piotr eventually managed to carry Gill to the farmhouse. By this time he was no longer aroused and looked as tired and dishevelled as Gill, giving the impression that they had spent the night together out in the fields.

Gill's mother recoiled in surprise and horror when she opened the door.

'Gill! Where have you been all night? I've had the police out. What happened to you?'

'Good morning, ma'am,' said Piotr.

'Who are you? Put my daughter down at once!'

'Certainly, ma'am, if you would just show me where.'

'Why? What's the matter with her?'

'I am here, Mother,' said Gill, mortified at their reception.

'Well, what's wrong with you?'

'I've hurt my foot and can't walk, which is why Piotr here had to carry me home.'

'Piotr! What sort of name is that?'

'Mother!'

Go and get the doctor right now,' she said, giving Piotr a long, hard look as she closed the door in his face.

'Who was that? You weren't with him all night were you? Where does he come from? He looked a bit foreign to me. He must be foreign with a name like that. Is he foreign?' Gill's mother continued as she settled Gill and made her as comfortable as possible. Suddenly, with a look of horror on her face, she said: 'He's not *German* is he?' *As far as Gill's mother was concerned, the only good German was a dead German.*

It took all of Gill's patience to answer her mother's anxious questions and put her mind partially at rest. She understood that her parents were under great stress as they awaited eviction and the destruction of their farm, which had been in her father's family for generations.

After the doctor's visit the pain subsided a little and Gill began to reflect on the turmoil of the previous twenty-four hours. *What had Allen been thinking when he tried it on with her? She had never thought of him in that way. How could two friends have such different views about their friendship?*

She knew Allen loved her in his simple, childlike way, but she hadn't thought it was anything more than that. He still seemed so young in many ways, whereas in her own innocence she was confused by the dramatic changes she was undergoing. She felt like a complete mess mentally and physically. And now there was Piotr. *How on earth should she behave with him? Allen was the only boy she had ever been close to.*

III

She had met Allen at primary school and they had immediately become friends as a result of their shared activities: running wild over the beautiful countryside, climbing trees, fishing, paddling and even swimming in the Pits: ancient lakes extended over the centuries by diggings to supply sand and gravel for roads and construction, and more recently the airport's concrete runways. They had grown up together: fit, fast, strong, tireless, lean and bright as buttons with barely a day's illness between them, or at least nothing that ever stopped them for very long.

They were closer to the wild creatures than they were to their contemporaries, who hung around cursing, mocking and throwing stones, usually at Allen. As a result, they were never drawn to the public swimming baths and cinemas where, to the terror of their parents, the nightmare of polio lay in wait for its young, susceptible victims.

During the war – which they had helped to win by eating their dinners, as they were constantly warned they wouldn't if they didn't – they had combined their adventures with earning money foraging for herbs; gathering potatoes; scaring birds from the crops with whistles and rattles; picking slugs, snails and caterpillars from the cabbages and sprouts; and, in the winter, running through the orchards with burning torches, shouting to discourage evil spirits.

More than anything, though, they had run for fun. They ran full tilt over the fields without putting a foot wrong, even across the exhilarating switchback undulations of ancient ridge and furrow work, usually singing along to their favourite verse:

> *The hare is running races in her mirth*
> *And with her feet from the plashy earth*
> *Raises a mist that, glittering in the sun,*
> *Runs with her all the way, wherever she doth run.*

After the war, on the occasion of the annual village fete, she and Allen regularly entered the three-mile foot race through the village, which was open to all. On these occasions, Gill and Allen never bothered to warm up. Living in the fields as they did, they were permanently warmed up. Gill used to get quite nervous, but Allen never suffered pre-race nerves as such because he suffered from nerves all the time, which once a year occurred, appropriately, moments before the race. Gill was faster over less than a furrow's length, but Allen had speed and stamina and always won.

Gill always got very angry when spectators, most of them drunk, used to sing the song "Run Rabbit Run" when Allen went by. She was particularly annoyed when they also shouted, 'Come on Wilfred', as this was a reference to her favourite book as a child. Wilfred was a rabbit adopted by a penguin that had escaped from the zoo and a stray dog; all of them outcasts.

As a result of the huge odds offered against anyone other than Allen winning, some challengers sought every advantage they could: drinking beetroot juice for stamina; nibbling on puff balls against cramp and willow bark against the pain. As a result, quite a few challengers always retired with stomach trouble.

Some even risked nibbling fairy ring fungi to enable them to 'dance' over the ground, like the elves and fairies within the fairy rings in the meadows, but they suffered such hallucinations they couldn't find the start. Once a challenger had arrived so crazed on herbal potions and festooned in vegetation to promote speed and stamina that the villagers were terrified the Green Man was upon them and he ran off in the wrong direction.

Safe in their virtue, simplicity and youth, Allen's relatively benighted state had yet to enter Gill's mind. As they parted at the end of each day and made for home like rabbits scurrying to their burrows, they would shout to each other: 'Do you still love me?' To which the answers would come: 'Still,' reassuring them both that nothing had happened in those last few seconds to change their hearts and minds.

Gill, however, had learned from her parents' disapproving reaction not to speak about the fun she had with Allen. Her parents had done all they could to keep her away from him. Their lovely daughter was too good for that strange boy. In their eyes, anybody was too good for him. Gill had said nothing and had carried on meeting Allen, but more secretively. They couldn't have known that they were each undergoing a metamorphosis, from which Gill would emerge perfectly formed and fly away, while Allen would emerge further damaged and beyond repair.

When Gill had recoiled in horror from his attempt to kiss her, Allen had also taken off running, not in pursuit of Gill, but, for the first time in their shared adventures, in the opposite direction, overwhelmed with shame.

Although he could follow a trail over the countryside with the quarry nowhere in sight, Allen couldn't have followed Gill even if, like Olwen of Celtic legend, she had left a trail of white clover behind her wherever she trod. He had lost Gill while she was in plain sight, and now, unlike Gill, what he was about to run into had no substance and would draw him in.

What had he been thinking? He had never kissed anybody in his life and should have known that it would be an inevitable disaster. But he had forgotten himself in that critical moment. They had been out together, roving the fields as usual, and had paused to rest. Looking at her lying next to him with her head on a cushion of soft moss, he had been overcome with a new sensation and, as if under a spell, had leant forward to kiss her. But the glimpse of an unknown adult paradise he observed in Gill disappeared more quickly than it had appeared as a local warning burst into his consciousness: "Ware the hare, lest it kiss the lip,' and he recalled girls in the village telling of nightmares about being kissed by the whiskery warmth of a nibbling hare.

After a painfully slow start to his life, Allen had grown to be thin, wiry and eventually tall enough for his age. He had hair that bleached yellow in the sun, but he wished was thicker, and green eyes he wished were set wider apart. But there was something elusive about his mouth that even the curious struggled to catch a good look at. It took a great deal of ingenuity and most of Allen's time to ensure that they didn't. Those that did catch a glimpse behaved as if he might not have noticed, despite it being in the middle of his own face. 'You should get that seen to,' they said. People were very helpful that way.

He had been getting it seen to for years, and the final bout of torture had been the last he could endure. Somebody with needle phobia would have considered him brave beyond belief that he preferred injections of what they called cocaine to the gas, when the stinking rubber mask enveloped his face and the terrifying humming filled his head. It certainly should have given him a sense of achievement over those who had known no real physical pain, no matter what the drama of their stories implied they might have suffered; especially over those who claimed the suffering of their ancestors as their own.

While still a young boy, Allen had learnt that something had been left too late and that as a result he was different and would be so forever more. Some in the village whispered that it must have been a case of 'mother-impression', when his mother had startled a hare from its scrape when she was pregnant with him. As a result, he had always felt he was beneath contempt, which of course he wasn't as it was always aimed very accurately at him.

As he had grown older he had gradually become aware of a vague sense of unease; a gradual rise in background anxiety that eventually emerged into his everyday awareness. It had crept up on him quietly and unexpectedly, giving no warning of the finality of its grip. He could clearly remember the point at which he could ignore it no longer. He had been looking out of the window at the garden of his childhood when there seemed to be more than just the glass between him and the view.

The stress of his prolonged fearful introspection caused by his unresolvable problem had intensified, until bewilderment and fear of the strange feelings and thoughts it brought had become as much a part of the suffering as his original problem.

He was surprised his reaction hadn't been one of fear and panic, but only of slight bemusement. He couldn't have known the impact it would have on the rest of his life and the lives of others. It was the relative calm before the storm.

IV

After his dramatic encounter with Gill, Piotr could not get her out of his mind. He had never felt like this before. Nothing else seemed to matter other than to see Gill again as soon as he could. Although he had lived through terrible things it took all his courage to overcome his nerves and return the next day to the farmhouse to try and see her.

After dithering outside the door – much to Gill's amusement, who was spying on him through the half-closed curtains – he finally managed to knock on the door.

'What do you want?' asked Gill's mother when she opened it.

'I'm terribly sorry to bother you, ma'am, but I would like to ask how Gill is. I've brought her some flowers,' he said, handing over a posy of sweet violets he had gathered along the way.

Initially, Gill's mother could make no sense of it, until she realised it was the young man who had carried Gill home after her accident. Now he looked very presentable, distinguished even, so against her instincts she invited him in. She was beginning to realise that, although he was foreign, he was a decent-looking young man with good manners, who spoke English with only the slightest accent. More importantly, he was a huge improvement on that dreadful, strange-looking Allen boy Gill had spent so much time with growing up, despite her best efforts to stop them meeting.

'Gill says you're from Poland,' she blurted out.

'Yes, that's right, ma'am,' he replied with a slight bow.

'Why are there so many Polish people around here now?'

'Well, we did help win the war,' he said, unable to bring himself to add the word 'you'.

'Don't be ridiculous. We saved you when we declared war on Hitler when he invaded Poland. There weren't any Polish troops in the victory parade.'

'That was because the Russians objected,' said Piotr as calmly as he could in the face of this unexpected hostile reception. He was barely able to stop himself telling this ignorant woman that nearly a quarter of a million Polish armed forces had fought under the British. He managed to check his anger when he remembered dismissing the West Indians and other Commonwealth countries' contribution to the Allied war efforts, which he now deeply regretted.

'Why would they do that?'

Piotr thought about answering, but gave up.

'Why, didn't you go home after the war?'

'Because Russia has taken over our country and they would kill us.'

'Don't be silly, they were on our side.'

There was a brief lull as Gill's mother took a deep breath and looked him up and down, before saying: 'Anyway, what church do you go to?'

'The Roman Catholic Church over in Fletham, madam. It's near where I live.'

A loud cough from Gill in another room interrupted her mother's terse, rude grilling.

'All right, you can see Gill, but I'll be nearby. Follow me.'

When Gill's mother moved out of the way and Piotr saw Gill sitting there, he could barely stifle a gasp. He had thought that he would never experience much emotion after everything he had been through, but he certainly did when he laid eyes on her. *Was this love at first sight, or at least at first proper sight?* He had heard about it and wondered whether he might actually be experiencing it. He was more acquainted with fear, loss, hunger, malaria and extreme privation than he was with girls.

'You look so different,' he stammered.

'That makes two of us, then,' replied Gill with a grin.

He had heard locally of Niamh of the flaxen hair, a Celtic goddess of nature, whose 'golden hair hung in tresses; of complexion as fair as a summer morning; her body slender and exquisite as a birch tree, the glory of all lands; the fairest woman in the world, conjured out of blossoms'.

Well, here she was, sitting in front of him with her big purple foot up on a stool. The only additions to the description were that her eyes were emerald green and her smile lit up the room.

Gill had no idea that she was a Celtic goddess. She had no vanity. She had only ever envisaged herself in a negative light and was only slowly becoming aware of how attractive she was to men. Her first concern on meeting anybody was always whether her hair was covering her ears or not. She was acutely embarrassed by the fact that, like her mother, she had no earlobes. 'Cagot ears,' she had heard a doctor say. She had been surprised to see a Spanish worker at the airport – a refugee from the Civil War – with the same condition.

She imagined that everybody she met immediately noticed them, which of course they never did – except the Spaniard – until her fiddling drew attention to them.

'You must forgive my mother. She doesn't mean to be rude, but she's under terrible stress with the eviction and the destruction of this place. Like we all are, of course.'

'That's terrible,' said Piotr, studiously examining his bitten fingernails.

'Yes, it's very sad after so many years. My parents are at their wits' end, but they've given up the struggle now that all the other farmhouses have gone.'

'When did it all start?' asked Piotr.

'During the war, 1944. Even while the bombs were still dropping! Hadleyrow Hall was the first to go to make way for Runway One, which also obliterated the remains of Caesar's Camp.'

'Was it falling down anyway?' asked Piotr.

'What, Caesar's Camp?'

'No, Hadleyrow Hall!' said Piotr, unable to suppress a grin, despite the seriousness of the topic.

'No! It was a beautiful old building. There were tall bay windows either side of the front door and French windows that opened directly onto a springy camomile lawn. A huge Cedar of Lebanon shaded the front of the house on summer days. Opposite, there was a beautiful borrow pond, dug for the brick-earth that was used to make the bricks to build it.'

'That does sound beautiful.'

'By the way, did you know that Caesar's Camp predated Caesar by centuries?' asked Piotr, proud to have the chance to impress Gill with some of his local knowledge and to shift the conversation away from the present situation.

'Yes, and when that was discovered some of the villagers wondered how the ancient Britons had known Caesar was coming so much later,' said Gill with a grin.

'They couldn't have known,' said Piotr, before catching up. 'Ha! And I bet some of the villagers wondered how the ancient Britons knew an airport was coming when what looked like a three-mile-long runway was uncovered during the same excavations,' said Piotr.

'How do you know about that? Lizzie thinks it was a spiritual runway to the stars.'

'Lizzie? Isn't she that weird old woman everybody thinks is a witch?' asked Piotr.

'She's not weird, just old-fashioned, and she's the kindest person I know. Some people do think she's a witch, but only because they're stupid.'

'Well those old earthworks are all well and truly buried under the concrete runways now,' said Piotr, looking guilty again.

'At least they'll be preserved there,' said Gill, knowing that before the airport had even been thought of, the vicar of the parish church across the main road had had the remains of Caesar's Camp almost ploughed flat for fear of its pagan associations, leaving only low, grassy banks marked out by bracken and gorse.

Gill was puzzled when Piotr visibly relaxed when she said this.

'By the way, do you know anything about that old cannon sticking out of the ground near where those earthworks were? I'm surprised people don't call it Caesar's Cannon,' continued Gill.

'That's William Roy's Cannon, marking one end of a line he surveyed in 1784 for the first accurate mapping of Britain,' said Piotr, amazed that his surveying knowledge was proving so useful during his first proper conversation with a beautiful girl.

'How do you know all this?' asked Gill.

Piotr flushed with embarrassment as he realised he had talked himself into a corner.

'Well, it's to do with my land surveying job,' he said, regretting having to reveal his connection with the airport development so soon.

'Oh! So you work for the airport, then?' asked Gill.

Piotr stiffened. His heart thumped. He had hoped to keep that quiet, at least until he got to know Gill better, if he was lucky enough to do so.

'I'm afraid so. What do you think?' he asked rather desperately, his mouth souring.

'Well, it's not your fault, and one way or another all of us younger people will end up working there if we don't move away.'

'What a relief! I thought you might see me as the enemy,' said Piotr, immediately panicking anew at the thought that

Gill might move away.

'Not at all. Now tell me about your life in Poland.'

There was a long silence, during which Piotr's heart continued to hammer in his chest.

'Well, where I come from had a lot in common with this area. Before the war it was largely agricultural and people made a living like they do around here by growing fruit and vegetables and selling them in the city.'

'Which city?'

'Warsaw. We lived near Warsaw Airport, which got busier and busier, so the peace was increasingly disturbed. During the war it became a battleground when the Polish resistance fought the Germans. On the land though, not in the air like around here.'

'Were you there then?'

Piotr paused before answering. 'No. Look, I'd better go now, but could I see you again, while your ankle is getting better?' he asked, trying and failing to appear casual.

'Of course, although I'd have to ask Mother. I heard you winning her over with your impeccable manners, so it should be OK. Just you being a Christian would have pleased her, but she'll think it's almost too good to be true that you're Roman Catholic. That might even make up for you being foreign,' Gill answered with a grin.

V

By the time Allen reached the freight warehouse at the airport – where to his dismay, he had been working since losing his agricultural work as a result of the airport developments – he looked as if he had been running all night, which he had.

He had to accept that things could never be the same

again with Gill, but he couldn't accept that her rejection of him meant that his love was of no consequence. He was convinced that, if anything counted, everything counted. True, he would never really know what he was missing, but he knew well enough for it to leave him with an aching hole in his chest.

He couldn't believe the sequence of events that had resulted in him working at the airport. He had tried fieldwork, but despite this being among the hardest of all jobs, it was mainly seen as women's work and the women had got rid of him as soon as they could. This wasn't as unfeeling as it might have appeared. Although he had inhibited their hilarious and bawdy conversations and songs, including one about 'The Bonny Black Hare', they were also trying to save him from himself. If he was seen doing 'women's work' for anything but a short-term emergency – when a crop had to be got in quickly, for example – they knew he would be even more ridiculed and isolated than he already was, if that were possible. However, he remained vulnerable as he continued to assist in chopping wood, which, though heavy labour, was also seen as women's work.

In fact, Allen had been relieved when he was edged out of the fieldwork, as it was so hard and the hours were so long that he hadn't been sure he could have stuck it anyway, women's work or not. Even the Land Army girls, who came from more privileged backgrounds than the local field girls, had soon toughened up, with some even living in temporary straw-bale houses thatched with nettles on the edge of the village.

The field girls worked in all weathers. Whatever the weather, they were totally swaddled in clothes, with headscarves that masked their faces to protect themselves from the ageing effects of the weather. They were not worn out of modesty, religious or otherwise, as their conversation revealed. The voluminous folds of their dull coloured clothes – only a fast hussy would wear red and green was considered unlucky – protected them from the cold, heat and rain in equal measure, like Bedouin in the desert.

They worked on a variety of tasks in the most awkward positions, usually bent over sowing seeds, planting seedlings, and cutting and pulling crops of every description. Hoeing was about the only task in the open fields they could carry out standing up, albeit lopsidedly. The harvesting of root crops such as potatoes was semi-mechanised, but they still had to be gathered up from the mud or dust by hand. In good years, immigrant potato lifters from Ireland would be hired and the field girls were allocated to more skilful work such as picking soft fruit, which had to be carried out with great care for it to arrive at market in near-perfect condition early the next morning.

However, picking red, black and white currants from the under-planting in the orchards when it was raining was still a hard, miserable job. Even if there was a break in the rain water continued to drip from the top fruit of apples and plums above, and because the trees were earthed up there was a furrow between every row that filled with water, through which the picker had to slosh. They had half-bushel and peck straw baskets, on which they would perch in order to reach the under fruit. At times, the pickers were so tired they would slip off or into the basket fast asleep, only to be woken by the overseer firing his sporting gun at irregular intervals under the pretence of potting rabbits.

After the fieldwork, Allen had tried mucking out the turkey sheds. This was done when the turkeys had been slaughtered and the doors were thrown open to the light and the air after several months. Inside, the compacted droppings, several feet thick, gave off an overpowering, eye-stinging smell of ammonia. Whenever he forked a 'fossilised' turkey that had died and been trampled flat like a sheet of cardboard in the muck up onto the cart, the manure carried on it showered back over him.

This was followed one bitter winter by a short stint on the brine tank in the bacon factory on the small industrial estate next to the airport. Here, even the brine, saltier than seawater, froze, adding its glitter and sparkle to the granite floor. Although he wore rubber gloves, the brine soon filled them and his florid, inflamed, salt-encrusted hands throbbed rhythmically in time with the machinery.

Allen had been surprised that nobody had told him he was luckier than a deck-hand on a North Sea trawler, battered by freezing winds and waves. To pre-empt this, Allen thought of suggesting to management that they have a wind and wave machine fitted on the brine tank. However, Allen realised only too well that among the damaged minds finding refuge in the bacon factory, there were broken survivors from some of the most horrific wartime experiences imaginable, to whom the brine tank job would be heaven on earth. So he got on with it.

Eventually he had accepted a temporary labouring job in the freight warehouse of a major American airline, despite his dislike of the airport. It was the least tiring job he had ever had. He found moving the freight so easy he moved it around just to tire himself out, to the complete astonishment of other workers and the annoyance of those trying to sleep in the cubbyholes they had built in the freight.

Originally, he had made the foolish mistake of assuming that his physical abilities, energy, tirelessness and fierce determination were a natural reaction to his afflictions. He had failed to realise that they were a blessing, a gift that was almost equal to the curse; that he had been given a fighting chance; that he could have had the same problems without his other physical and mental advantages, which had always enabled him to settle for exhaustion rather than total despair.

He constantly drove himself to the point where he could achieve some sort of peace. He contrived to do every job in the most physically awkward, tiring way. If he could lift something with one hand he would. If he could lift something in an awkward position he would. In his ignorance, it never occurred to him that he could get injured.

Those who sought to teach him to work in a more efficient way assumed that he was a very slow learner. On the other hand, many people had pointed out to Allen that he wasn't as stupid as he looked. This hadn't been obvious at school, as he had been so distracted by trying to maintain an illusion of normality in his appearance. He realised, however, this did not necessarily mean that he was clever; just that he looked more stupid than he was.

Outside work he increased his mileage, covering huge distances on foot deep into the countryside, never putting a foot wrong. This was in direct contrast to his internal world, in which his mind stumbled and tripped over even imaginary obstacles.

The worst part of the airport job was the air pollution, especially from the eye-searing unburnt kerosene in the exhaust of the aircraft engines as they revved up outside the warehouse. Allen had begun to notice the disappearance of once-familiar plants from the margins of nearby cultivated fields, as well as the thinning birdsong. There were no birds in the rafters of the airport hangers any longer, despite the massive doors being open more often than they were shut.

Added to this, there was the periodic stench of the Monkey Specials, freightliners crudely modified to contain crates packed with rhesus monkeys from Africa for use in medical research. More than half died in their own excrement en route, but nobody seemed interested in opposing this foul trade. It was widely assumed that if the trade was for medical research it must be a good thing, despite the obvious cruelty involved, to which people gradually became conditioned. However, there were those in whom it raised the spectre of recent wartime horrors, to which they had seen people become conditioned in the name of a greater good. These workers didn't last long at the airport.

The stench from the Monkey Specials created further problems at the small industrial estate next to the airport. One of the factories on the site bottled expensive perfume, so it was necessary to keep its doors and windows firmly closed all year round. On one occasion, the factory's salesman, when putting his hat on outside the building, had trapped some monkey-polluted air underneath it, which had remained there until it was released when he doffed his hat to the perfume buyer in the cosmetics department at a London store. Its effect was accentuated by the slight bow he gave, which brought the released sample close to the delicate and highly trained nose of the buyer. At the same time, his patent leather shoes made a squeaking noise, causing her to jump to the obvious, but erroneous, conclusion. This incident hadn't cost him his job as the buyer was too refined to articulate her complaint, but she had swiftly changed suppliers.

So potent was the toxic cocktail from the airport that it carried for miles, staining the neighbouring fields before losing itself in the fresh country air. At that time the acceptable solution to pollution was still considered to be dilution.

VI

'Bloody 'ell, Allen! What 'ave you bin up to?' asked Prof, his unlikely workmate.

Allen had found Prof in one of the cubbyholes in the freight. There was a fanciful story about Prof falling asleep in one and being flown out to Paris with the freight before waking up.

Prof was an ex-gangster from the Polish Jewish community that had settled in the East End of London at the turn of the century, many of whom decried the recent post-war immigration, especially that of the West Indians.

He had a huge head and a pale, fleshy face that betrayed a violent past, criss-crossed as it was with the furrows of old knife, axe and razor wounds. It was beyond belief that somebody with a face like that should have been employed in a relatively high-security area such as the airport. However, he had turned these scars to his advantage during the interview by describing them as war wounds, thus gaining guilty sympathy from the interviewing panel, none of whom had seen active service either.

He had been nicknamed Prof for his ability to hold forth with great authority on any topic, which was always linked, however tenuously, to boxing, horse racing, market spiel, partying with film stars in the West End or his scars.

They both recoiled from the enveloping stench of a Monkey Special that filled the warehouse.

'God, what a stink those grease-arse monkeys make,' said Prof, screwing his scarred face into an even more macabre pattern, paisley-like in its complexity.

'Rhesus,' said Allen.

'I should 'ave got a gun and shot 'em,' said Prof, ignoring the correction.

'Well, half of them are dead on arrival, anyway,' replied Allen, pretending not to understand the underlying meaning of Prof's peculiar sentence.

When Prof had come out with that curious phrase – 'I should 'ave got a gun and shot 'em' – Allen knew Prof didn't really mean that he should have shot the monkeys. Rather, that he felt he should have shot those he held responsible for his expulsion from gangland; those whose actions had resulted in him having to swap Savile Row suits for the old overalls he wore at the warehouse. In fact, virtually every sentence he uttered was followed by: 'I should 'ave got a gun and shot 'em.' This led to considerable apprehension in those who were unfamiliar with this quirk.

Conversely, his only other catchphrase: 'Nobody loves you like yer mother,' always created the impression that he was a gentle, caring person, no matter how much it was taken out of context. A good deal depended on which of these phrases burst out at any specific time.

As it happened, a gun was readily accessible at the warehouse. It was a big, heavy handgun that, to Allen, whose only experience of guns came from watching cowboy films, looked just like a Colt 45. It was kept in the safe to frighten off anybody who might try to steal valuable cargo, such as diamonds, gold or platinum bars, while they were in transit. The trouble was, the safe had to be opened to get at the gun, which would achieve a large part of any villain's purpose. Besides, none of the warehouse workers knew how to use it. The close juxtaposition of diamonds, gold, platinum and other valuable cargo, an actual gun and an ex-gangster who repeated 'I should 'ave got a gun and shot 'em', seemed like a recipe for disaster to Allen, which it turned out to be.

The rest of the shift kept clear of the warehouse, not only due to the periodically overpowering smell, but also due to a general aversion to hard work and the frequent presence of coffins in transit. During the night shift the others marvelled at what they saw as Allen's self-control and bravery as he sat alone on a coffin, without a thought of its grinning contents, in the ghostly light of the flickering fluorescent lights high up in the steel girders of the warehouse.

As a result of his self-absorption – his mind in turmoil with intrusive, persistent and unacceptable ideas, thoughts and images arising from and reinforcing his anxious state – Allen was impervious to any fear of what the coffins contained. He was anaesthetised by his own state of anxiety. He treated the coffins like any other freight, and had been surprised to learn of the special handling allowance the shift leaders claimed for this cargo. Despite his sensitivities, it didn't even occur to him that sitting on a coffin might appear disrespectful to many.

The offices at the front of the warehouse were always busy with uniformed permanent staff known as 'the Perms'. They concentrated on the paperwork, much of which involved organising the various scams that had already earned the airport the nickname 'Thief Row'. This reputation had developed rapidly, despite the caraway plants that grew locally with their fern-like leaves, the seeds of which, according to some locals, could prevent theft.

Many believed caraway seeds could even hold a thief in custody. This belief had been reinforced when a villager had taken some caraway seed biscuits Lizzie had prepared to a prisoner held at the police station and he hadn't run away when left unattended. Case proven. This was clearly because of the caraway seeds he had consumed, rather than because he had been so tired and hungry when he was arrested that he had welcomed the hospitality. The fact that he had endured and survived the horrors of the Great War, physically, at least, didn't arise when he appeared before the magistrates the next day.

Prof paced up and down in front of Allen looking distinctly uncomfortable.

'Allen, I need your help.'

'In what way?' Allen replied suspiciously.

Prof avoided Allen's gaze. 'Well, some old mates of mine want me to help them with a job, and if I don't they could make things difficult for me.'

'Some mates,' said Allen, staring across the remnants of the beautiful fields of his childhood, wondering what Gill was doing and how fate had led him to become the confidant of an ex-gangster from London.

'Yeah, I know. I should 'ave got a gun and shot 'em.'

There it was, the use of that phrase in its place of origin.

'Nobody loves you like yer mother,' he continued, spoiling the effect.

Allen groaned quietly.

'They've found out that I got this job and they want to get at the safe,' said Prof.

'How am I supposed to help you?' asked Allen. 'Anyway, it would make me an accessory.'

'Well, I won't tell nobody,' Prof replied unconvincingly. He couldn't even convince himself that he wouldn't, as when the gang had ousted him in an internal struggle he had grassed on them to the police, which had further exiled him.

Allen continued to gaze out over the fields, wondering what he was doing at the warehouse. Things could go badly wrong in this place. Responsibilities were dispensed recklessly to naive newcomers – typically temporary workers who were anxious to please and perhaps attain permanent status – with scant regard for the fact that criminal charges would result if anything went amiss.

In fact, it suited the Perms for the odd Temp to go down on some criminal charge from time to time, as it diverted attention from the criminal activities they themselves coordinated. The airport police also understood the situation. They needed prosecutions but couldn't procure anything major against the Perms, as some of the airport police were complicit in the scams. So they went after the Temps.

Their most recent triumph had been the sending down of a poor Temp who had signed for a lorry load of registered mail from a nearby US army base, which had been one bag short. A large army driver had dumped the load at the warehouse, pushed a pen into the Temp's face and demanded a signature before the Temp could count them, let alone identify each one with its lengthy code number.

A Perm would never sign for a lorry load of registered mail if there was a Temp around, and if there wasn't, a Perm would spend all day checking the load. Others signed using a creative nom de plume. Frank Sinatra and Ava Gardner caused some trouble, as management failed to believe the pair had rushed across from the airport VIP tent to sign, separately, for two loads of registered mail. Nevertheless, one of the clerks had turned a profit by selling the information to the press.

'Sorry, Prof, I can't help you.'

Allen was determined to try and curb his natural impulse to help everybody whether they asked for his help or not. He had to reluctantly admit that no good turn ever seemed to go unpunished.

VII

At his previous meeting with Gill, Piotr had lied about having to leave. Things had been going so well between them that he had lost his nerve and wanted to leave before he ruined it by telling her any more of his story. Even for someone who had been through so much, this polite, tentative, introductory conversation had been a rollercoaster of emotion for him. So great was his reserve and watchfulness as a result of his disrupted life that Piotr could hardly believe he had dared to ask to see her again, let alone that she had said yes without hesitation.

Having had so many disappointments, he wasn't used to looking forward to things. It was much easier to be wary and to expect the worst, although in this case he feared there was no surviving the worst. He also felt that looking forward to something was to enjoy part of the pleasure of it in advance, decreasing the contrast between the event and what led up to it, so that the more he looked forward to something the less he seemed to enjoy it when it came; if it came at all, which it rarely had during his lifetime.

If he hadn't met Gill, he could have struggled on in his lonely misery, but having met her he realised he would be finished if his feelings weren't reciprocated. The enormity of the situation stunned him. He realised for the first time that there could be more security in despair than in hope. Despair self-perpetuated and reinforced itself on disappointment. It was reliable and provided a strange security. For Piotr, hope didn't spring eternal.

Piotr could see how, at first sight, his overwhelming feelings for Gill could be dismissed as a predictable reaction to his previous deprivation. He had apparently fallen in love without any intimacy, warmth or emotion in their exchanges. They hadn't really chatted informally or flirted, but he didn't care. To him, she was a miracle of salvation. It was natural in this cruel world to lose one's parents, but it wasn't natural to meet the absolute fulfilment of one's dreams in a girl, despite what the fairy tales might say.

Also, after all his travels, loss and alienation, he was beginning to feel increasingly at home in Hadleyrow with its parallels to his homeland in Poland. But the more at home Piotr felt, the more appalled he was by the ruthless way in which even the landed farmers were being evicted.

He had sat in as an observer on the airport planning meetings, where his obscure origins and lowly job as an apprentice surveyor rendered him invisible to the senior management, enabling him to glean a great deal of restricted information. Despite his status as a displaced person – of no fixed nationality, let alone of no fixed abode, who was supposed to owe allegiance to no one and no place – he had begun to feel guilty by association for the destruction that was being wreaked in the area.

He had learned that the civil air lobby, planning for a new post-war civilian airport near London during the war, had disguised its intentions with the claim that the new airport was essential for the wartime needs of the Royal Air Force. This had enabled The Defence of the Realm Act to be invoked, allowing the requisition of land and the bypassing of lengthy planning regulations.

As the land had been requisitioned and not compulsorily purchased, rent should have been paid and the land returned to the owners after the war. However, the villagers had received no rent. It was beginning to look suspiciously like there was no intention of returning the land, and the villagers were still waiting to receive derisory compensation at pre-war prices.

No detail was too small to escape the authorities' mean vindictiveness. Piotr had spoken to one farmer who had been accused of stealing his own gates rather than leaving them to be destroyed. Unable to harvest his crops before eviction, another had been told: 'The crop of broad beans is seriously affected by black fly, and the lettuce crop has not been watered.' Both had had their compensation reduced by the maximum amount allowable, which remained unpaid in any case.

Any prior knowledge Piotr had of crucial developments, especially of planned evictions, he leaked to the locals at The Three Magpies. As he was seen as a total outsider with no connection to the local population, he was never suspected of being the source of these leaks by the authorities.

In reality, it was the vicar – the one who should have been their shepherd – who was the total outsider with no connection to the local population. He had been pleased when, in 1929, the Church Commissioners had sold seventy-one acres of land held by the church in lieu of tithes, as the proceeds had been invested to provide a good income for him and his successors.

The land had been sold to a pioneering aviation company for an airfield to test their new-fangled flying machines. Once they had got used to the sight of flying machines the locals had not been too concerned. The airfield was not a commercial operation; it remained within its original boundaries and consisted of little more than a single hangar and a nicely mown field.

They couldn't have known that it would be the catalyst for the rapid development of civil aviation in the area and become part of the largest international airport in the world.

The vicar wasn't too concerned about the destruction of Hadleyrow. He had nothing but complete contempt for the miserable God-forsaken hamlet, which didn't even have a proper church. 'Just that non-conformist tin shack with a snuff-snorting harmonium player,' as he described it.

But the monster he had loosed was threatening to turn north across the main road to destroy his own beautiful vicarage, the Norman church with its Tudor brick tower and the finest medieval tithe barn in England; a timber cathedral compared with the hovels of the poor, who had paid for it with their hard labour. The vicar was beginning to discover that, once released, monsters were hard to control.

VIII

While her foot was still mending, Gill was sitting in the sun as it shone through the leaded bay window of the downstairs back room when she heard tapping on the glass. Looking up, expecting to see a bird feeding on the small spiders that spun their webs there, she was surprised to see the wrinkled, weather-beaten face of Lizzie, as brown as a berry, pushed up against the window as if somebody was trying to clean it with a piece of old leather.

It was widely held in the countryside that walnuts resembled the human brain and that eating them improved intelligence. Lizzie hadn't been too upset to learn that the villagers held that walnuts resembled her weather-beaten face and therefore nobody would touch them. She was upset, however, when others said her face was more like a brown, wrinkled, half-rotten or bletted medlar; especially as she knew better than anybody that a bletted medlar had ancient bawdy names, one of the least offensive being 'dog's bottom'.

Gill opened the window.

'Lizzie! What are you doing here?'

'I've come up to see youm. What's wrong with yer leg, love?'

'I hurt my foot running across the fields.'

'That don't sound like youm.'

'It was in the dark and I was upset,' said Gill, too tired to explain about the cow.

'I'll bring some comfrey root fer it.'

Lizzie was known for her encyclopaedic knowledge of plants. Gill had once made the mistake of asking Lizzie the alternative names for great mullein, an imposing plant that grew up to six feet tall, with bold yellow flowers and leaves that were covered in thick, woolly down.

'Woolly mullein, or candlewick, candle flower, 'edge taper, torches or torch weed, 'cos its leaves be used fer tinder and wicks,' Lizzie had answered immediately.

Gill was happy with that, as it made clear sense. She had thought that was that, but, Lizzie, after rather aptly refilling her thin clay pipe with her home-grown and cured tobacco, lighting it and clamping it upside down between her leathery gums blurted out a torrent of names, as if she couldn't control herself:

'Aaron's rod, Adam's flannel, Our Lady's flannel, flannel petticoats, flannel flower, donkey ears, beggar's blanket, blanket herb, blanket leaf, clot-bur, clown's lungwort, Cuddy's lungs, duffle, feltwort, fluffweed, hare's beard, Jacob's staff, longwort, rag paper, shepherd's club, shepherd's staff, velvet plant and wild ice leaf.'

Gill was overwhelmed by Lizzie's knowledge, but she was saddened by a telling omission – 'hag's taper' – which, because of its dramatic nature, was the only alternative name Gill remembered. It was impossible that Lizzie wouldn't have known it.

'When youm were out there in the fields that night, did youm 'ear the bluebells ring?'

Gill's heart sank. 'Of course not. What are you talking about?! Why don't you ask me about the harebells as well?'

'Only them 'ares can 'ear them.'

'Stop it, Lizzie!' said Gill, becoming increasingly agitated.

Gill knew of the local belief that hares were mystical animals of ill omen with supernatural powers; the devil's servants; changelings shape-shifted from human form that could only be matched for speed by a black hound without a single white hair and could only be shot with a silver bullet or crooked sixpence, which confusingly was also known locally as a Black Dog.

'Did you see an 'are dance across the moon?' Lizzie continued, unabashed.

'Of course not! It's the wrong time of year,' said Gill, immediately regretting lending the legend any credence by proposing a reason.

'All the seasons 'ave gone mad round 'ere since those new-fangled airyplanes started messin' up the sky, so that's no reason.' said Lizzie.

'How do they do that, then?' asked Gill, despite herself.

'Well, when them takes off, them leaves them black exhaust trails. When them 'igher up on clear days, them scratch the sky with them white lines, and them make holes in the clouds with white streaks coming out of 'em. That's why there's been more rain and snow round here at funny times, messin' the seasons up,' said Lizzie.

Gill kept quiet, knowing that although Lizzie had lived

a life that the earliest inhabitants of the heath would have recognised, she had also been among the first in the world to observe the development of aviation when she had seen the early flying machines over the heath, and she was also very observant about the weather.

'Did youm see many rabbits?'

'Yes, of course I did. They're all over the place, despite the hunters.'

'Them brought down that airyplane that crash-landed that night some months back,' retorted Lizzie.

'How could they do that? The runways are concrete and they get squashed easily enough if they're run over by a plane. They can't dance across the moon either,' said Gill in exasperation.'

'Them droppin's attract them field mice, which attract owls, one of which got 'it by that plane.'

Gill fell silent. That was the trouble with Lizzie. It was difficult to dismiss her completely as she talked a lot of sense amongst all the superstitious nonsense.

Despite the contempt Lizzie was held in by most of the villagers some of her observations were of huge economic importance, not that she ever got any credit for them, let alone reward. To help control the field mice, she encouraged villagers to let their cats hunt in the clover fields. As well as reducing the number of owls hunting over the runways, it also reduced the destruction of bumblebee nests by the mice, which improved the pollination of every insect-pollinated crop, especially the tomato plants in the greenhouses.

When Isle of Wight Disease destroyed virtually the entire population of the native black honey bees throughout the land, Lizzie had nursed the local colonies through the epidemic with grease patties made from one part vegetable shortening with three parts powdered sugar and some menthol placed on the top bars of the hive; and by encouraging farmers to plant mixed wild flowers in their fields and glass houses to provide a variety of pollen and nectar, which helped keep the bees healthy.

'Did youm see the man in the suit and bowler hat, with a briefcase and rolled umbrella?'

'No!'

'He's about, youm know.'

'Lizzie! Will you stop all this stuff? If he's a ghost, why is he carrying a briefcase and rolled umbrella?'

'Because when youm see a ghost you see 'em in their time.'

Gill went to retort but couldn't. She had not anticipated that answer.

'Did youm see the Ghost 'Are?' asked Lizzie without a pause.

'No, I didn't! All that hare stuff is rubbish and you know it,' said Gill.

'Where do it all come from then?' asked Lizzie.

'Mostly you around here,' said Gill.

'Weren't me that made the hare constellation look like a reversed swastika, low in the scythe of Horion the 'Unter in the war.'

'Orion the Hunter,' said Gill.

'What love?'

'Never mind. You know some people think you can change into a hare and back,' said Gill.

Gill was worried for Lizzie because by country standards the evidence that witches turned themselves into hares was irrefutable, based as it was on first seeing an old lady and then, when she was out of sight, seeing a hare. When Gill had challenged a villager over this, he had claimed that once, when a hare was about to be ambushed by a cunning fox, someone had shouted, 'Run, Nanny, run!' providing further proof of its true identity.

'Yes, but I can't 'elp what them thinks.'

'No, but don't encourage them,' said Gill.

'Allen told me to tell 'em they're mistakin' corlation fer cosaneffect.'

'What?!' exclaimed Gill, before realising what Lizzie meant. 'Do you know what it means?'

'No. Didn't work anyway. Made them worse as them just thought I was puttin' a spell on 'em.'

Gill had to admit to herself that she sometimes failed to distinguish between correlation and cause and effect, especially when she thought about something and then it happened.

'Never mind all that, just youm be careful.'

'Why?'

'There's an 'obgoblin about,' said Lizzie.

'Lizzie! A hobgoblin?! What are you trying to do? It's me you're talking to!'

'I tell youm, I seen it,' said Lizzie with an earnestness that unsettled Gill.

'Now stop, it's gone beyond a joke. 'It's those herbs you're always chewing,' said Gill.

'And the inn signs 'ave been changin',' said Lizzie, completely unperturbed.

'When?'

'Over the years. The Plough and 'Arrow be The 'Are and 'Ound now.'

'Well that's because of that old battered painting on the wall of the bar; the one of the hare being chased by a pitch-black hound without a single white hair,' said Gill.

'Yeah, but nobody knows 'ow that got there. Then there's The Three Magpies. Them could change a team of four coachin' horses in two minutes there once, you know.'

'Well it's always been called The Three Magpies.'

'Only in your sweet life, love. It used to be The Three Pigeons, then it became The Magpie and Pigeons, before two more magpies turned up and the pigeons disappeared. Everybody knows pigeons aren't scared of magpies, so why should they leave? A man died there, y'know.'

'No! When?'

'1798.'

'1798? What are you talking about, Lizzie?'

'Don't matter 'ow long ago, still 'appened. He was shot just down the road outside The Old Magpies by 'ighwaymen and carried to The Three Magpies. Magpies everywhere!'

'Hares, hobgoblins and now magpies. What next?' asked Gill.

'I see youm 'ad a young man come avisitin',' said Lizzie, as if she hadn't heard.

'Yes,' said Gill resentfully.

'Do youm like him?'

'Yes, he seems very nice.'

'Well tell him be careful, too.'

'Why?'

''E's in 'arm's way.'

'Stop being so mysterious, Lizzie. Who would want to harm him?'

'A boggart.'

'A what?!'

'A boggart. One whom dwells near weeds.'

'Shut up!'

'One worthy of appeasin' with a posy of dog's mercury in

February.'

'What? Those tiny green flowers?' said Gill.

'Ah! Youm 'ave learnt somethin' after all then.'

'Shut up!' Gill repeated, angry but also frightened, despite herself.

'By the way, 'ave youm seen Allen?'

Gill tried desperately not to let Lizzie see her discomfort, but by doing so, ensured that she did.

'What's the matter, love, 'ave youm two fallen out?'

'No, it's just my foot's hurting a bit.'

They fell quiet and gazed out over the remnants of the fields.

"Ave them Germans landed?' Lizzie continued relentlessly.

'What?' asked Gill, completely thrown by this sudden change in direction.

"Ave them Germans landed?'

'No, of course not! The war's been over for years now,' said Gill.

'I heard a villager saying there are some Germans about.'

'The're POWs.'

'No, them say them are definitely Germans.'

'POWs means prisoners of war,' said Gill in total exasperation.

'Is it them knockin' down the old farmhouses and diggin' up our fields?' asked Lizzie.

'Yes, but they're being told by us to help do that. They're on our side now,' said Gill.

'Against who?'

'The Russians.'

'I thought them were on our side.'

'They were, but now it's different,' said Gill, too tired to explain further.

'Why were them bombers still goin' off to Germany after the war then?'

'They were dropping food and supplies for them.'

'Who?'

'The Germans.'

'Hmmmm. Are Germans dark brown?' Lizzie persisted.

'No! Why should you think they are?'

'I saw a dark brown man up there in an RAF uniform and thought he might be a German spy.'

'If Germans were dark brown, it wouldn't be much use them just putting on RAF uniforms,' said Gill.

'So 'e were one of ours, then?'

'Yes,' said Gill wearily, realising her mistake.

'Well, if ours can be dark brown and Germans were dark brown, it would be some use them puttin' on RAF uniforms, wouldn't it?'

'Germans aren't dark brown!'

'Whom shot that farmer when he refused to plough up his pasture for plantin' taters in the war, then?' asked Lizzie.

'The police, but he shot at them first,' said Gill.

'Why? Was 'e German?'

'No, he was English.'

Lizzie looked unconvinced. 'Can Russians be dark brown?' she asked.

'No! Anyway, Lizzie, who's still down at the Rookery with you?' asked Gill, desperate to return some sense to the conversation.

'Only Allen and Kate,' said Lizzie.

'Are you all right down there?'

Gill wasn't worried about Lizzie's personal security, as she was wily enough and the flock of geese on permanent patrol would have given any stranger short shrift at any time of day or night. Gill had even seen one of them force a Jersey bull, which have a somewhat evil reputation, to concede ground by latching tenaciously to its lower lip with its beak. But she was worried about the bulldozers and Lizzie's state of mind.

'No, love. I'm worried fer Kate's coughin'. I can 'ear 'er all night from next door. And I'm worried for meself. I'm not up to the fieldwork any more and I only get by cos Kate 'elps me. I don't know what I would do without 'er.'

Gill knew only too well how hard the field girls worked, as she had given Lizzie a hand once when Kate was off with the coughing. They had worked out in the field from eight a.m. to five p.m. and then gone into the packing shed where they stood around a long table, sorting and packing sprouts until eight p.m. It had been cold and sleet had come down all day, but despite their soaking clothes they had still sung and laughed their heads off.

It had become so cold in the evening that their aprons froze to the sorting table. To get free they had to untie themselves, leaving the aprons looking as if they had stayed behind around the table for a meeting to protest at the harsh conditions to which they were exposed.

As Gill had passed the packing shed the next morning she had heard a rustle that sounded like a sigh as the aprons lost their icy grip on the table and slowly slumped to the floor as if overcome with exhaustion after their all-night meeting.

'The only chance I've got of makin' extra money is with me 'erbs and potions. That's why I try to keep up the mystery,' Lizzie continued.

'Well, don't overdo it. At times like these, people get frightened and can turn nasty. I've heard people talking about you and the hares and I don't like it. So for goodness' sake don't start going on about hobgoblins,' said Gill.

'I've seen it. But don't youm worry your pretty little head about me, love.'

'Why won't you leave, anyway?' asked Gill.

''Cos I got nowhere else to go.'

'What about Kate?'

'She won't leave me, even though she's coughin' night an' day.'

The sound of an aircraft overhead distracted them.

'Be that one of ours?' asked Lizzie, repeating a question that had been posed frequently throughout the war.

'Yes, of course it is. Although it wouldn't make much difference if it wasn't as far as the destruction around here's concerned.'

Gill was starting to worry that her mother might find Lizzie with her. Her mother didn't approve of Gill having anything to do with anyone from the Rookery, particularly Allen and Lizzie.

'I'll get goin' now. Remember to warn yer new friend,' said Lizzie as if reading her thoughts, which, despite herself, Gill suspected she might have done.

Gill shut the window and didn't even attempt to watch Lizzie leave, knowing she would see nothing. Gill could see why some of the villagers, and the vicar particularly, treated Lizzie with such fearful suspicion. She wished Lizzie wouldn't play up to them so much. Lizzie was one of the kindest people she knew, but she didn't seem to realise how much hostility her ways generated in the more superstitious villagers.

'Who were you talking to?' enquired Gill's mother, looking around suspiciously as she entered the room.

'Nobody,' said Gill.

'I can smell smoke. It wasn't that Lizzie, was it?' Gill's mother asked, gazing out over the fields.

Gill didn't answer, confirming her mother's suspicions that she was lying.

'She's trouble, you know, just like that Allen. You really shouldn't have anything to do with them.'

'I know, Mother, you tell me often enough.'

'Well, you know what they say about her, don't you?'

'Yes, Mother,' said Gill, steeling herself to be told yet again.

'You know she was found between the rows of gooseberry bushes in one of the fields?'

'Yes, Mother, just imagine. Gooseberry bushes, too.'

'Straight after a huge balloon with its crew in a wicker basket made a forced landing in the next field. Some claimed Lizzie had been thrown out to prevent its crash landing and that her arrival was a portent of things to come.'

'That's rubbish, Mother.'

'Then they saw a gypsy girl out in the fields suckling a baby on one breast and a baby hare on the other.'

'Mother! That's even worse. You'll be telling me next that Mary Tuft was telling the truth when she claimed to have given birth to eighteen rabbits!'

'No I won't, although some would. Especially those who claim to have known her.'

'How could they?! That was in the 1700s!'

'Just you be careful who you mix with,' said Gill's mother.

Gill glanced out of the window. There was no sign of Lizzie, of course, but she only just managed to control herself when she saw a hare speeding away in the distance. She had to get a grip.

Many animals were suffering the destruction of their habitats as a result of the airport development and could be seen more frequently, but it was the hares that were discussed nightly at The Three Magpies.

'Beware the Levere of March,' had been heard again for the first time since the Roman legions marched past the already ancient Caesar's Camp. Those same Legionnaires knew Boudicca, the Celtic warrior-queen, had taken a hare into battle beneath her cloak. But they didn't know that it was the hare, not Boudicca, that had screamed like a woman when wounded.

Even the vicar had started to hear stories about those dammed hares again, and about, that old hag, Lizzie. He had always had his suspicions about the fieldworkers of Hadleyrow. Not the farmers, of course, whose houses he frequently visited for evenings of fine food, wine, music and conversation; although even then not without a small prayer as he crossed the main road, especially at night.

He was tired. His nerves were exhausted. He was losing his grip. These days he shuddered when he saw a hare. He knew all about the Celts and their God-forsaken so-called culture and beliefs. He had made a study of them. He had become obsessed with them. Despite himself, he had fallen under their spell.

CHAPTER TWO

I

Allen and Prof crouched in the darkest corner of the warehouse awaiting a signal to open the side door. Allen was astonished by his weakness in agreeing to go along with it all. He could see that his help wasn't really needed other than to keep Prof company and to share the risk, but he had felt sorry for Prof; a man who had bashed, slashed and stabbed people on the orders of others and still regretted not shooting them! So here they were.

Allen's tension was building as the enormity of what he was about to be part of began to dawn on him. He would now be an accessory for not having blown the whistle whatever happened. He was amazed that such tension seemed to have no upper limit and that he hadn't yet heard a mighty 'twang' inside his head as he finally broke. Not yet, at least.

'Nobody loves you like yer mother,' intoned Prof.

Just then there was a scratch at the side door. Prof quietly unbolted it and two shadowy figures slid in.

'Well then, me old mate, that was easy enough,' said the bigger of the two.

'Yeah, and it would have been even easier to walk in the loading doors, which are always open, and not get us two involved,' said Allen.

'Who's this funny lookin' geezer,' said the bigger of the two.

'He's a mate of mine. He's alright, don't take no notice of 'im,' said Prof giving Allen a look.

A few years earlier Prof would have taken them both on, but now he was at their mercy. He had lost his nerve after the last big battle, not before, not during, but after he had fought like a hero with his bare hands against razors and axes, with the skin of his forehead flapping down over his eyes.

When he was least expecting it, the world had lost its certainty. In a fraction of a second, all his sense of invincibility and indestructibility had drained away, and he knew he was lost. He had heard of the same happening to servicemen who had records of outstanding bravery under fire, but he couldn't draw any consolation from that. Fear and panic were personal.

He was no longer the man who had helped his boss terrorise half of London and carry out what he liked to call his 'Robin Hood visits' on behalf of beleaguered Jewish businessmen in Birmingham, Leeds and Glasgow, where he had been surprised to hear a razor scar from the corner of the mouth to an ear being referred to as the Glasgow Grin, rather than the Chelsea Grin. He was no longer the man who had never backed out of a fight because he was never afraid.

Prof led the way to the safe, which was wide open as usual. 'Now, lads, don't get jumpy. There's a gun in the safe, but it isn't loaded. It's just for show,' he said.

He placed the gun on a nearby shelf as his mates started rifling through the contents of the safe.

Allen had hung back, determined to make his escape, but as he turned to slink away his sleeve caught the barrel of the gun, which was overhanging the shelf. He just managed to catch it, but as he juggled with it, it went off with a deafening bang. The bullet ricocheted from the steel shelving in a shower of sparks and killed a feral chicken that had flown into the rafters through the large sliding doors which were open. The chicken tumbled down, followed by a shower of drifting feathers. It fell between two coffins where, out of sight, its still-twitching legs made a scratching sound against them as if the occupants were trying to escape.

The two villains immediately took off. Like all who depended on physical strength for their self-confidence they were terrified of the supernatural, against which their strength was useless. Several Perms rushed through from the offices to see what the commotion was about, while others locked themselves in the toilets. When the fluorescent lights finally flickered on, the scene that greeted them resembled a *danse macabre*. Huge, black, misshapen shadows – including that of a hare that had been chased into the warehouse by a fox – danced distortedly over the racks of cargo.

'Prof, this could look like we foiled the raid. Just don't say anything to the police. Pretend you're shell-shocked,' said Allen.

Allen didn't have to worry, as Prof was indeed shell-shocked. As he was calming Prof down, it occurred to Allen that the villains might come back to make sure he and Prof didn't give evidence against them if the case ever went to court. He needn't have worried. The villains' terror at the scratching sound they swore they had heard coming from the coffins was enough to ensure they would never return.

What Allen really would have to worry about, though, were the sinister rumours that subsequently sprang up that implicated Lizzie in the apparent ritual slaughter of a chicken, along with the associated scratching that more and more people claimed to have heard coming from the coffins and the presence of a giant hare. Also, given the air of mystery associated locally with magpies, it wasn't long before those noisy black-and-white birds entered the story when it was discussed in the local pubs. They pushed in everywhere.

Allen knew all the folklore attached to magpies, especially the chant about the significance of how many of them were seen at any one time. There were several versions, but no matter which was believed, a walk in the countryside could be very disturbing as they all began with: 'One for sorrow' and continued with references to death, hell and the devil himself, amongst a few more cheering ones.

In order to placate these ominous birds, people would doff their hats to the first magpie they saw before noon, saying: 'Good morning, Mr Magpie, and how is your lady wife and family?' Some wore a hat specifically for this purpose.

Superstitions apart, magpies were also thieves of bright, shiny objects including jewellery, and were notorious killers of chicks and smaller birds. As a result, nobody liked them anyway, even though some villagers themselves were thieves of bright, shiny objects including jewellery, and also collected chicks from the sparrow pots for eating.

II

Allen's relief that the robbery had been thwarted was short-lived. When the airport police arrived to interview him he was toying with some of the complimentary packets of four cigarettes that were offered to passengers on the aircraft.

He was shaken by their first question: 'Where d'you get these from, lad?'

'They're just free samples,' said Allen, not dreaming that possessing anything that was normally given away could be considered stealing, especially among this den of thieves.

'OK, sonny, you're coming with us,' said another policeman.

'What about the attempted robbery?' asked Allen in complete bewilderment.

'Your mate can tell my colleague about that.'

Allen's mouth soured as he realised that, as usual, the police were going for the soft target to boost their statistics with the minimum effort or risk to themselves, while vanloads of high-value goods were ferried out of the main gate on a Sunday afternoon with a nod from the gatekeeper.

He had barely marshalled these thoughts when he received a stunning blow to his head. In his hyped-up state, and because he had a thick skull, a strong neck and a high threshold to physical pain, the blow didn't hurt at all. It had, in fact, been dealt by accident when one of the policemen had slammed the back door of the car shut as Allen was halfway in with his head still sticking out.

'Bloody hell! Was that your head?' enquired the copper as the door rebounded with a loud thud.

'Yes,' said Allen, without any fuss.

This incident turned out to be a blessing in disguise, as it put the officers slightly on the defensive. They couldn't understand how he hadn't been knocked out, or even worse. That type of blow could have killed some. Nor could they understand why he didn't make more of a fuss.

On reaching the airport police station, the questioning continued. 'So where did you get these?'

'Like I said, they're free samples. They get swept up by the cleaners, like the barley sugar passengers suck to clear their ears on take-off and landing.'

'But you work in a bonded area and are not allowed onto the aircraft, so how did you get your hands on them?' enquired the policeman, idly making a little house out of the slender red and white packets.

The warehouse was an HM Customs and Excise bonded area. Freight in transit escaped import and export duties as long as it stayed in the warehouse before it was transferred between aircraft. To oversee the movement of these bonded goods, HM Customs employed 'Watchers' to hang around the warehouse watching things, becoming closely involved with the Perms and their scams in the process.

One such scam involved a Perm putting a foot through the side of the cardboard crates of champagne destined for the first-class passengers, and the complimentary cigarettes destined for all passengers. When alerted, a Watcher would wander out and sign them off as damaged in transit and the contents would fuel a party in the office, be taken home or sold on.

During one night shift, Allen had surprised a Temp – who had ambitions to become a Perm and as a result had been recruited into the rackets – kicking in the side of a crate of cigarette packets. On seeing he was being observed, he had thrown a handful of packets to Allen. Not wishing to embarrass the Temp-Perm, Allen had pocketed them and thought no more about it.

But now that Allen's brain was up to full speed, he could see that accepting goods from a bonded warehouse was completely different from picking up a few discarded complimentary packets from an aircraft. And even though a Watcher had signed off the crate of cigarettes the Temp-Perm had kicked in, Allen realised he could still be accused of stealing them if everybody involved closed ranks, as they were certain to do. Those who imposed the law on bonded goods also regularly sought out a relatively innocent victim to give themselves a spurious reputation for ruthlessness.

'Come on, laddie. If you don't come clean we'll have you inside overnight.'

Allen was catatonic at the thought. His stomach turned and his mouth soured again.

'And we can go to your place and see what else you have stored up there.'

Allen felt the sweat beginning to run down the small of his back as he frantically tried to make the right guess. He was astonished that a problem of the real world – the world to which he thought he was so indifferent – could banish his inner demons in a flash.

The thought of a police car pulling up outside those little cottages and poor old Lizzie looking on as they searched the place horrified him, even though it wouldn't take long to establish that there were no hiding places in those tiny rooms. Lizzie was rigidly law-abiding and her poverty was accompanied by the highest standards of morality. Allen couldn't bear the thought of the shame this would bring upon her.

Neither could he risk prison for something he still saw as trivial. So he said that one of the Perms had given them to him, and he couldn't un-say it. Most Perms were involved in stealing from the warehouse and they couldn't risk any sort of investigation there, so they also needed the cigarettes to have come from the aircraft, which meant the Perms would close ranks and finger the Temp-Perm as the link between the aircraft and the warehouse.

Allen had calculated the odds and traded the risk of going

to prison and finishing off poor old Lizzie against somebody else possibly losing their job, as taking cigarettes from the planes was unlikely to be treated as a criminal offence.

He then played the only card he had left. He started to rub his head and moan quietly as if he were in great pain. It worked. The coppers shot furtive glances at one another and Allen immediately detected a slight easing of their aggressive attitude.

'OK, sonny, we'll need to see you again when we've interviewed the Perms.'

The police realised that, despite their threat, being in possession of a few packets of complimentary cigarettes wasn't enough to hold him overnight, no matter what they might learn in the morning. They also knew that this 'weirdo' still lived with his grandmother or whoever she was, and never left the village.

Allen felt a wave of self-recrimination and guilt at having become so easily drawn into the culture of the warehouse. As to his standing with the Perms and the security of his job, he didn't have any as a Temp, so there was nothing lost there. But he had, in effect, shopped the Temp-Perm to save his own skin, possibly still in vain.

All his theoretical morality about standing up for what was right had been exposed as a sham and he instantly realised that, had he been exposed to sufficient threat, he could have stood by in the face of war time atrocities and might even have become entangled in them himself. So he was, in effect, no better than an informer; a collaborator; a war criminal, and had only escaped those fates by avoiding the circumstances through chance of birth and geography.

But who could point the finger at those who betrayed others? Allen wondered. *Not those who had never been so tested and who had comfortable, self-satisfied lives without any doubt that they were good, brave people, which was how he had felt before this petty debacle. And what was the point in all his reading and thinking when, in the heat of the moment, he behaved according to the basic instincts of self-interest?*

All he did know was that he would have to go to Lizzie's at the first opportunity to warn her in case the police still intended to go there and search the place.

III

Allen paused at Lizzie's old, grey, weather-warped oak door to gather himself before going in. He glanced up at the model weather-house that sat on a shelf and saw that the brightly dressed woman was swinging out rather than the man in the dark suit with the brolly, but no briefcase. That would save Allen a lot of time misinterpreting the sky and consulting the unreliable weather plants later. Lizzie came bustling through from the garden.

'Hello Nanny. Sorry I didn't get back earlier. Have you had any visitors?' he asked, looking around nervously for any signs that the place had been searched.

'Yes, the gen'leman in the back.'

Allen's heart missed a beat. *So they had come down! But if they had, where was their car? They would never have walked down here.*

Allen moved tentatively through to the back room.

'What 'appened to you?' asked Prof.

Allen remained speechless with surprise at seeing Prof seated at the table.

'The coppers were leanin' on me. I think I managed to convince them we 'ad nothin' to do wiv the raid, but I'm not sure we're in the clear yet, mate. Either way I've 'ad enough of it down 'ere so I'm off back to the Smoke.'

'The smoke?' Allen managed to squeeze out.

'London, you nutcase. I come down 'ere to see if you wanna come? We should stay together 'til all this is sorted. Otherwise they'll try and set us against each other. I know what they're like.'

Once again Allen remained speechless with surprise. Things were happening too fast, he didn't have a clue as to what he should do. He had been to London before with the window-box crew on Sunday mornings. They had left the plant nursery in Hadleyrow at three in the morning to empty and replant the window boxes of the big city buildings. They would totter up wet and muddy ladders with nobody steadying them at the base on wet and muddy pavements, before inching along narrow, wet and muddy ledges with heavy window boxes on their shoulders. Any slip would have been fatal or at least crippling. After twelve hours of this dangerous, backbreaking work, they would return to Hadleyrow slumped on a pile of mud and vegetation in the back of an open truck, usually in freezing cold rain.

'It's not far and you can always come back when all this is cleared up down 'ere. I'll sort things out for yer,' said Prof.

Allen was beginning to realise he didn't have much choice. He wanted to move as far away from Gill as possible following his humiliation and he was still not in the clear from the botched raid and the cigarette fiasco.

'OK then,' said Allen, in pure desperation.

As Lizzie busied herself getting them some tea, Allen saw one of the old books he had rescued from the rubble of a demolished Elizabethan farmhouse on the table. He loved these old books: the leather binding, the foxing, the musty smell, the silverfish and, above all, the friends he found within them.

He had increasingly retreated into these books in an attempt to calm his inner world of chaotic thinking, which was becoming more frightening by the day. He devoured everything he could understand and much that he couldn't.

He was surprised by how much he found was relevant and appropriate to his personal experience, as if it were written by friends especially for him. Allen had been greatly relieved to find that he had so much in common with a galaxy of famous and respected people spread over centuries and even millennia, especially as he appeared to have nothing in common with anybody in the village, apart from Gill, not that they had ever spoken of such things.

Initially, he had only looked at books about nature and farming. The first had been a slender volume written by John Woodward, published in 1699, entitled *'Some Thoughts and Experiments Concerning Vegetation'*, about the culture of plants in water rather than in soil, and the discovery that plants in less pure water grew better than plants in pure water. Centuries later, before it was bulldozed, the same farm had been investigating using modern hydroponics, involving similar principles, to grow tomatoes.

He had then found an earlier volume by the same author, published in 1653, which contained a collection of notes and observations in which Allen had read with a jolt:

> *It is the nature and property of that principle to disturb the thoughts, pervert the reasoning power, and present melancholy and vexatious ideas and images of things. So that to advise them to think rightly, or to be cheerful, is just the same as to advise a man under a severe fit of the gout to be easy and to be in no pain.*

It was the first time Allen had had an inkling that his terrified state of mind was not his fault; that it was not a sign of weakness, but as much an affliction as any physical illness. It wasn't very optimistic, but the fact that his condition had been recognised several hundred years earlier was of huge reassurance. John Woodward had died aged sixty-three, but his message reached across the centuries to help him while those around him taunted him on a daily basis.

Allen shook himself out of his reverie. He wasn't sure how much he could trust Prof, but he had no one else to help him get away. He had isolated himself from any idea of friendship as part of his campaign to alienate himself before people could alienate him, a sort of pre-emptive alienation.

The one exception was a chap called Briscoe from the Caribbean who worked at the airport as a van driver, delivering to and collecting from the warehouse. Allen had been surprised to find he had a lot in common with Briscoe. Despite their differences in appearance and origins, they shared the experience of being outsiders and had the same intelligent interest in everything around them. But he couldn't ask Briscoe for help as it would bring him under suspicion from the police.

No. It was Prof or nobody. He had no choice. He couldn't manage it by himself.

IV

To Piotr's huge relief, the conversation with Gill had continued with the same warm humour during his next visit, as if it had never been interrupted. However, Piotr was no more relaxed as seeing Gill in a dress was more disorientating than it had been previously. He knew he was in love with her, even though he had no previous experience of what that meant. He just knew he wanted to spend every single second of the rest of his life with her. *If people wanted to deride that, it was their problem*, he decided.

'How did you get over here today?' asked Gill.

He paused momentarily, only just managing to avert his gaze as she raised her knee to scratch her mending ankle.

'My lovely new motorbike. Well, new to me.'

'Oh, so that was you roaring up. It sounded like one of those V1 flying bombs in the war that landed around here.'

'Yes, it makes as much noise, but it doesn't crash like the V1s did when their engine stopped. Perhaps when your foot's better I could take you for a ride?'

'I'm not sure. I've never been on a motorbike before. Is it dangerous?'

'It can be, but so far it's been less dangerous than running across a field in the dark can apparently be,' replied Piotr with a smile.

A comfortable silence fell between the two as they gazed out at the remaining countryside.

'Do you notice anything about the ivy growing up the trees?' asked Gill.

'No,' said Piotr, puzzled but relieved that they were chatting about less distressing things than his story, or the destruction of the village and his unwitting role in it.

'It never reaches the top,' said Gill.

'I can't believe that.'

'Well, now you can spend the rest of your life checking, like the rest of us do,' said Gill with a smile.

'I'll try not to,' said Piotr.

'You won't be able to stop yourself, and the harder you try the less you'll succeed.'

'Anyway, I thought most of the tall trees had been felled by now because of the aircraft,' said Piotr, unintentionally returning to the airport development. 'I've even seen woodpeckers reduced to drumming on chimney cowlings to attract a mate.'

'There are still some tall trees near the Rookery down towards the Pits. But that's the fascinating thing. Ivy never reaches the top of any tree and it applies everywhere.'

'The Rookery? I've never been down there. Why do they call it that?'

'The cottages are built out of wattle-and-daub, which the villagers call sticks and mud. And it's inhabited by dark, noisy flapping shapes that to outsiders all look the same. The villagers even take it as a sign of rain if the residents swirl close to home, just like rooks do.'

'I heard they're all a bit strange,' said Piotr.

'That's just what outsiders say. Some of the nicest people I know live down there, especially Lizzie and Kate,' said Gill, feeling bad that she hadn't mentioned Allen.

She knew that if modern life met some cataclysmic end, which it could do at any moment now that the Russians had the atom bomb, the rookeries of the world would survive while civilisation collapsed around them. But not this particular rookery, as it was about to meet its cataclysmic end without any help from an atom bomb.

'Doesn't that Allen still live down there with those two?' asked Piotr, as if, like Lizzie, he could read her mind.

'Yes, I think so,' said Gill, compounding her guilt.

'I heard most of them down there have never left the area, let alone the country,' said Piotr, whose travels up to that point matched those of the migrating birds that passed through Hadleyrow as they followed the sun on its annual travels.

'That's not their fault,' said Gill, slightly flushed in

response to what sounded like a hint of superiority from Piotr, particularly as she had never left either. But it was true; those who lived down at the Rookery were like the local grey partridges, which spent their entire lives in the fields, where they could disappear when huddled in a tail-to-tail circle, giving an all-round view of the open landscape; ever watchful.

'Do you feel up to telling me more of your story now, Piotr?'

Piotr looked up at the timbered ceiling. 'Those beams look old,' he said.

'Yes, they're older than the house. They're timbers from an Elizabethan ship. She kept her pigeons in the dovecotes here.'

'Who did?'

'Queen Elizabeth.'

'*The* Queen Elizabeth?'

'Yes, and in living memory King Edward VII had his lunch here on a hunting trip from Windsor.'

'All that royalty,' said Piotr.

'Yes, but the real royalty were the RAF fighter pilots billeted with us during the war. They used to spread them out of the camps for safety. They would tilt their wings over us on the way back if they'd shot down any enemy aircraft.'

There was a long silence, during which the old beams could be heard to creak, as if they were still at sea with a storm approaching.

'What about your story, then, Piotr?'

Piotr gripped the arms of his chair. 'Well, when I was ten, my mother and I were deported by the Russians to a Siberian labour camp.'

He had wanted to soften his story, but had learnt that if he ever attempted to tell anything other than the truth he got in such a mess it wasn't worth it. However, it was such a dramatic tale it sounded like anything but the truth. In fact, it sounded like something one would make up to earn the sympathy of a beautiful girl. He couldn't win.

'That's terrible,' said Gill, looking shocked and suddenly understanding Piotr's reluctance to tell his story.

'Look, Gill, it is terrible. And once I start I can't stop.'

Piotr's past always returned to haunt his present. He would have preferred to delay the telling of it until a lot later, but he wasn't sure there would be a lot later, and she had asked.

'I don't want to ruin our precious time together,' he added.

Piotr immediately felt he should have been more restrained about revealing his feelings for at least a few weeks, but he wasn't calm. He was desperate and he was losing control.

'No, go on,' said Gill, shyly ignoring his flirtatious compliment.

'Well, when the Nazis invaded Poland from the west, my father, who was a pilot in the Polish air force, joined his unit to fight the Germans.'

'What happened to him?'

'I don't know. We never saw him again.'

'No! That's terrible.'

Piotr showed no sign of a reaction and pressed on as if in a trance. 'At the same time, the Russians invaded Poland from the east. When they arrived at our village they gave us half an hour to pack, including food. We were taken to the station in the freezing cold and loaded thirty-odd to a cattle wagon, for what was to be a three-week journey to Siberia. Once our own food was finished there was only a slice of bread a day and sometimes a bowl of watery soup. Any dogs, cats or rats that could be caught around where we stopped were eaten. People's hair froze to the sides of the wagon while they slept. The toilet was a hole in the floor. Hundreds on every train died from cold, hunger and disease.'

'I don't know what to say,' said Gill.

'Don't worry. That's just the right thing to say. I'd better stop there for now.'

Piotr felt that telling his story at this point was potentially disastrous, as it would emphasise his foreignness and introduce alien horrors to Gill's mind. Also, as well as telling Gill, he was retelling himself and the story was not much better in retrospect.

V

'I saw you,' Gill said, while out with Piotr for her first tentative walk on her nearly mended foot.

'What?' replied Piotr, fearing he had done something to upset her. No pretty girls had walked by, and even if they had he wouldn't have looked. Not any more. There were no other pretty girls now that he had met Gill. He had been relieved that his story hadn't stopped Gill from agreeing to see him again and amazed that Gill's mother had agreed to let them walk out together.

'Checking the ivy on those trees,' she said with a smile.

'Guilty,' he said with almost tangible relief.

To his astonishment and delight, Gill slipped her arm through his.

'Piotr, I know telling your story upsets you, but now you've started I just have to know how you ended up here. But only if you want to.'

'OK. As long as you're sure.'

'Yes, I'm sure,' said Gill.

'Well, we arrived at a labour camp near Archangel, about seven hundred miles north of Moscow, just south of the

Arctic Circle. We were already in a terrible state and we were put in unheated huts infested with lice and fleas. I discovered pregnant females don't hop… fleas, that is,' he added, in a weak attempt to lighten the mood a little.

'That's just what Allen said! They didn't have lice, but he used to clear fleas from rooms by tempting the fleas onto him by crawling around on the floor every night for a few weeks in his, er, shorts,' she said hesitantly, not wanting to say underpants.

Although he was intrigued as he knew the Romans had used their slaves in the same way, Piotr was visibly irritated.

'Where was that, then?' he felt obliged to ask. He couldn't imagine what sort of camp Allen had ever been in.

'In their cottage down at the Rookery during the war. They also had bedbugs and they used to be painted purple all over to get rid of itch mites, which cause scabies,' said Gill.

Despite himself, Piotr was irked to have his story compared to that of someone who hadn't been through what he had. Such were the extremes of his experiences that it was hard for him to credit English people's suffering if they hadn't seen any of the war in Eastern Europe. He should have taken the opportunity to shut up, but he couldn't now that he had started.

'Sorry, Piotr, please go on.' Gill understood that it might have sounded as though she was trying to make Piotr's story sound less dramatic, which was the last thing she intended. She was just surprised by the parallels. *Remember this isn't a conversation*, she warned herself. *All you have to do is listen.*

'In the winter, the mercury in the office thermometer usually froze, which meant it was below minus thirty-nine degrees centigrade. People estimated that it went as low as minus seventy. When the air was still, a fog of frozen breath could hang in the air, and if someone walked through it slowly their silhouette was left cut out of the icy cloud. Tiny ice crystals called diamond-dust fell sparkling to the ground from a clear blue sky with a tinkling sound we called *shopot zvyozd*; the whispering of the stars.'

'Diamond dust!' Gill exclaimed at the familiarity of the phrase. In the winter of 1946-7 she and Allen had tossed hot water out the door to watch it freeze before it hit the ground. They had called that diamond dust, but that had only been at minus twenty.

'Yes, what were you going to say?' asked Piotr.

'Nothing. I just thought it was a lovely description,' said Gill.

'In the summer it was hot and infested with mosquitoes. We all contracted malaria, which plagued us for years. You would start shivering and sweating. You would have a violent headache and keep vomiting. Then the symptoms would ease until the next time. For us it was another fact of life, like the weather and the fleas, and we just accepted it. There was no quinine.'

'What about Herb Bennet?' asked Gill.

'Herb who?' replied Piotr, puzzled and again irritated.

'Not who. What. It's a plant. Allen told me the spicy roots were used by the Romans against malaria,' said Gill, mad at herself for interrupting again and disconcerted by the strength of her memories of Allen.

In turn, Piotr found himself struggling to curb his irritation at the repeated interruption to the flow of his story and the mention of Allen.

'We were always starving. The main food was a sort of slurry or watery soup with a few grains of barley at the bottom. The daily bread ration was eight slices for workers and four for non-workers. We were allowed to cultivate a patch of land in order to keep us working, but it was very difficult to grow anything worthwhile.'

'Yes,' said Gill, remembering, against her will, how she and Allen had struggled with gluts and poor storage when growing vegetables in their gardens.

'Yes, what?'

'Yes, I imagine it must have been difficult,' Gill said, not entirely convincingly. She felt helpless. The harder she tried, the less she could stop recalling parallels with Piotr's story, especially parallels involving Allen.

'During the summer and autumn, people used to collect nuts, berries – mainly cranberries – and edible fungi to be dried and saved for the winter months. But we still all suffered with deficiency diseases.'

Gill sighed in exasperation at herself, as she recalled the days they had been given off school in 'nut years' to gather hazelnuts from the hedgerows, and how much trickier it had been in the generally alternating 'berry years' as so many were poisonous.

Puzzled by Gill's response, Piotr continued hesitantly. 'We heard stories of people finding frozen salamanders and mammoth remains in the melting permafrost, and thawing and eating them. The meat was still fresh after tens of thousands of years.'

Gill, now nearly at her wits' end, grimaced, as she couldn't stop herself remembering the diamond-dust winter once again, when the gravel pits, ponds and small local rivers had frozen almost solid. They had chipped out fish, which were locked like jewels in the ice; 'chip 'n fish' the locals had called it.

'Are you OK? Are you sure you want me to go on?' asked

Piotr, startled by Gill's grimace.

'Yes. Of course. It's just my foot hurting.'

'Well, the lack of sanitation meant dysentery and cholera epidemics occurred. Heart attacks and cancer were common, even in the young, which everybody believed were stress-related. The birch trees for miles around were stripped of their fungus-induced cankers or chaga, which were used to make an infusion people swore cured cancer, especially of the stomach.'

Gill just stopped herself from saying: 'Lizzie does that.'

'There were lots of horses for pulling timber out of the forest. We gathered hay for winter fodder for them during the summer. When the adults asked to be treated as well as the horses, we were threatened with reduction of rations and told that the horses were more valuable than us.

'All they were worried about was making sure we kept working. They threatened the women that if they didn't fulfil their work quotas their children would be put into Russian orphanages. Only a parent could ever imagine the terror that would induce. What monsters could threaten that?'

Gill bit her lip. It had broken her heart when she had seen children from a children's home just down the road waiting on Fletham Station for a train to London, from where they were to be shipped out to Australia, either to orphanages or for adoption. They couldn't have known what fate awaited them. Rumours had rippled back about some abuse at the hands of some of their so-called carers. Some evacuees from London during the war had similarly failed to find paradise awaiting them in the beautiful countryside. She felt sick to her stomach at the thought of it all.

Completely confused by Gill's obvious discomfort, Piotr fell silent and stared resolutely out of the window, biting his nails.

'Can hares be black?' he asked after a while.

'Yes, although they're very rare. The old villagers sing a song about 'The Bonny Black Hare' that hid up a girl's apron, but I don't understand it. Why do you ask?' enquired Gill, grateful for the respite from the relentless hardship of Piotr's story and the thoughts it provoked.

'I think I just saw one.'

Gill followed Piotr's gaze out over the fields, hardly daring to look. Over towards the Pits she could make out a black shape, but she could tell from the way it moved that it wasn't a hare, nor was it Lizzie.

'Shall I go on?' he asked despondently.

'Yes. You must now you've got this far.'

'One of the worst things was when my mother had to have a tooth out. There was no anaesthetic, of course. Two people kept their feet on the stool where she sat and the third person pulled,' continued Piotr abruptly.

Gill winced as she listened to this description. She was done for. It was about the worst subject Piotr could have touched on. She knew all about bad teeth from Lizzie and others of her generation from the Rookery. It was perhaps the most terrifying experience of all for those benighted inhabitants.

Gill had been horrified to read an account written by an early traveller who had noted about the Rookery:

These forlorn cottages house the sorriest collection of residents concentrated in one place imaginable. Largely, they have no teeth, and those that do use them to chew tobacco, squirting the brown expectorate accurately at the vermin that share their miserable hutches.

Gill had been overwhelmed by the descriptions of the crude dental practices Lizzie had suffered as a girl without anaesthetic, other than the occasional use of the deadly henbane. She too had been held down in a chair, but with a string tied between the bad tooth and the handle of an open door, which, when slammed, pulled the string taut, extracting the offending tooth. As she had grown older she had been left to do it by herself – or not.

As was traditional in the area, Lizzie had had the remainder of her teeth pulled out to celebrate what was guessed to be her twenty-first birthday. At least those extractions had been performed by a dentist and not, as in earlier times, by the blacksmith. She was also lucky to have been fitted with plastic dentures rather than wood, bone or ivory ones; nor those set with 'Waterloo teeth' extracted from the dead of the Battle of Waterloo and later battles, which had still been going around in the countryside when she was young.

Lizzie only lost her false teeth in the mud once. She never found them again and that was that.

Gill gripped the arms of her chair and squirmed as she recalled Lizzie telling her that in the old days pretty girls who wanted work as servants at the Manor House were forced by the lady of the manor to have a front tooth pulled out to render them less attractive to the lord of the manor. And once she had noticed that when a local lad had had just one of his front teeth knocked out his girlfriend would have nothing more to do with him.

Piotr was totally distraught by Gill's silent facial contortions, which he interpreted as signs of disapproval.

'Sorry about the horror,' he said, unaware of the horror that she, in turn, was struggling to keep from him.

'Don't be silly. You did warn me, after all.'

VI

After Piotr's desperate disappointment over their most recent conversation, he was astonished and quite overcome when Gill agreed to meet again as if nothing was wrong. Apparently he had also won over Gill's mother, as she agreed to let him take Gill on her first motorcycle ride.

On his arrival, Gill virtually leapt across the pillion and, to Piotr's delight, held him tightly around the waist; not that she had any choice if she was to stay safely on the bike. They rode across to the big river and sauntered along the towpath. It was a beautifully bright, clear, cold day, and the river flowed darkly in the sunlight.

Despite the difficulties she had experienced previously, Gill was determined to hear the rest of Piotr's story. Even if she hadn't been falling in love with him, she had always felt a responsibility to learn about other people's experiences.

'Are you ready to go on with your story?' asked Gill quietly.

'I hope you don't think I am going on,' replied Piotr, seeking further encouragement. He didn't want a repetition of their previous conversation.

'No, don't be silly. Go on.'

Piotr coughed nervously, cleared his throat and continued in a rather more formal manner as he prepared to keep tight control of his emotions.

'Well, when Russia was attacked by Hitler, Russia became an ally of Britain and they released their Polish prisoners for the men to be recruited to a new Polish army to fight the Germans.

'The camp commandant didn't want to let us go. He was terrified as his work quotas stayed the same and he knew he couldn't fulfil them without us. It wouldn't surprise me if he ended up like his predecessor, who shot himself when he lost his Party membership card because he was so terrified of the consequences.

'Curiously, being deported by the Russians most likely saved us from the Nazis; almost definitely so for the Jews among us. Anyway, we somehow made our way thousands of miles south in an endless blur of illness, dirt, hunger and fatigue to Persia, which was then under British control.

'The Polish army under General Anders went to fight the Germans in Italy, and many of the Jewish men eventually went to Palestine, while the women and children were held in Persia before being dispersed throughout the world.

'We stayed in a huge tented camp on the outskirts of Tehran. It was hot in summer and freezing in winter, but compared to Siberia it was like a holiday camp. We used to get Red Cross food parcels. I remember my first egg and my first taste of cheese, which we called soap. We swallowed the eggs raw so as not to destroy the vitamins.'

By this point it was easier for Gill to resist mentioning that they had reacted in the same way when they received similar Red Cross food parcels from Canada during the war.

'But I hated the lavatories, which were deep pits with planks slung over them.'

'The earth privies…' started Gill, silently completing '… are still a bit like that down at the Rookery.'

'What about the earth privies?' asked Piotr.

'That's what they would be called in English,' said Gill deceptively.

It was getting dark and a light drizzle was falling.

'So much for: "Mackerel sky, twelve hours dry." Or is it: "Three days neither wet nor dry"?' said Gill with a grin.

Piotr felt relieved that the elements would prevent him

from going on and on, which he could so easily have done as his brain attempted to rationalise its chaotic memories and emotions.

A duck quacked.

'That's a female,' said Gill, seizing the opportunity to return to the present.

'How on earth do you know that?' asked Piotr.

'Only female ducks quack,' she said with a smile.

'So are those honey bees,' added Gill.

'What?'

'All worker honeybees are female. And that mosquito, which is just about to bite you.'

'So all mosquitoes are females, too?' asked Piotr, slapping at the offender.

'No, but all the ones that bite you are.'

'OK, so what do the males do?'

'Drink fruit juice.'

Piotr had a flashback to the pestilence of the camp and could not imagine benign male mosquitoes drinking fruit juice or even finding any in that hellhole.

'So is that cat,' said Gill, pointing to a cat that was just disappearing over a fence about fifty yards away.

Piotr had another flashback to the railway stations, where it would have been caught and eaten irrespective of its sex.

'Go on, tell me.'

'All tortoiseshell cats are females,' said Gill, not being completely truthful, but finding it too complicated to explain.

Gill reflected on the ridiculousness of posing as an expert on the subject of sex; a topic that was finally entering her life with great urgency. Her innocence was a product of the times; her religion with its prohibitions; her upbringing throughout which sex had been a taboo subject; and her sensitive, self-conscious and introverted personality. She couldn't have known that Piotr's situation in this regard exactly mirrored hers.

'I know that pregnant fleas can't jump,' said Piotr again, in a weak attempt to follow the thread.

'I know you do,' said Gill, reassuring him that she had been listening carefully to his story.

'Your story sounds so terribly sad. Did you ever have a happy time?'

'Oh yes, in the camp outside Tehran, even though it must have been terrible for my mother, worrying about me and not knowing my father's fate. I feel guilty about that now, but it was such a relief after Siberia. We had enough to eat, I had lots of friends to play with and we had the occasional treat. We had no toys, but any old bits and pieces would do.'

'Yes, you don't need much to be happy. We had no real toys either, but we had each other and the freedom of the countryside,' said Gill, relieved that that did not necessarily mean her and Allen, which it did.

'Were you ever physically attacked in all the terrible places you were moved to?' asked Gill.

Piotr thought for a while, tempted to make up some incidents, but rejected the idea as disrespectful to the memory of those who had suffered them.

'No. Nobody laid a hand on me, but our lives were permanently under threat from the conditions and people died all the time. Nor did I see or hear any explosions until I got to England during the war. It was the mental stress and illness – especially the fear of an unknown future and the malaria – that were so unbearable.'

Gill thought of those in Hadleyrow who had been killed and injured by the bombing during the war, but said nothing.

'Let's look for ivy growing to the tops of trees for a while,' Gill said.

As they wandered along, inevitably failing in their task, Piotr could not suppress his urge to reach out to hold her hand. To his delight she did not withdraw it. It was the first time in Piotr's adult life that he had ever held hands with a young woman. The deprivation heightened the impact and he found it difficult to continue speaking.

No boy had ever held Gill's hand in this way either. She had been equally isolated from contact with boys other than Allen, who nobody seemed to think counted as such. She had been brought up as a strict Catholic in an isolated, rural community where some still believed that a girl could get pregnant just by touching the provocative flower of the cuckoopint, which, according to the whispered rumours, resembled the human sex organs.

'What happened next?' asked Gill, finding herself holding his hand tighter as she steeled herself for a return to Piotr's story.

Piotr's heart leapt. The pressure on his hand reassured him more than any words ever could have done.

'We were in that camp for about eighteen months until the summer of 1943, when we were sent to Karachi, more than a thousand miles away. It took weeks in convoys of lorries with Indian drivers. From then on it was an endless blur of events. From Karachi we were put on a British ship, *The Old City of London*, to Bombay. There we were transferred to an American passenger ship, *The Hermitage*, for a six-week voyage to Los Angeles.

'When we arrived in America we were shocked when military trucks took us to an internment camp holding Japanese Americans, where, even worse, our section was enclosed by barbed wire. The conditions were much better than our previous camps, of course, but we were prisoners again.

After four days, we were loaded onto a train with sealed windows. A military guard was posted at the door of every carriage and no one was permitted to leave their coaches. Some panicked and started screaming, fearing a repeat of what they had seen and heard of in Europe. One never regained her sanity on the very threshold of freedom.

'After a journey of about seven hours we reached the Mexican border, where we changed to a train with no guards and we could open the windows and wander from one compartment to another. We were in Mexico and we were free again. The Mexican railway workers were on strike, but as a gesture of solidarity they let our train through.

'After another long journey we arrived at a station decorated with Polish and Mexican flags, where we were greeted by a welcoming committee and a small band playing the Polish national anthem. For the first time in years we felt like human beings. We were overwhelmed by their hospitality.'

'Where on earth were you?' asked Gill.

'The Hacienda Santa Rosa near León. It was completely renovated, with a communal dining room, schoolrooms and accommodation for families and the couple of hundred orphans that were among our number. There were flower gardens, ponds, play areas for the children and a theatre. We were showered with gifts from charity organisations. To us it was paradise on earth.'

'How wonderful! Why did you ever leave?' asked Gill.

'We wanted to stay there forever, but after the war was over in Europe in 1945 various attempts were made to move us on, until the camp was finally shut down in 1947. So once again we were heartbroken and homeless.'

Piotr stopped speaking and tried to avoid Gill's gaze.

'You can stop if you like,' said Gill, sensing his distress.

'No, I might as well finish and get it out of the way.'

By now the pressure of Piotr's grip was becoming uncomfortable.

Piotr shifted uneasily, took a deep breath and continued in a wavering voice: 'We hung around the camp for as long as we could, working locally, and found lodgings with a family who had worked at the camp and were grateful for the rent. Eventually, my mother learnt that some relatives had managed to survive the war and had got to London, and she decided I should go to them.'

'Just you?'

'Yes. I don't know why, but it must have been for the best as she saw it, after the way she had fought to protect me all those years.'

'Where is she now?'

'I haven't heard from her since.'

They stopped walking and turned towards each other, now holding both of each other's hands.

'I've tried everything I can, but I've been unable to find out what's happened to her yet. But I'll never give up trying.'

They resumed their walk in silence, watching the dark river flow by.

'How ever did you get to England?'

'Well, my mother and I had been working at odd jobs and had managed to save enough money for me to take a bus for a seven-hour journey to the port of Tampico, where I bought a one-way ticket on the British ship *Empire Windrush* for passage to England. There were about sixty other Polish passengers en route to London, mostly women, some already on board. It was basically a troop ship and we travelled on the lower deck they'd opened up for all the West Indians who'd already boarded in Trinidad and Jamaica. I'd never met people like them before, but they were a great bunch, mainly young men. There was a cabin class, but they didn't mix with us. We called in at Cuba for two days, and Bermuda for three, before crossing the Atlantic to London.

'During the voyage I discovered that it was originally a German cruise ship for Nazi Party members, called the *Monte Rosa*, then a Nazi hospital ship in the war, before being captured and eventually renamed by the British in 1947.'

'That's amazing. Everybody in Britain thinks the *Windrush* only carried West Indian immigrants,' said Gill.

'Yes, I know. That annoys me. That voyage was the only one it ever made to the Caribbean.'

'Everybody over here thinks that was all that it did,' said Gill.

'Curiously, there are West Indians of Polish descent,' said Piotr.

'What?'

'Yes. A Haitian on board told me about descendants of Polish troops sent by Napoleon to help quell the great slave revolt in Haiti. Following the victory of the slaves, the 1805 constitution forbade white people to live on the island. But some Polish soldiers had deserted and fought with the slaves for their independence, and these were allowed to stay and preserve their Slavic customs if they accepted being officially categorised as "black". Their descendants still live in the villages in the mountains and they proudly call themselves "Lapologne". They are also known as "moun rouge". But try telling somebody from the Caribbean with African slave ancestry that white people were among the first to be officially called black and that their descendants are called red!'

'How did you get on when you got here?' asked Gill, feeling a bit lost.

'I lodged with my relatives, who all had terrible stories to tell. I slept in the kitchen until I could get a job and rent my own room. But overall, I experienced great kindness from strangers and found most British people friendly, helpful and trustworthy. More so than many fellow Poles.'

To her annoyance, Gill remembered that Allen still slept in the small room that passed as the kitchen in Lizzie's tiny cottage.

They wandered along in silence for a bit.

'By the way, Piotr, do you have any enemies?' asked Gill, thinking back to Lizzie's warning.

'Yes, millions in Central Europe.'

'No, seriously. I mean here.'

'Yes. Strange you should ask. There's a man up at the airport called Burian. He tried to pretend he was Russian.'

'How did you know he was pretending?'

'When the locals went on about their soil being the best in the world he boasted that the black earth "back home" was so good the Germans had shipped it back to Germany by the trainload during the war. He also boasted of the sugar production "back home" being among the greatest in the world. The West Indians thought he was mad when he said that. When he referred to people from the Caucasus as "chorny" or "black", and I noticed his soft consonants when he was talking, I realised he must be Ukrainian. I knew he was Catholic and hated me for no good reason, so that almost certainly made him Western Ukrainian. When I tried to force him to admit it, he went mad.'

'Be careful,' said Gill, without fully following Piotr's

explanation.

'I'm always careful. Especially with him, as he gradually moves behind anybody he's talking to. I saw the camp guards do that when they were interrogating people.'

'Yes, but especially so,' said Gill.

'Why?'

'Well, Lizzie seems to know something about him somehow,' said Gill.

'I'm watching him, anyway,' said Piotr.

'Maybe I'll meet him. I've just applied for a job in catering at the airport,' said Gill.

She hoped against hope that she wouldn't meet Allen there. The airport was sucking them all in, one way or another.

'Let's sit here and enjoy the river,' said Piotr, anxious to get as physically close to Gill as he could and soothe the tension generated by telling his story. The seat was enveloped by a curtain of branches from a weeping willow tree on the bank of the river, so they were virtually invisible from the path and those cruising by on the river. They sat in the dappled sanctuary, arched over by the delicate, pale green tracery of the rustling willow branches, tentatively exploring what each would allow, while hoping they wouldn't be allowed to explore too far.

VII

Some days later, Piotr was wandering along, lost in his thoughts about Gill and what her reaction would be to his story, when his reverie was interrupted by a shout.

'Hey, man! Did you hear the news?'

Piotr looked up to see Denzil waving at him over the waist-high chestnut-paling fence that surrounded a field that was grandiosely called the Airport Public Enclosure. In one corner was a wooden, shed-like café with an ex-army, brown canvas marquee acting as an extension, which served the huge weekend crowds. One Sunday in June 1947, seven thousand people had paid three pence each for entry to the enclosure to watch the aircraft; more than the number of outsiders who had visited the village in the previous hundred years or more. Everybody who worked in and around the airport used the enclosure café as their unofficial meeting place, avoiding the entrance fee by exploiting a gap in the fence.

Denzil was from the Caribbean. He was as tall as Piotr, with a stronger build, straighter hair, lucid green eyes and only slightly darker skin.

'I heard Prof and Allen have disappeared,' said Denzil.

'What?' exclaimed Piotr.

'Yes, man. Rumour is Prof knew one of the gang involved in that failed robbery, which also puts Allen in the frame. If you fly with John Crow you'll eat dead meat,' said Denzil, letting slip a traditional phrase from the West Indies about keeping bad company.

'Well, that puffy old Pole!' said Piotr in disbelief.

'I didn't know Prof was a Pole like you,' said Denzil.

'Yes. Like you and that other lot are West Indians,' snapped Piotr as he wandered away, not wanting to be grouped with Prof and knowing Denzil did not want to be classed as a West Indian.

In Caribbean terms, Denzil was a 'face-man' of high colour and good hair. Some would even say a 'red-man', like the *moun rouge* in Haiti. This was about as ridiculous as calling him black, which, to his utter astonishment and burning resentment, had happened several times since his arrival. He was certainly no darker than Piotr, nor most of the field girls; especially Lizzie, who was as dark as a Romany, with her scaly, weather-beaten face like that of a bletted medlar or lizard. Terrified of being labelled black and of lizards in equal measure, Denzil couldn't repress his horror when it came to Lizzie.

Whenever possible, he would pass himself off as South American. If pressed, he had to remember that Guyana was the only English-speaking country in South America. Even this often misfired badly for him, as most people thought Guyana was in Africa.

Despite being healthy, strong and good-looking, with many healthy children, Denzil's life was poisoned by obsessions with racial status – especially those related to skin colour and hair texture – as he struggled to avoid what he considered as racial taint. He had ensured that his passport photo had been developed 'light', even though most photographic studios back home did so anyway. But the problem with photographic bleaching was that it was a 'face card'. Its benefit was largely psychological, as, while the subject could deceive him or herself, it wouldn't fool anybody else. At times he had even contemplated going for the real thing and lightening his skin with cake soap – a detergent containing bleach – but he feared for his fine complexion. Even though Denzil took great pride in the fact that his good hair was straighter than Piotr's, this still wasn't enough to assuage his dented pride.

Denzil worked as a van driver for one of the airlines. Having known better times back home, he was deeply ashamed of his job. When he had to deliver to West Indians darker than himself it made him squirm. Even they told him that a man with his high colour shouldn't be doing delivery work.

'See di man deh who want to be blacker dan he is,' they

said in disbelief.

His shame was deepened by the fact that Briscoe – whose appearance spoke of Africa across oceans and centuries, and who Denzil considered to be, and called, a 'nayga' – had the same job. He couldn't believe some bracketed him and Briscoe together as black and even treated Briscoe as an equal. It made him seethe inside.

However, despite being from opposite ends of the pigmentocracy in the Caribbean, Denzil and Briscoe had both experienced similar shocks on arrival in the 'mother country', as they had been brought up to consider it. When Allen had first heard mention of the mother country, he had asked where it was, and Briscoe had looked at him incredulously.

Local accents, especially the whining estuarine English of Londoners, jarred compared to the refined English spoken by whites back home. White women with fine, straight, tall hair wearing rollers were a complete puzzle. Black women in the West Indies did the same, but for the opposite effect. The sight of white road sweepers, dustbin men and even white people riding bikes shook them to the core. As for handicapped white beggars, many of them casualties of the First World War, they had never seen their like before.

Neither had they seen a double-decker bus in real life, let alone ridden on one, feeling as though they would capsize when going around corners. Nor had they seen white people queuing in the freezing wind and driving rain, or a white man on a bus. A white man on a bus back home was either mad, broke, a misfit, a loser, or a combination of all of those things, like 'the walk-foot-buckra who had not horse in days of slavery'.

However, Denzil derived some consolation from the fact that, as far as he knew, none of the British he had met so far could drive, and nor could Piotr. Denzil had never met a man of high colour at home who couldn't drive, except the Germaicans – descendants from German-indentured labour – who didn't really count as far as Denzil was concerned. This slight consolation would have been denied him if he had known that Gill had learned to drive a tractor at the age of ten and her dad's van at fifteen, and that when she was seventeen she had once driven up to Covent Garden market at four thirty in the morning.

VIII

Before their arrival on the *Windrush*, Denzil's personal story was as different from Piotr's as could be imagined. Denzil had grown up as free as a bird in a tropical paradise, despite being surrounded by dire poverty. Day length and temperature varied little all year round, as did the height reached by the blue sea up the beaches of silver sand. Tide and time appeared to wait for all men on Denzil's Caribbean island.

Denzil belonged to a large extended family that was successfully involved in building, haulage, retail, farming and teaching. He also had children all over the place by more 'baby-mothers' than he could name, let alone the children. Some would say he was perpetuating his ancestors' white slave-owner genes and conforming to the missing father stereotype and the matriarchal model of a former slave-based society.

He was genuinely surprised if he was ever criticised over his multifarious affairs. *That was what real men did.* He didn't have the slightest sense of guilt with regard to his treatment of women. He also believed that these women had a completely free choice in the matter, as nobody forced them to sleep with him. He believed he was doing them a favour and that without him they would be a lot worse off, which economically was true. He was flattered when people used to say: 'Im cyaan lock im hose off.'

In contrast to Hadleyrow, which was set in a pan-flat landscape a few feet above sea level, Malvern, the small village in Jamaica Denzil came from, was perched high up on the edge of the western mountains, overlooking the coastal plains to the blue Caribbean beyond. Malvern's cool, fresh climate had attracted the original plantation owners to have their houses built in these hills, overlooking the plains from which they had made their fortunes from the horrors of slavery. Some of their descendants remained there, while others had returned to Britain with their poisoned wealth, both groups still privileged and financially advantaged, living off their ancestors' sins well into more enlightened times. These days, the plains were dotted with the ruins of old sugar plantation buildings, which were disappearing under the relentless and overwhelming power of vegetation. Nothing could withstand it; not even airports in cooler climes, let alone in the tropics.

Denzil had lived in a large new-build bungalow in the hills below the great houses, to which he was never invited. Even so, the veranda of his bungalow looked west over the plains to the coast from a height greater than that attained by sightseeing flights over Hadleyrow.

His numerous business activities around the island had waned during the war. He had tried 'higglering' crops to the hotels on the north coast, but he didn't like to be too closely associated with the peasant growers in the hills, or to the men at least. The wives and daughters were another matter. As far as Denzil was concerned, it didn't matter how black they were as long as they knew their place.

It was warm, windy and dry when Denzil – with his fine hair and a big white smile on his handsome face, a white rum in his hand and a beautiful woman on his knee – decided to take up the offer of a ticket on the *Empire Windrush* to England, in order to seek his fortune in the mother country. The island newspapers of April 13, 1948, had carried an advert offering one-way passages to England on the *Windrush* sailing on May 24. Passage was available for anybody who wanted to work in the UK, as immigration restrictions for citizens within the British Empire had just been lifted.

To his dismay, Denzil had had no luck with the white women on the voyage to England. To his surprise, they were not English but Polish DPs – displaced persons – about sixty of them, most of who had boarded in Mexico. The Polish women had been withdrawn and impervious to his advances, so he simply assumed they were prejudiced against him. It was their loss, as far as he was concerned. He invented a new name for them, 'the refusenikas', a description he was rather proud of.

The fact that there were few Polish men and boys with them signified nothing to him, except that he had less competition. He certainly didn't remember seeing Piotr among their numbers, but then Denzil had paid extra to travel cabin class. He would never have shared a cabin with a bunch of naygas like Briscoe on the troop deck.

On arrival at Tilbury in June 1948, Denzil and Piotr couldn't have known what to expect. Their individual receptions couldn't have been more different. With regard to culture and education, Denzil was virtually English, whereas Piotr was truly foreign. But with regard to their appearance, Denzil was treated by many as a foreigner of the worst type – a black immigrant who had arrived on the *Windrush* – while

Piotr was almost universally accepted. And it was those from the Caribbean rather than the Poles who caused MPs to raise questions, even though a good proportion of the West Indians were servicemen on leave who were returning to their units, ex-servicemen intent on re-enlisting, or potential new recruits, mainly for the RAF, one of whom would confuse Lizzie in Hadleyrow.

Those who were not destined for the forces were appalled by the temporary accommodation provided for them at the Clapham South deep bomb shelter, but it was close to the Employment Exchange in Brixton, enabling them to register for work, which most did on arrival.

Neither Piotr nor Denzil took into account the state of Britain when judging their reception. Britain was bombed out, bankrupt, exhausted and suffering a level of deprivation worse than during the war years, when there had been bitter winters the like of which had not been seen for sixty years.

It was said that the summer of 1946 fell on a Wednesday, as it seemed there had only been one sunny day all year. Cereal crops were badly damaged and in Hadleyrow hay, wheat and oats were spread on the aircraft hangar floors to dry. Bread rationing was imposed for the first time. During a sustained period of bitter weather from January to March 1947, Britain was left frozen, plunged into darkness and on the brink of famine under the 'hunger moon'.

The thaw that started early in March only made things worse. The ground was frozen so hard that the melting snow, swollen further by major rainstorms, ran off as raging torrents. Storms swept in from the west; hail, sleet, lightning, sun, rain and rainbows sharing the same sky in the wettest March on record. March was traditionally a dry month, the drier the better for ploughing, sowing and planting potatoes, which made the spring floods of 1940 and 1947 – in which thousands of square miles of rich farmland were flooded – a double disaster. Deep winter frosts had already destroyed a huge number of stored potatoes, and potatoes were rationed for the first time until the following spring.

Because Piotr's wartime experiences had been so extreme, it was unlikely that knowing the state of Britain in advance would have changed his view that civilian hardship, other than in the cities during the Blitz, sounded trivial in the face of those suffered by millions in Eastern Europe.

Piotr's view was strengthened when he heard of the so-called post-war period in Eastern Europe. There, the terror continued: a world of vengeance and violence, rape and looting. Seventeen million displaced people scoured the land, including twelve million Germans driven out of Eastern and Central Europe. Rival nationalists in Eastern Poland and Western Ukraine fought on in an undeclared war of horrifying savagery, displacing a further two million.

During the winter of 1946-47, the populations of Europe's destroyed cities were reduced to a Stone Age existence. People cleared the rubble of bomb-flattened towns with their bare hands as they scavenged for food and fuel. They would have given almost anything to be in Lower Hadleyrow, sitting around the fire eating Lizzie's rabbit stew.

Prior to his arrival, Denzil, in complete contrast to Piotr, had never suffered physical hardship or emotional trauma. Even with regard to the weather he had only experienced two seasons, wet and dry, both of which were warm. Unless 'windy' was included as a season, when from February to April the north-easterlies rustled the tender purple mango leaves. Some talked of summer when the mangoes ripened between the rains of May and those of October and November, but no one spoke of winter. Although hurricanes brewed at sea in August and September, they didn't always strike the island.

CHAPTER THREE

I

Prof and Allen stood waiting for the London train at Fletham station.

Intent on paying his way and having some money for the unknown events ahead, Allen had retrieved some cash from the old tin box hidden under his bed in time-honoured country fashion. He had made sure to leave more than enough for Lizzie and Kate should any emergencies arise.

The tin under the bed was not as vulnerable to theft as it might seem. Nobody from outside the Rookery would have had the nerve to poke about under Allen's bed with all the wildlife around. Bedbugs, fleas, spiders and rats were underrated as defences against burglars. It was the big houses with their locked doors and windows, guards and guard dogs that were much more vulnerable, as the owners often discovered when crop picking was at full tilt and the travellers were about.

'Bloody 'ell. There's Briscoe. What's he doin' 'ere standin' out like a sore thumb?' asked Prof.

Allen pulled himself out of one of his endless ruminations to see Briscoe standing well away from everybody else at the end of the platform. Briscoe waved and walked towards them.

Allen couldn't hide his discomfort as Briscoe approached. He realised that being seen with him and Prof on the train could be almost as incriminating for Briscoe as giving them a lift up in his van.

Allen's discomfort did not go unnoticed and Briscoe felt even more disconsolate than he always did in the face of such a reaction, as in this case it was Allen, who he considered to be the first white man with whom he had anything in common.

'What yer doin' 'ere?' asked Prof.

'Mi van block up,' said Briscoe curtly, showing his anger by not explaining any further.

Once on the train, the unlikely looking trio sat resolutely looking out of the window in glum silence.

'Raatid! Them treat wi like dog an wi still no get no bone,' said Briscoe breaking the silence despite himself.

'What's up?' asked Allen.

'I just see a notice in a window: "No Blacks. No Dogs".'

'Well, I've seen: "No Dogs. No Irish". In that order! So it's not just you, mate,' said Prof.

'That nuh make it much better,' said Briscoe refusing to be placated.

'It may not mean what you think,' said Allen.

'Nuh? What the hell could it mean then?'

'Well a landlady might be a war widow or spinster who is nervous about who she lets into her house, especially if she has never seen what you call a black man before. Also, she might not like dogs. It doesn't have to mean they're saying they don't like you, nor that you are like dogs. They're just afraid,' said Allen.

Briscoe and Prof fell silent as they contemplated this possibility.

'Anyway, how could they expect a dog to turn up on its

own?' Allen added in a vain attempt to lighten the mood.

'Yeah and me wife's bin called Black Irish,' said Prof.

'Black Irish?' queried Briscoe.

'Yeah, because of her dark eyes, skin and hair. She looks like that film star Ava Gardner, who I used to meet at parties. Supposedly they're descended from the crew of the Spanish Armada wrecked on the west coast of Ireland,' said Prof.

'I saw a book called *The Black Irish of Jamaica* about Irish prisoners shipped out by Oliver Cromwell as chattel slaves,' said Allen.

'Was that before or after you Africans?' asked Prof.

'Cha man, who yuh callin African? People in England nuh go round tellin each other where they came from centuries ago. Anyway, I've got Irish in me too,' said Briscoe, remembering a cousin called Dermat, who was some sort of 'ologist.'

'Keep yer 'air on. You're not black, anyway. Dark brown, I would say,' said Prof.

'All I know is, nobody here is black or white. We're all coloured,' said Allen, getting tired of all this divisive talk. He gazed out of the window at the increasing urban sprawl that was spilling over the countryside.

'Coloured! That's worse,' said Briscoe.

'Why? We're all some sort of colour,' said Allen.

Allen hated the appropriation of the words black and white with regard to race. He suspected this was because his contrary mind recalled the connotations associated with black and white centuries before different races were widely known about; not only in the local legend of the evil black hound without a single white hair, but also of the mythical white beasts that failed in their missions because of a single black hair. But it wasn't only about colour. He hated anything that categorised people into faceless groups, perhaps because that was what had been done to him, literally, throughout his life.

'Oh yeah! I saw the way you looked at me when you saw me at the station.'

Allen felt awful. 'It's not what you think,' he said.

'Oh no! What is it, then?' asked Briscoe staring defiantly at Allen.

'Prof and me are still under suspicion about that failed robbery and I'm suspected of being part of a bonded goods racket. You'll be a suspect too if you are seen travelling up to London with us.'

'Oh,' said Briscoe embarrassed at having jumped to the wrong but most obvious conclusion.

'No Dogs. No Blacks. No Irish. No Black Irish. No Black Dogs. No Irish Dogs. No Black Irish Dogs, No Poles,' continued Prof regardless.

'You OK, Briscoe?' asked Allen, sensing more tension.

'No,' snapped Briscoe, annoyed by what he saw as attempts to trivialise the racism with which he was regularly confronted. 'Black is not our colour. It's our core. It's what we livin, fightin and dyin for,' he said, inadvertently striking a rhythm.

'You're gettin' niggly,' said Prof.

'Nuh use that bad word to me,' said Briscoe, becoming increasingly angry.

'What word?'

'*Nigger.*'

'What yer talkin' about? I said "niggly". Anyway, even if I 'ad, when we were kids it didn't mean nothink to us,' said Prof.

'That show jus how much it soaked in yuh society,' said Briscoe.

'We couldn't have known. And, by the way, it's not "my" society, either, it keeps wantin' to lock me up,' said Prof.

Allen thought he had better not mention what he had once heard Denzil calling Briscoe.

'I get fed up with everybody staring at me,' said Briscoe.

'What do you expect if they've never seen anybody like you before? Anyway, it's not always them being rude,' said Allen.

'Huh! How come?' asked Briscoe.

'Well, the villagers and the Gypsies believe in "mother-impression", and when pregnant they stare at men who have the features they would like for their babies. So it can be a compliment.'

'They're black enough already, so what they hoping for?' said Briscoe.

Allen didn't answer for fear of being misinterpreted, but he guessed they were hoping for Briscoe's big white smile, which had survived years of chewing sugar cane as a lad, unlike his own, which had almost never been exposed to sugar, despite having grown up surrounded by thousands of acres of sugar beet.

'That's just a way to explain why a baby and a man other than the 'usband look like each other,' said Prof.

'Forget just looking at them. If one parent is black and one is white, as you call them, why aren't their children grey?' asked Allen.

Briscoe sucked his teeth.

'Mother-impression definitely affects an unborn baby's mind. A teacher told me children born during and after the war were more nervous than normal,' said Allen, ashamed of his attempt at a joke about grey children.

'Yes, I knew a man seem like him come this world ready

fraid by what his mother see them-time,' said Briscoe, sounding less hostile, but with his speech still all over the place as a result of the tension he felt.

'Briscoe, why do you speak so differently sometimes?' asked Allen.

'We make allowances for who we're talking to.'

'Are you doing that now?'

'Yes.'

'How?'

'Well, back home we also speak patois.'

'Is that a language?'

'Yes, but it's not standardised.'

'Why?'

'It's the language of the poor. It's more spoken than written. People dem argue all day bout patwah,' Briscoe said to illustrate his point.

'Why d'you expect so much of this country, anyway?' asked Prof.

'Cos them did tell wi so,' said Briscoe, continuing to demonstrate his point.

'Who did?' asked Allen.

'You English.'

'I never told anybody anything,' said Allen.

'And good Queen Victoria.'

'The Famine Queen?!' asked Prof incredulously, who had heard his wife going on about her.

'She did save wi from the planters.'

'Why didn't she save the Irish, then?'

'Yuh mean the potato famine?' asked Briscoe, surprising Prof with his knowledge.

'No, starvation. It ain't famine in the face of plenty. More than a million starved to death next to the richest nation in the world, good Queen Victoria an' all. And more than a million went to America on what they called coffin ships as so many died on the voyage,' said Prof, hoping he had remembered correctly what his wife had told him so many times, as it seemed impossible for such a small country.

'She mussy did try fi help them. Me know she went there,' said Briscoe.

'Yeah! They said her receptions lit the graveyards,' said Prof.

'Perhaps she did help through the government,' said Briscoe weakly, before remembering having read that the British government had granted three times as much money as compensation to West Indian slave owners after emancipation as they had to famine relief in Ireland.

They all fell quiet as the rattle of the wheels over a long section of points drowned out their voices.

A lot had been written on the subject of slavery in Allen's books, and he had been relieved that none of his old friends had served on the Defence Committee, which defended Edward Eyre, the murderous judge of the Morant Bay Rebellion in Jamaica, after he returned to England.

'And 'ow many West Indians died of starvation durin' 'er reign?' Prof asked when they regained the smooth rails.

'There's another one! "No West Indians",' said Briscoe ignoring Prof's question.

'Why do they call you that?' asked Prof.

'Cos "Christ-tief-come-rob-us" did think im sail round the world to India,' said Briscoe.

'Who?' asked Allen.

'Christopher Columbus. Im did bring the sugar cane, the cause of our sufferation,' said Briscoe.

'Well, we grow our own around here,' said Allen.

'What?' said Briscoe.

'Sugar.'

'I neva see nuh cane here, man.'

'Acres of sugar beet. There are miles of trucks piled high with it over the railway sidings in Fletham.'

'I thought them were turnips.'

'They look like turnips, but three of them give one pound of sugar,' said Allen, who had once watched Lizzie crystallising out the sugar in her tiny kitchen.

'Why do they call Red Indians Red Indians when they're not red or Indians?' asked Prof idly.

'Even them did have black slaves,' said Briscoe.

'What?' asked Prof.

'Everybody enslave us,' said Briscoe.

'I've never enslaved anybody,' said Allen, desperate to dissociate himself from any link with slavery and its consequences. But his contrary mind instantly reminded him that an old friend from one of his books, Montaigne had observed that:

Every man has within himself the entire human condition.

When he had first discovered friends in his old books, Allen had been afraid that, by living so vicariously through the writings of others, he would be accused of being even further removed from reality than he already knew himself to be. But his sense of relief had been almost tangible when, in Michel de Montaigne's essays – which were addressed as to an old friend who had died – he came across the timeliest quote, which freed him to rejoice in the wisdom of others without reservation:

They Couldn't Have Known

I quote others only to better express myself.

To Allen, Montaigne was still there beside him, on the train, now aged four hundred and seventeen. Whenever he could, Allen worked out the ages of the spirits of all his friends, or at least their messages. It helped prove their worth.

Another chap, Terry – Allen didn't know his second name – proposed:

I am a man and nothing human is foreign to me.

Naturally, Allen took this to mean that he was capable of doing evil and that, under certain circumstances, he might. It never occurred to him that these considerations applied to everybody and not just him; that he was no more susceptible to behaving in an evil way than anybody else. This would have been scant comfort, perhaps, but much more than he had ever allowed himself.

'Even the captin of the West Indies cricket team haffi be white,' said Briscoe,.

'What about George Hadley in 1948?' asked Prof, ashamed of his interest in cricket having once been a gangster.

'That was only for one match. For the series the captin haffi be white,' said Briscoe.

'Is it really like that?' asked Allen, despite himself as he did not want to prolong the discussion.

'Worse. Back home, black girls have white dolls with blonde hair and blue eyes, and draw pictures of themselves like that. Later, them straighten their hair and bleach their skin. Even me own mama buy the weave and try to get her skin more fair. She say black is lower; she never say black is power. Every John Crow think him pickney white. We still inna slavery inna wi own country. So what chance we have here?'

All the talk about race and then crows triggered an association in Allen's mind with Aesop's fable about a crow and a swan, but it had been used to promote racial prejudice, so he kept quiet. He also kept quiet about Aesop who, despite being white, had been a slave, although by now he guessed Briscoe would most likely already know that. Allen's interest in Aesop had been heightened by the fact that he had also reportedly been hideously ugly and even dumb. If he ever existed, that is.

'You've got a better job than me, and none of you West Indians are working in the fields over here,' said Allen, surprising himself with his forthrightness. Naturally he immediately remembered the British woman of African descent who had been refused entry into the Land Army four times during the war on the basis of her colour, until questions were asked in parliament.

Briscoe did not respond immediately. He knew nothing about the field girls living in greater poverty, suffering greater prejudice and working harder and in worse conditions than he ever had. He thought of them as coolies: dark and mean-looking, with narrow, pinched faces. He certainly didn't think of them as white. As far as he was concerned, white people never worked on the land. They only went near it to boss black people about.

Similarly, the field girls wouldn't have had a clue about Briscoe or his origins. Their knowledge of Africa came from *Tarzan* films at the makeshift cinema in Timbertown or the Fletham Playhouse; films in which there wasn't a single African. The supporting cast came from Hawaii and were paler than the field girls. Tarzan, a white man – King of the Jungle – had a beautiful white girlfriend called Jane and a very clever monkey friend. Tarzan swung through the trees, dropping down to fight lions, tigers, jaguars, leopards, pythons and crocodiles or alligators, while herds of dairy cows milled around.

'Trouble is, the pressure buildin. A big set of bouys now stormin Britain. Any corner you turn, odds on you bounce up a spade. These days every shipload is big news. It not like long time when forty or fifty straggled in. Now they comin by the hundreds. Worse, a lot are hustlers, spoilin it for us,' said Briscoe, revealing the typical prejudice of the pioneering immigrant.

'Why don't you go back then, mate?' asked Prof.

'When yuh go a foreign, yuh cyaan go back less yuh pockets full. An when us fellars who here long time see people runnin from there, is only logic it damn foolishness to go back,' said Briscoe.

'I've seen a notice in showbiz digs up west saying: "No Performing Animals. No Dancers. No Jugglers",' said Prof, ploughing on regardless.

'No Black and White Minstrels,' suggested Allen, who had seen pictures of them in a magazine, taking a risk, but finding it quite funny nonetheless.

When Prof chipped in with 'No Lodgers', Allen and Briscoe couldn't help laughing, whether he meant to be funny or not.

'Man, me dead from laugh,' said Briscoe, finally cheered by the madness.

It was the first time Allen had laughed with anybody but Gill.

II

Allen was overwhelmed by the crowds at Waterloo station, while Prof and Briscoe were completely relaxed.

'Ah! Home sweet home,' said Prof, sniffing the air.

They had just led Allen through the ticket barrier, when a thick-set bruiser moved in on them.

'Well, well, if it isn't our old mate Colmore!'

It was the first time Allen and Briscoe had heard Prof's real name.

'Teddy!' said Prof, shooting a glance at Allen and Briscoe.

'Who are these two weird-looking geezers?' asked Teddy.

'Just a couple of blokes I met on the train,' said Prof totally unconvincingly.

'Oh yeah! We 'eard you was coming up, let's all go and see Spot,' said Teddy.

Teddy raised a finger and a taxi broke out of the middle of the rank and came straight to them.

'Paddington. The Vienna Rooms,' said Teddy.

Briscoe and Allen looked quizzically at Prof, who just spread his hands and shrugged his shoulders in despair.

During the journey, Allen became increasingly car sick with the twisting and turning, so he was relieved when they finally pulled into the dingy courtyard at the back of a large, turreted, red-brick Victorian building.

'In you go, lads.'

The dimly lit, seedy-looking room, which contained several packed gaming tables, fell silent. The air was so thick with smoke that Allen thought the place was on fire and wondered why everyone was sitting there so calmly.

'Who the hell are these two?' asked an even bigger, well-dressed bruiser in a grey suit, looking at Allen and Briscoe.

'They came up with Colmore,' said Teddy.

'Right, stick 'em in the safe room till Spot gets back. We don't want no spade wandering about around 'ere anyway,' said Grey Suit.

Allen and Briscoe sat in the gloom of the small, windowless room, with a cluster of dusty filing cabinets and a large safe in the corner.

'Who's Spot?' enquired Allen.

'Jack Spot, self-proclaimed King of the London Underworld. Him control most of the gambling: on-course betting, horses an dogs; boxing an pavement. Nuh drugs or vice, though.'

'How do you know all that?' asked Allen.

'It's where we immigrants live, between the Arch, Water, Gate and Grove.'

'Where?'

'Marble Arch, Bayswater, Notting Hill Gate and Ladbroke Grove.'

'Sorry I got you into this mess, Briscoe, but I did try and avoid you.'

'No worries, man. I can see why now.'

'Well, it was the police I was worried about. I didn't see this coming. I should never have felt sorry for Prof in the first place. Talk about no good turn goes unpunished.'

'If yuh sorry fi mawga dog, him turn an bite yuh,' said Briscoe, quoting one of his traditional phrases with the same message.

'Spot sounds like a dog, anyway,' said Allen, not quite understanding.

They sat in gloomy silence for a while.

'It cold in here, mon. Nuff respect mi have now fi yuh rass climate,' said Briscoe, parodying his patois to emphasise his foreignness with regard to the weather.

'On the boat comin over we heard on the BBC the Colonial Secretary seh that cos we had British passports, they had to let wi land, but there was nothin to worry about, cos we wouldn't last one winter in England anyway.'

'You missed our worst winter ever.'

'When was that?' asked Briscoe.

'The winter of 1946-7. Lizzie told us it was coming.'

'How she know?'

'In the autumn of 1946 leaves still hadn't fallen by St Martin's Day, onions grew thick skins, bees blocked their hives deeper with wax, and ladybirds clustered in sheltered places.'

'Did it come as bad as she seh?'

'Not at first, but she also said: "As the light lengthen, so the cold strengthens." Which it did after Christmas. Freezing rain covered surfaces in glassy black ice. Trees crashed down under the weight of ice on their branches. Leaves of evergreens tinkled and rattled in the wind. When we trod on the frozen grass it snapped and crunched like breaking glass.

'Different types of birds huddled together in large groups, but still froze on the branches, as did our chickens on their perches. The January King cabbage crop was ruined. We were cut off for months, but we had everything we needed, perhaps because we were poor.'

Briscoe shifted uncomfortably. He hadn't heard a white man talking about being poor before, and he felt as if he were being robbed of something.

'We lived on Lizzie's famous rabbit stew she made in a pot hanging over the open fire. It was so cold we could catch the rabbits by hand, and sometimes even pheasants for a treat. We hacked potatoes and root vegetables out of the ground.

'The Pits froze nearly solid and we made a slide right across one. It was scary looking into the depths and seeing the long, green weeds frozen in the ice. On still nights, bitter cold air slipped down the slopes into every dip, so cold you couldn't breathe.'

'Must be relief when it over,' said Briscoe.

'No. When the thaw set in, there were massive floods. Those wattle-and-daub cottages that had no stone foundations were washed away in a mass of mud, straw and reeds, like giant drowning hedgehogs. We could only tell where the rivers and the Pits were by the willow and alder thickets on their banks.

'Spring sowing was delayed. Our famous pea crop is shallow rooting and needs a lot of water, but not that much. Lizzie used to say: "Get up with thy barley lande, dry as thou can: at March, as thou layest it, so loke for it than." But nobody had a clue what she meant. We didn't hear a thrush until March and the hawthorn didn't flower until June.'

'When should them have done?'

'Hawthorn normally flowers in May, which is why it's known as May blossom. Thrushes can sing all winter, but they usually start about February.'

'Our thrush birds sing all year round,' said Briscoe, upon whose island of origin most things went on all year round.

'Did you live in a town or the country?' Allen followed up.

'Country. Same area as Denzil, but he live in the hills.'

'Did you know him out there?'

'No chance. We no mix in the same places.'

'What was your house like?'

'Like your wattle-and-daub, but with tin roofs. Corrugated iron, that is. My wife and picknies still there. Nice place. Yet I get asked if I lived in the jungle,' said Briscoe.

'Well, if people genuinely don't know they have to ask and

then at least they learn. "The confession of ignorance is the beginning of knowledge,"' said Allen, repeating one of his favourite quotes and confusing Briscoe with his change of speech.

'What do you grow on your island?'

'There still some big sugar estates, the oldest in the world, and banana plantations. But up in the hills, where Denzil live, them grow vegetables like here: tomatoes, cucumbers, Irish potatoes, onions, and specially carrots and cabbages. More cabbage eaten than any other food on the island.'

Allen thought that was something The Cabbage King would have been interested to hear.

'But in the parish where Denzil and me come from, them tearin up the land for bauxite.'

'What's that?'

'Aluminium ore. Everything covered in red dust from the opencast mining, including us, so they call us "red men". They also call us that because many light-skinned people there with blue or green eyes. Descendants of Europeans.'

'Slave owners?' asked Allen, horrified at the implications.

'Some, but also them survivors of shipwrecks; prisoners from England, Ireland and Scotland; and planters, many from Glasgow. Campbell a common name in the island,' said Briscoe.

'There's an old phrase: "Never trust a Campbell",' said Allen.

'Raatid, man. Me thought it was: "Never trust a camel." Them one time on the island, yuh know.'

'That's better advice,' said Allen, who had read about camels' bad tempers and grudge bearing.

'Also, descendants of German and Polish indentured labour. They keep themself to themself, so many born with problems,' said Briscoe.

Allen recognised with a pang the parallel with the situation at the Rookery, although there it was the neighbours – who considered them stupid, diseased, mad, possessed of black magic powers and emitting a pungent body heat that would shrivel an apple in their hands – who isolated the inhabitants.

Allen knew such wretched and 'infectious' outsiders were invented by societies around the world to promote a feeling of wellbeing and identity for the insiders. But it was difficult, if not impossible given his anxious state of mind, not to fear that he could well be contaminated in the ways described.

The stranger, more unreal, grotesque and frightening his thoughts, the more he felt compelled to follow them through, almost as if he were mesmerised. He felt driven to find out the worst. In a state of sensitisation and fatigue, he would deliberately probe to see how bad his thoughts could be. Being so suggestible, he couldn't resist testing his suggestibility. He suspected there was no limit to how bad it could get.

III

The door crashed open.

'Right, the spade comes with us,' said Grey Suit.

'No he doesn't, fatso. He only travelled up with us,' said Allen, who, as usual, was less frightened of real dangers than his inner demons. His dramatic change in demeanour took Briscoe by surprise.

'Shut up, you funny-looking scumbag,' said Grey Suit.

'Shut up yourself, fatso,' said Allen, to Briscoe's total astonishment.

Grey Suit hesitated. He was as superstitious as everybody else and this bloke looked really weird.

'Hwat iss thin nam, uh?' hissed Allen, exploiting the hesitation.

Standing behind Allen, Briscoe heard only the strange phrase and thought it entirely responsible for Grey Suit backing off with a look of horror on his face.

At that moment, there was a bustle in the gaming room and a voice said: 'Spot's 'ere.'

An immaculately dressed man wearing a trilby and with a huge cigar in his mouth appeared in the doorway. Allen's attention was drawn to the large mole on his left cheek, at the same time noting the man's flicker of resentment as he noticed Allen's glance.

Allen couldn't believe he had been trapped by the same inherent attention to facial details as others by such a small blemish. *How could he blame people for being so repelled by him? He couldn't. It was pure biology, against which a wonderful life and friendship with Gill could not prevail.*

'Bring them both in here,' said Spot.

Grey Suit thrust Allen and Briscoe into the gaming room. There was no sign of Prof.

'Who the hell are they?' asked Spot.

'They came up with Colmore.'

'Did they now? Perhaps Colmore will be able to tell me what 'appened at that bloody airport fiasco. I haven't seen those other two wasters since they botched it up,' said Spot looking more interested.

Allen tensed. Spot was obviously the one who had sent the gang members down for the raid, but didn't yet know about Allen's involvement. Considering Prof's alienation from the gang, the gun incident and the total failure of the raid, Allen feared for Prof's safety. *He should never have helped him in the first place. Perhaps then Prof wouldn't have had the nerve to go ahead, despite the threats from the gang. If Prof let on that he, Allen, had been the one that had caused the gun to go off, there would be trouble for him and now Briscoe. Why had he not totally ignored Briscoe on the platform? He shouldn't have cared what Briscoe would have thought; he would have been much better off thinking it was yet another case of prejudice. But oh no, he had just had to let Briscoe know that he was not being discriminated against. Again, no good turn had gone unpunished.*

'Look, my mate here just sat with us on the train,' said Allen.

'Your mate? A spade?' said Spot with a look of surprise.

Briscoe was almost as surprised by Allen calling him his mate.

'OK. Let 'em go. We don't want no more trouble with the spades,' said Spot.

To their amazement, Allen and Briscoe were shoved out into the courtyard.

'You were a bit easy on them, Boss, especially the spade. You know the trouble they're causing us opening all those dumps they call clubs,' said Grey Suit.

'Yeah, and we don't want no more. It might be 'andy to 'ave one on our side,' said Spot.

As they stood outside in the courtyard, Allen and Briscoe couldn't quite believe their luck.

'Rass, man, that was close, what you seh to mek that bruiser back off? Some sort of Obeah?'

'No,' said Allen, not knowing what Obeah was, but guessing it was something similar to the witchcraft Lizzie was often accused of practising.

'I asked him what his name was in Anglo-Saxon. Lizzie taught me. By the way, Briscoe, what's your other name?'

'Taximan.'

'Taximan?'

'What's wrong, man? It's what everybody call me back home. No different from Butcher or Baker.'

'That's true. I wonder why you never come across a Candlestickmaker, though,' said Allen.

'What's yours?' asked Briscoe.

'Aglab,' said Allen.

'Aglab?' said Briscoe with some relish.

'Yes, I saw the name on some parish list. There were dozens in our village.'

'Where you goin now?' asked Briscoe.

'I don't know, now that Prof has disappeared. I hope he's all right.'

'Well we can try and find him,' said Briscoe.

'OK,' said Allen only too aware of how guilty he would feel if he just abandoned Prof to his fate.

'Good, let's get over to my area,' said Briscoe.

'Where's that?'

'Ladbroke Grove.'

They went by bus as Briscoe correctly assumed that Allen wouldn't have been able to face travelling by tube.

'Ah! Home sweet home from home,' said Briscoe breathing deeply on their arrival.

They strolled past huge bomb sites, which reminded Allen of Hadleyrow in miniature, except here nature was making inroads into man-made devastation, rather than the other way around.

In the short time since the war, life had flooded back into the bomb craters and burnt-out ruins of London. The deeper craters had water in the bottom and were indistinguishable from the small borrow ponds and marl pits in Hadleyrow. They teemed with life, which had arrived just days after the bombs fell: insect larvae, water boatmen, pond skaters, snails, fish eggs on birds' legs, frogs and newts.

The charred brick walls of the ruins were green with plants colonising every nook and cranny: mosses, ferns and flowering plants, including the aptly named gallant soldier and London pride. Buddleia, the butterfly bush, flourished even on brick walls. Rosebay willow herb or 'fireweed', rare in London until the Blitz cleared sites for it, grew tall. In a few weeks' time, its purple flowers would give the impression that the embers of the burnt-out buildings were still glowing, and later their fluffy white seeds would look like clouds of smoke as the embers died. At night, the sweet smells and ghostly white trumpets of bindweed, or hedge-bell, silently summoned the moths and, in their wake, the noisily silent bats.

Small thickets of willow, birch, sycamore and alder had sprung up, providing cover for birds including a newcomer from Europe, the black redstart or bomb-bird. City pigeons and house sparrows preferred the buildings. A crow flew overhead but Allen didn't see any rooks.

Here and there, people had cultivated small allotments, growing crops in the area for the first time since Anglo-Saxon times. A handful of chickens wandered about, pecking aimlessly, while others fluffed their feathers up in the dust bowls they had scratched out of the soil.

'That one look like a peel-neck, scraggy, red-feathered senseh fowl,' said Briscoe, pointing to a sorry-looking specimen.

'What's that?' asked Allen.

'A chicken which scratch up buried Obeah tricks.'

'Looks like a Rhode Island Red at the bottom of the pecking order to me,' said Allen with some feeling. He knew chickens to be intelligent animals with a complex social organisation that could break down under pressure, typically resulting in violent bullying of the lowliest; a position that was familiar to him.

A movement near his feet caught Allen's eye. Glancing down, he saw an injured lizard trying to crawl away. He could see that it had lost one of its back legs and its tail. But despite its pitiable state, it was still beginning to show streaks of green in vain preparation for the mating season. It seemed to so embody Allen's fate that he gathered up the lizard gently and put it in his pocket, where it seemed to settle straight away.

'What you doin, man?' asked Briscoe with a look of horror on his face.

'Well, it wouldn't have lasted long with those chickens around.'

'So? So?' stammered Briscoe.

'So, I'm going to look after it until it's stronger and let it go in a safer place,' said Allen.

'Raatid, man!' Briscoe shook his head in complete disbelief. Allen putting the lizard in his pocket was the equivalent of him, Briscoe, putting a huge spider in his.

A big reddish-looking bruiser sauntered up to them. 'Wanna try our new club, man?' he asked.

'I've never been asked to join a club before,' said Allen.

Briscoe grinned and nodded to the bruiser, who led them around a corner, down some stairs and into a dingy half-basement flat.

'What the hell are you two doing here?' a familiar voice enquired, as a plush office chair, quite at odds with the dingy surroundings, swivelled round.

'Denzil!' Allen and Briscoe exclaimed simultaneously.

Denzil was as dismayed to see them as they were surprised to see him. They were the last people he wanted to see up there. Apart from the loss of face he would suffer by being seen with that damned naygar and weird white man, they both knew too much about him, which was dangerous.

'Well?' insisted Denzil.

'We came up with Prof,' said Allen.

'Where is he now?'

'We don't know, but we last saw him at Spot's place,' said Briscoe, forgetting he was talking to a fellow West Indian.

'He knows Spot?'

'Yes. He was one of his gang,' said Allen.

'Hmmm. We could make a connection there that might tek some pressure off. So, welcome to my club!' said Denzil, with a grandiose sweep of his arm around the smoke-filled room.

'Your club?' questioned Allen.

'Where d'you think I've been shipping all that airport stuff to on Sunday afternoons? I've got nuff champagne and cigarettes to run for years. All profit.'

Allen and Briscoe were dumbfounded.

'This mi cousin, Big Radish,' said Denzil, nodding towards the big, red-tinged bruiser who had brought them in. 'He'll be keeping an eye on you.'

'Big Radish?' Allen queried, reacting to the familiar name.

'Because him big and reddish. Drinks on the house,' said Denzil.

IV

Briscoe had wandered off to the gaming tables and Allen sat in a corner nursing a glass of rum and observing the scene. Gradually, Allen sensed the presence of a huge spider on the wall near his face. He froze. It was his phobia. Even though he thought he didn't care about anything any more, his subconscious knew better. He looked around, but nobody was taking the slightest bit of interest in the spider until, uncharacteristically, Denzil spotted Allen's discomfort.

'*Cenus malvernensis*,' said Denzil, wandering across.

'What?' asked Allen, astonished that Denzil, who had never shown any interest in nature, knew the Latin name for this monster.

'They name it from where they did first find it, in mi village, Malvern. They come in with the bananas and people bring them here to keep the cockroaches down,' said Denzil.

Despite his terror, Allen couldn't help but recall that the word 'malvern' meant 'evil alder grove', many of which could be found around the Pits, according to the older villagers.

With a mocking laugh, Denzil grabbed the spider in one hand and dumped it into Allen's drink. Allen was paralysed with fear at the sight of the huge spider flailing its legs around in the rum and threatening to get a foothold on the rim of the glass. The commotion attracted a crowd. Nobody else appeared to be afraid of spiders and most took great pleasure in Allen's terror.

Allen remained catatonic as the big black horror finally got a purchase on the rim of the glass and crawled out onto his sleeve. Suddenly, a woman screamed, and chairs and tables were scattered as the crowd fled. Looking down, Allen saw the lizard with one of the spider's legs hanging out of its mouth.

Stunned by the swirl of events, Allen was left alone in the empty bar. After a few moments, faces tentatively reappeared at the door. When they could see no trace of the lizard, which had returned to Allen's pocket, they slowly drifted back, looking at him in some awe.

Their fear of lizards had obliterated any memory of Allen's fear of spiders. Fear was very personal like that.

Allen couldn't understand what was going on. His status seemed to change so quickly around here. Apart from white English, he barely knew what he was supposed to be any more. *Hero or coward? Perhaps both.* He had noticed that the Spaniard who had the same ears as Gill had spoken of somebody being 'brave on that day' or 'afraid on that day', rather than one or the other as a permanent state. He would try to settle for that.

Briscoe picked his way through the upturned furniture.

'Raatid, yuh a man of iron, fi sure,' said Briscoe in awe.

'What are you talking about?' Allen asked him.

'That lizard, man. Back home, lizard them incarnations, omens, warnins of evil. If lizard bite yuh, yuh must plunge into water or die, even though some did die doing just that. The "croaker" that walk on ceilings a national phobia on him own.'

Allen was bemused. He loved lizards; they were perhaps his favourite creatures. It was the contents of the lizard's stomach in his pocket that terrified him.

Idly looking around, Allen noticed that a new huddle had formed at the bar, with Big Radish sitting in the middle, arm-wrestling all newcomers for whatever they wanted to wager.

Big Radish was a legend back home and now in London for having wrestled and killed what everybody thought was an alligator. This was a reasonable assumption, as he had been working as a bouncer at Alligator Pond, a bauxite port on the south coast of his island. But, like most legends, it had little to do with reality. He had, in fact, concocted the story to impress the bargirls waiting for the next bauxite ship to dock. The story had gone around the island, and by the time it had got back the man-eater had clamped its jaws on Radish's leg, who, with his bare hands, had prised its jaws apart until they dislocated and penetrated its skull. He was so seduced by the story himself that when a government nature conservation officer had come sniffing around to investigate the rumour that someone had killed a protected crocodile – there being no alligators on the island – Radish had felt guilty and, despite the heat, had worn long trousers.

'OK, you de only one lef nuh,' said Big Radish with a grin.

Allen looked around to see who he was talking to. There was nobody else, just him. It was a frivolous challenge. Big Radish had only made it to involve the strange white man rather than in any seriousness. Big Radish always looked out for the underdog, which is why he took such good care of his girls. Woe betides anybody who abused them; more, that is, than the abuse they suffered in being there in the first place.

Allen's arms looked like sticks next to Big Radish's massive, overblown bulk, and Big Radish was surprised by the equanimity with which Allen accepted the challenge. Actually, Allen wouldn't have accepted if he hadn't been so preoccupied with the contents of his pocket.

Allen took up the strain, holding the tension easily, and when he felt Big Radish faltering, largely out of shock, he exerted just enough effort to put Big Radish's arm down. The only things that concerned Allen were being in such a close face-to-face situation and avoiding any extra distortion of his mouth through the effort.

It all happened so quickly that Allen didn't have time to realise that, having mistakenly accepted the challenge in the first place, it would have been better to have feigned losing. His reputation wouldn't have suffered, while Big Radish's certainly had in being beaten by this stringy white man. There were gasps of disbelief from the group of beaten participants amid much sucking of teeth; not only at Allen's impossible victory, but because it also meant that he would have beaten each of them as well. As a result, some decided Allen must be a Meki-man and shivered.

The barman turned away and wiped a few glasses. He didn't want to witness Big Radish's discomfort and embarrassment. Big Radish was a good influence around the place and his mere presence was enough to keep the peace.

'Try the other arm,' a man in the crowd said.

'Good idea,' said Allen, wishing he had always had second chances to put right the things he had regretted in the past. To him the past was not gone to be forgotten. It wasn't even past. Once created it remained to haunt him.

The barman turned back. He had expected this white man to brag about his unlikely victory and make the most of it in front of the stunned audience, but there wasn't the slightest sign of that.

Big Radish was in turmoil. *What had just happened couldn't have happened. But now he had a chance to put things straight.* This time Big Radish easily forced Allen's arm down flat onto the table.

'Try the right one again,' pestered the crowd, eager for the weird white man to be put back in his place.

Again, Big Radish put Allen down with ease. Big Radish shot Allen a glance as he and his group of acolytes moved away to play dominoes. Big Radish was mightily relieved that his public reputation had been restored, albeit a little tarnished. The arm-wrestling helped to maintain his invincible aura in a non-violent manner, and provided a good source of income. He also knew that it was a good indication of his overall strength.

At that point, Denzil emerged with a big grin on his face and a girl on each arm.

'What's up?' he asked Allen reluctantly, sensing the awkward atmosphere in the bar.

'Nothing. Big Radish has just beaten us all at arm-wrestling,' said Allen quickly.

'"Us?" You a fool yuhself. Leave dat fi de strong men dem,' said Denzil incredulously, forgetting to temper his patois for Allen.

Not able to sit around when there was any work to be done, Allen started tidying up the chairs and tables.

'Kiss me neck, look pan dat deh mashmout bredda, de alibotn work fi not'n,' one chap whispered to the astonished group, their entire history and personal experience having been based on white people exploiting their physical labour.

'Who dem callin alibotn?' asked Denzil.

'Me. What's an alibotn?' queried Allen. He had made out the sounds 'mash' and 'mout' well enough on his own.

'Alibotn satisfai wi enitin; alibotn work fi notn. Someone who thinks he's worthless, satisfied with anything, works for nothing. Someone stupid,' said Denzil, his speech finally under control.

Allen said nothing. He couldn't complain too much as that was exactly how he saw himself.

Denzil was embarrassed by the attention Allen was drawing to himself. He was beginning to suspect the worst of Allen, who never smiled, couldn't drive and, worst of all, hadn't yet taken the chance to go with any of the bargirls. Denzil had also noticed that Allen treated everybody as a complete equal, which he considered totally ridiculous.

Some things were essential for any male worth his salt as far as Denzil was concerned: good teeth, the ability to drive fast, and the ability to belly-wop women all night and make them cry out, although not necessarily in that order. Allen failed on all three, or four for those who counted the last one as two. Denzil could never separate them and therefore always counted them as one.

Denzil considered dumping Allen in the street, but with Jack Spot's men watching he didn't want to leave a loose cannon like Allen wandering around. Perhaps Allen would be his Yawsy-Bwoy, a character from Caribbean folk tales whose skin was scarred by 'yaws' – a tropical disease – and who, though ostracised, manages to save the day. Not that Denzil held out much hope.

He didn't care about Briscoe. Briscoe was so black nobody would take any notice of him, whatever happened.

V

Denzil had disappeared again and Briscoe had drifted away to watch the action on the gambling tables when one of the bargirls came over and sat with Allen.

'Buy me a drink, suh?'

'Yes, what would you like?' said Allen.

'Two double Scotches,' she shouted out to the barman.

'*Please*,' said Allen. 'You didn't say please.'

The girl stared at Allen in disbelief before breaking into peals of laughter.

'Weh yu carry come gi we yasso, Denzil?' she shouted across to Denzil, who was sitting with the two girls entwined around him.

'An buy me a patty, den,' she said to Allen.

'Certainly,' said Allen, not exactly sure what a patty was.

'Two patty deh ova deh so,' she shouted to the barman

again.

Allen opened his mouth to decline, but gave up.

'Dem a soon come, but nuh figet fi seh please an tanks,' the barman said, amid guffaws of laughter.

Allen was on his guard. He was becoming a figure of fun again, but this time for his manners. This had never happened in Hadleyrow. He had been denigrated for just about everything else, but not for his manners, which Lizzie had indelibly imprinted within him when he was young.

Allen could see that the girl was about to ask for something else, so he said: 'Order whatever you want, you don't have to ask.'

The girl looked at him askance. She wasn't used to this, and to her surprise she was even beginning to feel the slightest bit guilty about plying her trade on this innocent young chap with the funny mouth.

Duppy must ave boxed im dere, she thought.

He looked haunted and on guard, unlike the cruel, arrogant men who normally came in.

Briscoe came over, thinking Allen might need some support. He ordered a couple of rums for Allen and himself, and a Scotch for the girl, who was obviously trying hard to get drunk, as if she were preparing herself for some sort of ordeal.

'This is watered down, yuh know, man,' said Briscoe.

He looked pityingly at the girl and softly began to intone:

'Agnes o' de Village Lane
Fancy o' me childish will.'

'Do you know her?' asked Allen.

'No, man, she just remind me of me first sweetheart,' he

said, before continuing:

'Playin', now before me eyes
Sadly I remember still
How much once your love I prize.'

'Did you write it yourself?' Allen asked.
'No, man. It's a famous poem back home.'
The girl felt uncomfortable under Briscoe's gaze. She didn't want any black man getting between her and her white man. And she wasn't called Agnes, either. Taking her patty with her, she wandered off to find a friend to attract Briscoe away.

Allen stood up as she left the table.
'Nuh. Steh hya mi soon come,' she said, completely misunderstanding Allen's politeness and thinking he was trying to come with her.

'I know one about an Agnes. Saint Agnes,' said Allen.
'What does she do?' asked Briscoe.
Quoting from one of his old books, *Mother Brunch's Closet Newly Broke Open*, and sounding a bit strange as he tried to emulate Briscoe's style, Allen intoned:

'St Agnes, that's to lovers kind
Come ease the trouble of my mind.'

Encouraged by Briscoe's attention, he continued:

'Agnes sweet and Agnes fair
Hither, hither, now repair
Bonny Agnes, let me see
The lad who is to marry me
Now good St Agnes, play thy part
And send to me my own sweetheart

*And shew me such a happy bliss
This night of him to have a kiss.'*

There was a sudden, dramatic change in Briscoe's demeanour, and Allen realised he had somehow put the fear of God into him.

'Fi God sake, shet up,' Briscoe hissed. 'People deh bout who woulda kill a man fi a talk lika dat, an even me fi a listen. Dem tink we batty man dem for sure.'

Allen's first reaction was that the reference to 'batty men' was to do with cricket, and he wondered whether there were also 'bowly men' and 'fieldy men'. But his instincts told him it was yet another word for a homosexual man.

'I just recited it as it was written,' said Allen resignedly.

Allen had heard Briscoe and other West Indians bemoaning the welcome they had received in England, yet all the ones he knew had well-paid jobs in which they were treated as well as, if not better than, he had ever been. They found it hard to find good accommodation, but nobody was going to kill them for quoting poetry.

Realising that nobody had overheard them because of the cacophony of noise, mainly from those playing dominoes West Indian style, with much slamming of the 'cards' and leaping up and shouting, Briscoe calmed down.

The girl returned, having been unable to find anybody to attract Briscoe away as he was too black. Much to Allen's amazement, she plonked herself onto his lap, put her arm around his neck and started whispering into his ear. Allen couldn't understand what she was saying, but he could feel her warm breath on his ear, smell the whiskey on her breath and feel her firm bottom against his thighs as she wriggled about.

Allen was confused by this sudden intimacy.

Briscoe looked sad and returned to his soft refrain:

'Fus I saw your pretty smile
Loved your face so free o guile
An your soul so clear of stain
Agnes, Agnes o de lane
Agnes o de lane no more
For you went away, my pet
Agnes once so sweet an pure
To a miserable deat
Oh, de membrance brings me pain
Fallen Agnes o de lane!'

Allen had barely understood a word, but he sensed the sadness of it all. As far as he could tell, Agnes had fallen into debt, but that didn't seem to match Briscoe's sadness. The girl on his lap, however, understood only too well that it described her wretched situation as a bar girl. She wasn't dead yet, but she knew other girls who had once been just like her who were. She stopped wiggling about on Allen's lap and started quietly crying on his shoulder.

She whispered: 'Me did tink London town woulda be pretty-pretty and dat I could mek someting outta meself.'

'How can we help her?' Allen asked Briscoe, his heart breaking.

Briscoe stared at him long and hard to see whether he was making a cruel joke, and then looked around nervously.

'It difficult, man, she have nowhere to go. They take her earnins and keep her in debt so she can't run away. If we help her, they track her down and treat her worse. She not much more than a slave when it come to it. Same old business, no matter how it dress up.'

'What does she do for a living?' asked Allen, assuming from her behaviour that she wasn't married.

Again, Briscoe looked at him in blank amazement. 'Where have you been all your life?' he asked in as kindly a way as he could.

'Hadleyrow,' said Allen.

VI

Throughout this conversation, a fat, round-faced white man, with short, fair hair and thick, horn-rimmed glasses had been staring at Allen and the girl with his mean eyes. When he saw the atmosphere change between them and the girl start to cry, he got up and pushed his way across the crowded bar. He was wearing an untucked white shirt to hide his bulging beer belly. To Allen, he looked like a fat white toad, although Allen realised that wasn't fair to toads, which had beautiful golden eyes.

'Cheer up. Come with me, gal, eh,' he said in what sounded to Allen like an American accent. 'I'll show you a good time. Don't waste your time with this one, eh. He doesn't seem to know how to keep you happy, and we know what that means,' he said with a smirk at Allen. At this, he took her arm and pulled her off Allen's lap into a slow dance on the tiny patch of floor.

Allen was so surprised he was slow to react, but the girl didn't object and nobody in the bar took any notice, so he decided he would have to let it go. *Yet another insult to swallow.* If she had asked for help he would have stopped the man, but he seemed well-known to the other girls and the locals at the bar, so Allen thought it better not to make a fuss for Denzil's sake. There was something about the man to which Allen instantly took against: the self-assurance, the arrogance and the superciliousness.

> *'And after all, many gals richer than me*
> *Pretty white girlies of better degree*
> *Live as I do, an are happy an gay*
> *Then why shouldn't I be as happy as they?'* intoned Briscoe in his sad, singsong rhythm.

It finally dawned on Allen what had really happened to Briscoe's first love. She must have left their village and somehow ended up as a bar girl in a city, which was why this girl had triggered Briscoe's melancholy.

'Your Agnes reminds me of a girlfriend called Anne of Oxford Street,' said Allen.

'That's a funny name,' said Briscoe, relieved that Allen had at least had a girlfriend.

'Well, nobody knew her real name.'

'How did you meet her?'

'No, I never met her. I read about her.'

Briscoe's heart sank.

'How come she did in a book?'

'Well, she was a young runaway who lived on the streets of London and was kind to a homeless young man. He became a famous writer and wrote about her and her kindness, describing how he saw her in his dreams years later, more beautiful than she was by lamplight in Oxford Street and no older. Which is how I read about her and why I feel sad for her,' said Allen.

'Is she still alive?'

'No, the two of them lived hundreds of years ago.'
Briscoe's heart sank further.

In fact, this writer had been of great help to Allen with the observation:

For it may be observed generally that, wherever two thoughts stand related to each other by a law of antagonism, and exist as it were by mutual repulsion, they are apt to suggest each other.

Allen loved this quote. It was ingrained in his memory, but he felt that it could have been refined by the addition of the words 'in a contrary way'. In other words, only for the worse, never for the better; a 'bad' thought never being apt to suggest a 'good' one. But, with De Quincey there with him, Allen thought he had better not. Thomas De Quincey, English essayist, master of poetic prose and staunch abolitionist, would have been one hundred and sixty-five if he hadn't died aged seventy-four.

Allen had also discovered, beyond coincidence as far as he was concerned, that De Quincey was mentioned in a Sherlock Holmes short story, 'The Man with the Twisted Lip'. The fact that this story also highlighted the adverse effects of opium addiction and was inspired by De Quincy's account of his experiences with the drug, gave Allen pause for thought with regard to his admiration for De Quincy's work. He could never separate artists from their art.

De Quincey had become addicted to laudanum, a mixture of alcohol and opium, which he took to relieve chronic toothache. Lizzie knew of an ancient anaesthetic containing opium, mixed with the juices of various herbs, which was supposed to produce a sleep that lasted several days. But some of the ingredients were so dangerous she never dared to try it.

Instead, Lizzie had prepared a powder from the bark of alder, willow and birch to dull the pain of toothache – as Allen had read the ancient Greeks had done – which actually worked. Yet Saint Apollonia, virgin and martyr of Alexandria from the third century, was still invoked locally against toothache.

To offset the imbalance between science and religion, when he had read that Horace Wells was the first to use nitrous oxide to pull a tooth painlessly in 1884, Allen had carved 'Wells' deep into the smooth, grey bark of a sycamore tree near the Pits. It wasn't much of a memorial, but it was better than nothing.

One of the German refugees wandering past some time later couldn't believe his eyes, assuming that it referred to Otto Wels, leader of the only party in Germany to vote against the granting of absolute power to Hitler. Allen had unwittingly commemorated two heroes for the effort of one.

Briscoe had left to get some more cigarettes in little red and white packets of four when the girl wandered back to Allen's table.

'Yuh nuh eat yuh patty yet,' she said, sitting down close to him.

Luckily, Lizzie had taught him: 'Be not 'asty eatin' pie or pasty.'

As a result, he always looked inside a pie or pasty before eating it. When he prised the patty open he was faced with a pastry boat full of squirming blowfly maggots, which, on exposure to the light, wriggled out all over the plate with amazing speed and agility.

The girl screamed and recoiled in horror, but Allen wasn't

too put out. He was used to maggots. In fact, Lizzie had once said: 'Always choose them apples with the maggots. Better the maggots youm see than the poison youm don't.'

In response, he would trot out his one and only joke: 'What's worse than finding a maggot in your apple?' To which Lizzie would in turn dutifully reply: ''Alf a maggot.' Although she really wanted to say: 'No maggot'.

The girl looked on in astonishment as Allen attempted to catch all the maggots and put them back, but each time he caught a few he couldn't get the pastry lid back on quickly enough before more got away. On returning the patty, he apologised for letting some of the maggots escape and meekly accepted another one in the way of compensation, as he didn't want to make too much fuss.

The girl, who by now was getting drunk, started urging Allen to go into one of the rooms with her. Allen grew increasingly uncomfortable. Even if he hadn't been damaged, he was so innocent when it came to sexual matters that he wouldn't have known what to do anyway. The only thing he did know about the subject was that 'protection' was important if you didn't want a baby. So, when he was out with Gill, he had always carried a Brussels sprout stalk as a cudgel, not that he knew what he was supposed to be protecting them from.

It didn't occur to him to go next door with the girl and offer her twice the money just to sit with him for a suitable length of time before returning to the bar in order to do her a favour — to save face, for want of a better phrase — and perhaps even to learn something. He didn't think like that. All of this was too sudden and too new for him to act with any guile. Anyway, it was Gill he yearned for, not just any girl.

'Sorry,' said Allen.

The girl downed her drink in one go, pulled a face and

moved over to a group of soldiers who had just arrived.

'Rhaatid, yu a wutless bwoy,' she said as she moved away. 'What yu need is a good Front-End-Lifter to big yu up nice.'

She had persuaded the kitchen staff to keep a pot of 'mannish water' – a salty soup of entrails, testicles and head of goat – to feed to her customers, but the kitchen staff had drunk it all themselves. So she used horse tonic whenever she could get it and kept some small spiders in a jar for the same purpose. She and the kitchen staff, were wasting their time, of course, as these were about as effective as other such remedies around the world, including those used in Hadleyrow. Generally it wasn't a problem, as most of her customers were sex maniacs anyway.

Allen settled further back into the corner and longed to be alone in a hedgerow in Hadleyrow watching the hares in the rain amid the cool, green countryside, or at least what was left of it.

He wondered what Gill was doing.

VII

Allen became aware of the Big Fat White Toad standing next to his table. 'You see that weirdo on the next table, eh? He doesn't go with the girls. He only hangs around these places because he's covering up the fact that he's queer. Q-U-E-E-R,' said the Big Fat White Toad with a smirk on his face.

Caught by surprise once again, Allen involuntarily turned to look at the next table. It was empty. Puzzled, he turned back to see the Big Fat White Toad waddling back to the group that was gathered around the bar. The anger Allen had been suppressing for weeks for the sake of other people's peace and quiet began to well up to bursting point. *What right had that Big Fat White Toad to call him anything?*

He had overheard enough to know that queers were men who went with men rather than women. At first he couldn't imagine what men might do to each other, and when he had heard, he wished he hadn't. Either way, he had the sense to realise that queers could no more choose to be who they were than he had chosen to be who he was; that they could choose their actions but not their instincts.

Despite Allen's unfamiliarity with patois, it was becoming apparent that, in Denzil's club, the hatred was fiercer and the language more creative with regard to homosexuals than towards any other group. Any man with a fenky-fenky, mincing walk, even if he was suffering from ingrown toenails, bunions or any foot problem that prevented him from walking in a manly way was – as it was 'a mixed race ting; a white people ting' – an effeminate white pussy hole.

Allen suspected that those singing the songs would have approved if landladies had put up notices saying: 'No Effeminate White Pussy Holes'.

This hatred was even expressed in songs: 'We dreamin of a new island, when batty man fi dead.' And, more puzzlingly: 'Bun a fire pon a kuh pon mister fagoty, ears ah big ben up and a wince under agony, poop man fi drown a yawd man philosophy.'

Briscoe had refused to translate, but Allen guessed that it was something like Guy Fawkes Night, only with some paradoxical drowning involved. He wondered what sort of philosophy could celebrate such horrors. In Hadleyrow, Hallowe'en and Midsummer had been celebrated with bonfires, but both had been extinguished by Guy Fawkes on the Fifth of November, when the burning of a Catholic was celebrated. As a lad, it had never occurred to Allen that there was anything barbaric about burning the effigy of a man, but when it did, he winced at the thought and couldn't watch the flames as they consumed the Guy. But at least he had never tried to rescue it.

Similar venom was aimed at women who only loved women. Allen hadn't heard of these in Hadleyrow and found the idea even more unfathomable. But here they were a similar source of artistic creativity, as expressed in a song he heard in Denzil's club:

When yuh hear a Sodomite get raped
But a fi wi fault
Two women gonna hock up inna bed
That's two Sodomites dat fi dead.
Bwoy dem kinda gal naasti, sah!
But dis caan happen, two shutpan caan join.

When Allen had asked Briscoe to translate, Briscoe had nearly choked. Allen knew Sodomites had come from Sodom near the Dead Sea in biblical times, but he wasn't sure how they had arrived in the Caribbean.

And now the Big Fat White Toad, without ever having met Allen before, had exposed him to this potentially deadly threat. When the Big Fat White Toad got back to his gang at the bar, they all turned to stare at him. One of them started wiggling his nose like a rabbit, while another made strange, limp-wristed movements with his hands. Again, in innocent surprise, Allen looked around to see who all this was aimed at.

Because he had been mocked all his life, and because he was insecure, Allen was vulnerable to every perceived slight and insult. But because he was competitive, he felt the need to meet every challenge. And because retaliation had to be suppressed in everyday life, he simmered with resentment and bore grudges, which was like swallowing poison for a prolonged period in a bid to cause the offender to suffer.

Whenever he could he had always taken off on a long run over the fields. The relief of doing something so natural in such beautiful surroundings had always worked its magic, so that, although he couldn't forgive or forget the insults, his anger was dissipated. Even in the sphere of emotion the solution to pollution was dilution.

But he couldn't do that in this case, so the anger built up like a pent-up volcano. He wanted to disfigure the Big Fat White Toad so he would know what it was like to be alienated, insulted, mocked and attacked; always by a stinking, cowardly mob that had to outnumber its victims, like the hounds and the hare. *Well, this hare had had enough. He would take on the hounds around the bar. He would take on the whole lot of them.*

Allen pushed his chair back, stood up and squeezed his way across the crowded dance floor, involuntarily saying: 'Excuse me please,' as he went. He couldn't help himself.

He grabbed a glass of white rum from the table of a surprised customer, intent on driving it into the face of the Big Fat White Toad. However, even in his anger he realised as he drew near that he couldn't do such a thing and lost his resolve. Even in the heat of the moment he remembered a line about 'bold action being sicklied over with the pale cast of thought'.

Coming upon the sniggering group at a pace, focused entirely on the Big Fat White Toad, he still didn't know what to do. *What could he do? What should he do?* He saw the Big Fat White Toad getting bigger and fatter and whiter.

Allen was nearly upon him when the decision was made for him. He slipped on the tiled floor, wet with spilled drinks, and as he fell he grabbed the Big Fat White Toad. As they both crashed to the floor in a writhing heap, Allen's main concern was to avoid dislodging or harming the lizard in his pocket.

Disentangling himself and springing up, leaving the Big Fat White Toad heaving on the floor like a beached seal, Allen was angry that he hadn't carried out his plan to inflict serious damage on the Toad's face, even though he knew he would have spent the rest of his life regretting it.

Nevertheless, Allen's ill-conceived attempt at getting back at the Big Fat White Toad had been partially successful. By the time the Big Fat White Toad had been helped up, the story that he had been involved in a public demonstration of affection in Denzil's club with another white batty man was already out the door and on its way around the tenements and clubs. So for a while the Big Fat White Toad's reputation was in tatters and he was exposed to the same potentially fatal consequences as Allen. Even when the true story caught it up, the reaction amongst most had been: 'Yu nebba see sumoke widout fiyah.'

The estranged husband of one of the bargirls, embittered with jealousy and resentment towards Denzil, whom he blamed for his wife's cruel fate, took his cue from the furore, and tried to start a rumour that Denzil was a batty man, but it never made it out the door; unlike the husband, who was slung out for being such a 'fool-fool fi troo'.

On hearing of the incident, Denzil turned a deathly pale. Normally he would have flaunted this natural bleaching in his frantic efforts to distance himself from those dammed naygas, but on this occasion he kept out of sight in his private room at the club, wondering how the hell he could sort out any damage to his reputation. Even as his mind raced, however, he admired his temporary 'high' complexion in the mirror.

Denzil need not have worried, as everyone knew only too well that he would never have had anything to do with batty men. Luckily for Allen, this also proved to the crowd that he couldn't possibly be a batty man either, although all agreed he was the weirdest white man they had ever seen.

Cheered by the reassurances shouted by his friends through the door regarding his bigotry and prejudices, Denzil re-emerged into the front bar, downed a couple of glasses of cowneck, grabbed a spiced pickled herring and shouted to one of his women to cook him up some salt codfish fritters, peppered shrimp and fried cassava bread. He had no trouble sourcing supplies.

Denzil had an irrepressible character and immediately worked on further retrieving the situation. He didn't waste time wallowing in the aftermath of bad luck or mistakes. Generally, this was a good life strategy, except for the young children playing in dusty yards back home without a daddy in sight. He might never see any of them again, except perhaps for some of the daughters he might unknowingly meet in a bar some time in the future.

VIII

Allen staggered outside, desperate for a breather and for some contact with nature. He took a deep breath and realised that, since leaving Hadleyrow, he had experienced fewer of his terrifying thoughts. This proved that, born as they were from the internal world of fearful imagination, the chance of obtaining relief from them increased the less it was sought and the more he was distracted by real experiences.

One of his old friends turned up to share this wisdom:

Richard Baxter, English Puritan church leader, poet and theologian, who would have been three hundred and sixty-nine if hadn't died aged seventy-six. Allen had read that his ghost was still seen in Kidderminster. Not that he had to go up there to see him, as Richard Baxter always arrived when he was needed to advise Allen to:

> *Take less notice of your troublesome thoughts. If you answer them, they will never be done with you. Take no notice of them and they will become weary. Be sure that you keep yourself constantly employed as far as your strength will bear.*

The sun shone weakly through the city gloom. He had no idea how long he had been away from Hadleyrow. In terms of new experiences, it felt like a lifetime.

He wondered what Gill was doing.

Briscoe and Radish had seen Allen leave and followed him out to keep an eye on him. The unlikely trio sat in silence, which hinted at friendships forming through shared experiences, despite their disparate origins.

'Do you know anything about that fat white man?' asked Allen, only now realising that referring to him as white suggested there were similarities between his own situation and what Briscoe termed being black.

'Yes, man. He live in Jamaica and when he come over on business trips he's always in here. Him one of them white fellas who must live in a black country to get somewhere. The only other place he lived is South Africa. He wouldn't do so well among his own kind.'

'Raatid, they're at it again,' said Radish.

'Oh no, man!' said Briscoe.

Allen looked up and saw that they were gazing over at a group in a far corner of the bombsite, where loud music had started thumping out.

'Wait here, mon. Deh need stoppin,' said Radish.

Briscoe had no intention of waiting there and followed at a distance. Left alone, Allen took the opportunity to check on his lizard. It was sluggish and very cold to the touch, so, finding himself alone, he slipped it into his mouth. It was nothing unusual to him. He had done it before in the fields to revive a lizard caught out in a cold snap. His mouth lacked the normal sensitivities as a result of the damage inflicted upon it over the years. He had even astounded people in the past by putting a large bumblebee in his mouth so they could hear it buzzing about inside. He had never been stung.

The music stopped and Allen saw an altercation between Radish and the group, with Briscoe hurrying up to join him. Allen followed and nobody noticed him as he joined one end of the group.

Egged on by the others, one of the gang was urinating against a grimy, semi-basement window, through which he just caught sight of the pale face of an old woman recoiling in horror.

Allen saw Radish confronting the apparent leader of the gang, a giant of a man who was built like a gorilla. Radish looked as though he sensed he had met his match even before he was felled by a huge blow. Briscoe, following up, was simply brushed aside. Allen rushed forward and grabbed one of the Gorilla's arms, unable to reach around the Gorilla's biceps even with both hands.

'Coo deh, look wot we got here,' said the Gorilla when he became aware of Allen hanging onto his arm. Pinning Allen down on a pile of rubble, he pushed his face right into Allen's and said: 'Come den, rabbit man. Mek we look pan yu mout.'

Sensing more trouble than they had bargained for, the gang

began to break up. At great personal risk to his reputation, one ran to the police station for help. A few thought they should help the strange white man but weren't sure why or how. They spent some time trying to work out their best plan of action and came to the conclusion that: 'Kakruoch no bizniz iina faul fait.' So, like cockroaches, they didn't interfere in a fowls' fight.

Despite his apparently desperate situation, Allen couldn't believe his luck. Emitting a weird gurgle through his clenched lips, he gently aligned the lizard up with his tongue towards an avenue of escape from the dark, warm, wet cavern in which it had mysteriously found itself.

The lizard tentatively poked its head out through the hole between Allen's lips. If Allen hadn't gently blocked off its retreat with his tongue and forced it forwards, it would have shot back into its sanctuary at the screams that greeted its appearance. When the Gorilla and the remains of the group saw the lizard emerge from Allen's strange mouth they all recoiled in utter horror. They knew they were in the presence of Great Evil.

As soon as he felt the Gorilla loosen his grip, Allen unleashed all his pent-up fury to break free and leap off the heap of rubble. He was so quick that everyone who witnessed it convinced themselves that not only had this male version of a white witch spewed out a lizard, but that he had also flown across the yard. Briscoe shoved the shocked Gorilla backwards over Radish's slumped figure, causing the Gorilla to crack his formidable skull on an even more formidable piece of concrete, knocking him clean out. Radish came to and was unable to make any sense of the turmoil that surrounded him.

'What was all that about?' asked Allen as they staggered

back to Denzil's.

'That mob works for a Jamaican landlord who's getting rid of all the old lodgers so he can pack a load of West Indians in and charge them a fortune in rent,' said Briscoe, without a trace of patois in his subconscious attempt to dissociate himself from the offenders.

'Yes. British and Polish slum landlords do the same,' said Allen, trying to ease Briscoe's embarrassment.

'Yes, mon, dem all bastards, no matter weh dey from,' said Radish.

'What happened?' asked Denzil when they returned to the club.

Denzil had his suspicions that Radish was losing his powers and had been looking at the leader of that gang to replace him at the club.

'Him mash up de big man,' said Briscoe quickly.

Radish looked bemused for a moment.

'Yes he did, good and proper,' said Allen.

'Yuh see nuttin like it, man. Radish give im a beast lick. Me sey me cyaan believe it. Them jump an kick an gwan like a coolie duppy pon them,' said Briscoe, using his patois to increase the dramatic effect.

Radish couldn't remember a thing, but he had the distinct feeling they were covering for him somehow, so he kept quiet. He knew his powers were waning, and had already resolved to get out of the business as soon as he could. Things seemed to be getting more and more violent. He also knew there would be no end to it. *In de bad-mon bizness peace is beside de point. How cyaan yout set demself up, distinguish demself inna dere area, widout violence?* he pondered.

'When have you got to go back to the airport?' Allen asked Briscoe.

'Tonight. You comin?'

'No. I've got nothing to go back for. I'll try and get a job up here,' said Allen.

Briscoe looked doubtful but didn't say anything. He resolved to keep a lookout for Allen through his network of connections, just in case.

'Denzil's got other properties. I'll ask him if he can find you a room. Walk good, tek your time, less you buck your foot.'

PART TWO

CHAPTER ONE

I

Denzil didn't respond well to Briscoe's request to find Allen a room. As far as he was concerned, that weirdo had caused enough trouble and Denzil didn't want him in the area. But as Allen knew too much about him stealing from the airport, he reluctantly agreed.

'How far is it?' asked Allen.

'A couple of chains.'

'What's a chain?'

'The distance between the stumps,' said Denzil, to Allen's bemusement.

When they arrived at the rundown block of flats, a slim young woman ran out to greet Denzil. Despite carrying a young child, and with others hanging around her feet, she moved beautifully. With a pang, Allen was immediately reminded of Gill.

'Dis a mi woman an mi pickney dem,' said Denzil with a smirk, forgetting whom he was talking to.

Amid all the kissing and hugging, Allen saw Denzil say something to the woman as she looked back at Allen. 'Try don't look pon him mouth,' he had whispered, covering his embarrassment at being associated with such an obvious misfit Englishman. 'Im nuh skin im teet.' With a flash of inspiration, he added: 'Him did be a pilot in the war, but get badly wounded inna de face.'

'Poor brave man,' said the woman, duly impressed that Denzil had befriended such a distinguished man. Not that Denzil had to impress this woman; she was already sufficiently impressed by him.

Denzil beckoned Allen forward.

'Very pleased to meet you Mrs...' started Allen, before he was cut off by a huge guffaw from Denzil.

'No man, this not mi wife. She just have some of mi pickney them. One of mi baby-mothers.'

'Just call me Sonja,' the woman said to Allen with a smile, showing no resentment on hearing Denzil's description of her.

Allen was astonished that this wasn't Denzil's main family scene. Millions settled for much less.

To Allen's surprise he was immediately accepted into this large, noisy family and, even more to his surprise, he felt completely at ease. Sonja smiled at him warmly from time to time, and children of all ages scrambled around him.

It was the first time Allen had experienced such a large, uninhibited, happy household. The happy family scene coupled with the music and the spicy scents of cooking threatened to overwhelm his senses. He had always agreed with one of his old friends that life was a task to be worked off, but a crack had opened in his defences. *He had better be careful. Something terrible could happen; was bound to happen.* Lizzie used to say: 'When the chicken cluck the hawk is near' and he had been surprised to hear Briscoe say: 'When chicken merry, hawk deh near.'

Allen chatted easily with Sonja about the herbs she was

using in her cooking, some of which were completely new to him. However, Denzil didn't like the easy way they were getting along. Even though he didn't care too much for any woman, he made it clear with a glance that she had better restrict her attentions to him, or else.

He couldn't understand how any woman could even look at Allen, let alone talk to him. It was obvious Allen knew nothing about women and never would. He was also irritated by all the talk about plants between the two of them. He didn't want Allen to look like an effeminate white pussy hole when he, Denzil, was with him. He had only just recovered from the debacle at the club.

Even Denzil had been annoyed by the 'No Coloureds' notices in the windows of the houses around London, but he would definitely have put one up himself that said 'No White Batty Men Who Like Plants'. That would have been different.

With the inventive use of the Caribbean's rich language, constructing creative insults – even outside the dangerous subject of sexual orientation – was a national pastime on the islands. But although their mutual insults could sparkle, the islands could be baneful, grudging places of shadeism, rankings, skin bleaching and hair straightening. Racial profiling was ingrained in Caribbean society, as could be heard in the weary phrase: 'Everybody have prejudice, is so life go.'

Fine hair, high colour, and thin noses and lips were prized; all the racial legacy of slavery and colonialism in small, hierarchical societies that were riddled with anxieties about social class and colour through absolutely no fault of their own.

Light-skinned 'brownies' like Denzil formed a racial and economic middle class that was well off, even prosperous. However, being the least certain of their identity, isolated as they were between the two defining poles of the colour spectrum, they propagated a vicious form of colourism and class snobbery in a desperate attempt to distance themselves from the masses of destitute 'blacks', who were hard broke and desperate, with little stake in the so-called national identities of the islands.

References to 'adulterated beings' could still be heard throughout the islands. Denzil had made a comment once about sorting the sheep from the goats and had grown angry when Allen had innocently asked him which Denzil considered himself to be. Allen never got an answer, so he was still none the wiser. Allen had always been called a rabbit, so at least he knew he was neither sheep nor goat.

'Let's go. Me haffi pick up a new sign fi mi club,' Denzil said to Allen, not wanting to leave him alone with Sonja.

Allen marvelled at Denzil's helter-skelter life, while not feeling entirely sure that he should. Denzil lived for the moment to such an extent that it would be difficult to diagnose the onset of dementia in him.

Allen was puzzled by the fact that he was actually beginning to like Denzil, despite his shortcomings. There was just something likeable about him. Allen occasionally longed to be likeable, but realised that likeability had no moral value. Some of the most evil people had to be likeable in order to perpetrate their crimes.

Denzil parked up in another tenement yard, where a group of men spanning every age, colour and description sat around a central table thick with paper plates of half-finished rice and yellow curried goat; rum and beer bottles; and overflowing ashtrays. They all sat looking outwards at the surrounding fence, where there was an array of advertising signs of various shapes, sizes, colours and materials for every product and business imaginable: cigarettes, rum, beer, West Indian sauces and menus, alongside larger signs for cafes, restaurants and clubs.

They were greeted by a large, yellow-tinged man with a head like a big round breadfruit.

'Big Ben! Me come fi mi sign man and me want it quick,' said Denzil, pulling the man to one side and whispering the same explanation about Allen's appearance as he had done to Sonja.

Allen would have been mortified to know that Denzil had lied about his activities during the war, when in reality he and Gill had often lain in the fields watching the white vapour trails of the fighting aircraft criss-crossing the deep blue sky. They had lain in paradise on earth looking up at a scene in which young men, not much older than they, were being burnt alive in their cockpits.

Once he had had this thought, Allen had been no longer able to watch, so he had looked at Gill instead, with her head resting on a mossy cushion. The summer of the Battle of Britain had been glorious, the third-driest August of the century. Gorse and vetch pods had burst in the heat and scattered their seeds over her like black pepper, while tiny spiders drifted in the breeze on gossamer threads, presagers of 'goose summer'. Allen had stared at Gill's beautiful mouth and teeth as much as her eyes or her body. He was funny that way.

Perhaps because of his problems, Allen was obsessed by beauty, but he could make no sense of it. However, his observation that there was no correlation between beauty and fertility brought him some solace. *If beauty in mind and body was just a matter of chance with no reproductive advantage, could not the physically and mentally disadvantaged be seen to be carrying the burden of chances that failed to produce perfection? You couldn't have one without the other.* If this was true, it allowed him to imagine that, in a way, he had contributed to the lives of those he had envied from afar.

'Respect,' said Big Ben, thinking Allen looked a bit young to be a war hero. He hadn't had a white man at one of his sign-checking parties before, let alone a war hero. If he could make up a sign to mark the occasion it would help his business.

It was to be the only memorial Allen would have in the whole wide world: a pilot with a perfect white smile – with a diamond-shaped star representing a glint of reflected light, which Big Ben had copied from a toothpaste advert – giving the thumbs up from the cockpit of a Spitfire. Allen in an aircraft with a big white smile on his face! Big Ben was an artist. Picasso would have struggled with this particular assignment, as Allen already looked like one of his abstracts in real life.

Not that anybody ever knew who was depicted on the sign. More than ten thousand West Indians had been in the RAF during the war and those who saw the sign supposed it to be the legendary World War Two bomber pilot, Group Captain Leonard Cheshire of the famous 617 Dambusters Squadron, who was well-known in the islands for his Cheshire home for disabled people in Jamaica.

'OK, but if yuh find a mistake yuh will have to live with it, as me cyaan change tings in a hurry. Not pon a checkin day,' said Big Ben.

Big Ben knew from bitter experience that it was impossible to get text right every time. Allen thought such things about the Bible, but immediately felt guilty and, despite himself, asked forgiveness; from whom he wasn't quite sure.

Having discovered that the secret of checking signs was the number of people checking and not the time one person spent checking, Big Ben tried to maintain a high turnover of guests at his parties. He was not too worried, however, if some stayed all day, as their personalities changed as they got increasingly drunk so they often spotted mistakes they had previously missed.

II

Allen spotted a mistake immediately: 'Jumble Sale: Support Prostrate Cancer Research'.

Allen determinedly stifled his amusement. The mistake was funny in itself, although it referred to a condition that caused terrible suffering. The first time he had heard this common mistake made, he had actually laughed out loud. That conversation had been interrupted and he hadn't had the chance to explain that he wasn't laughing at the idea of the disease. Devastated by guilt, his stomach turned every time he thought of it, until the guilt was displaced by the onslaught of another crisis of paranoid self-consciousness.

A fine-featured brown man wandered in. He had long, matted hair held back with a red, gold and green headband. He was as tall as Allen and had the same wiry build. They could have been brothers; one just a little darker-skinned than the other.

'Televicion. Dat not right, but tell-lie-vision a true de same,' he said with a laugh to nobody in particular.

Big Ben came back with Denzil's sign which read 'The Koleidoscope Club' in bright yellow letters on a green background. Big Ben spotted the mistake immediately, as he always did once the paint was dry.

'Quick, mon, have a drink,' Ben said, pulling Denzil over to the makeshift bar.

'Dat not right,' said the man in the headband. 'But it too a true de same. De world a collide-o-scope of race an religion,' said the man.

'What's wrong with it, Rastaman?' asked Denzil, who had wandered back with a drink in his hand that the barman had poured from a full-strength bottle under Big Ben's covert instruction.

'It spelt wrong.'

'I know that,' lied Denzil. 'Now gwan about yuh business.'

Denzil couldn't stand Rastafarians with their talk of Africa being their Zion. He didn't want to be reminded of Africa.

'Nuh worries, man. Me leave you to your Babylon. But remember if you are a black man, no matter where you come from, you are an African.'

'Babylon?' enquired Allen. He had read of Babylon in the Bible and would have liked to go there to see the beautiful gardens.

'The way everybody other than them lives, in what they call "uncivilisation",' said Denzil seething with anger.

A middle-aged man in a maroon T-shirt strolled up. 'Nuh tek nuh notice, him call mi way of life Babylon too. Me! A Maroon!'

'Maroon?' Allen was puzzled as to why the man should refer to himself in terms of the colour of his T-shirt.

'Yes. Nanny come up and lead us in the wilderness. We did lead slave rebellion them in the islands. She keep wi strong an safe with her spirit. She Ashanti; a warrior nation with mighty women.'

'Nanny?' queried Allen, shaken by the familiar name.

'Queen Nanny. Queen of resistance, rebellion and survival.

She still run in the wilderness.'

'Where?' asked Allen, fascinated by the idea of a Nanny who ran like his in a wilderness, although Lizzie was now limited to a few fields and the Pits.

'Jamaica, in the Blue Mountains. Them find old clay pipe them an dream-drawin with her clay pipe clamped upside down inna her teet.'

Following the bizarre image that flashed through his mind, Allen realised Maroon-T, as he now thought of him, must have meant *teeth* and not *teat*. He thought of Lizzie regularly breaking her cheap, thin, clay pipes clamped upside down between her leathery, tortoise-like gums. Even the Irish clay pipes up to a third of an inch thick could still be bitten through quite easily.

It was against orders to smoke at work, although everybody did. In a bad week Lizzie had as many as six pipes confiscated by the foreman, together with whatever 'shag' she wasn't quick enough to hide up her skirts. She had once stuck a lit pipe up there when caught by surprise and would have set light to her underskirts had they not been soaked through from the rain. Instead, smoke and steam seeped out, as if she were a giant tea cosy sat over a steaming pot of tea.

The pipes and tobacco were usually returned at the end of the shift, as their young foreman was a decent type. He enforced the rules but was fair in all his dealings. He didn't try to be friends with the field girls and they respected him for not blurring the lines. He worked hard and prided himself on the fact that he never asked anyone to do anything he couldn't do himself.

'We master of camouflage, clad in vines.' Maroon-T broke through Allen's reverie.

Again, Allen's mind took off and he thought of the coating

of mud and the dusting of pollen and powdery green algae from the branches he accumulated as he pushed through the alder thickets around the Pits. This rendered him invisible if he remained motionless, which he could do for extraordinary lengths of time.

'Some seh Nanny neva need clad herself in nuh vine. She disappear when she want.'

Now Allen's attention was riveted. He thought of Lizzie disappearing in the wide, open, pan-flat fields, which had brought so much suspicion upon her.

'Nanny a mystery, a mystic, a martyr, a myth, a fighter, a leader, a spirit of freedom, a legacy, an earth substance. She our Grand Nanny. Ya-Ya. She did lead us Maroons against the forces that did rule the sea, and did burst black bondage asunder. An odyssey of courage and endurance; an inspiration. Mi Maroon heritage mean more than life to me,' said Maroon-T, who sounded as if he had learnt this passage from somewhere, just as Allen did.

Allen finally realised that the chap's use of the word maroon was a reference to a group based on something other than the colour of his T-shirt. In fact to Allen, according to what he had read, Maroon-T could have been describing the Celts, for whom the essence of the universe was female and women were the spiritual and moral pivot, equal to men in all things. Although he didn't like quoting the Romans, whom he considered evil tyrants, he knew the Romans had written of Celtic women:

> *The women of the Celts are nearly as tall as the men, who they rival in courage. A troop of foreigners wouldn't be able to withstand a single Celt if he called his wife to his side.*

Allen had also read that they were 'warrior queens, who taught boys the arts of love and combat'. *Oh, how he would have loved that. It had the potential to bridge the chasm that had opened up and isolated him from the world of sexual love so quickly and apparently forever, and to make him even better able to defend himself.*

Allen's reverie was brought to an abrupt halt with Maroon-T's next pronouncement: 'Our herbal remedy them heal an cure.'

Allen couldn't suppress a groan, although he was tempted to ask whether they had any aphrodisiacs, before pulling himself together just in time. He hadn't tried eating a ladybird yet.

'What happened to your Nanny?' asked Allen.

'Some seh she did get shot by a black-shot.'

'What's that?'

'A black man with a rifle.'

'A black man?!'

'Yes.'

'That's terrible. Where's she buried?' asked Allen.

'If you aks where Nanny bury you did miss the point of her life.'

'Aks! That's Old English,' Allen blurted out in surprise.

Maroon-T ignored Allen. 'We know she still run free. Nobody see the body. That black-shot Cuffee did a lie to get him reward. Him neva have nuh silver bullet.'

'Silver bullet?!' exclaimed Allen.

'Yes.'

'Run, Granny, run,' said Allen, to his own surprise.

'Yes. Guan, Nanny, Guan. But when you see old lady run, no aks what the matter. Run too!' said Maroon-T, not finding Allen's utterance in the least bit odd.

'But afta the treaty yuh left we alone to this day,' said

Maroon-T.

'Who left you alone?' asked Allen, deliberately enticing the expected retort and getting it.

'Yuh English. This slavery you white man visit pon wi cruel beyond imagine,' said Maroon-T.

This was dangerous territory for Allen. Given his precarious state of mind, there was a danger he might begin to think that perhaps he might be personally responsible. But Allen felt Maroon-T's accusation was the equivalent of him, Allen, going to Rome and accusing a beggar of enslaving him in the notorious underground slave dens on the grain-growing estates the Romans had established in Britain.

Allen had also read that before the transatlantic African slave trade, so many different races were enslaved that no one saw slavery in terms of race; and that black kings in Africa believed the slave trade was ordained by God and rejoiced in reducing their enemies to slavery. But it was all too horrific, so he kept quiet.

Anyway, he didn't consider himself white. If he was to use that term, all of his enemies were white. He had grown up being tormented by whites. The Germans were white, despite what Lizzie thought, and they had killed villagers with their bombs. Whites had destroyed his village, his way of life, and his countryside; right now, in his personal lifetime, not hundreds of years ago. By the same measure he had never seen a black man, or even one that was close to black.

He settled for saying: 'My people were enslaved, too.' But even this jarred, as he didn't really identify with any group.

'Who them?' demanded Maroon-T, a defiant look on his face.

'The Celts,' replied Allen.

'Neva heard of them,' said Maroon-T, visibly losing

They Couldn't Have Known

interest as the conversation moved away from the type of slavery he understood. The notion of white people being slaves was beyond his comprehension. It was obviously just more white man devilry. Maroon-T sniffed. He didn't want to listen to this strange-looking white man anymore.

'Hey man, yuh nuh tell im dat in return for dere freedom de Maroon dem return runaway slaves to de English, including Three-Finger-Jack, de famous black highwayman!' said Rastaman, who had been hanging around, eavesdropping on the exchanges.

On the mention of a highwayman, Allen recalled the legends of the highwaymen Dick Turpin and Sixteen String Jack, who reportedly haunted the heath back home.

'Nor dat yuh even catch and return Paul Bogle, leader of de Morant Bay rebellion, for execution! Nor dat you had slaves, too,' continued Rastaman.

Allen was mortified by these revelations. To him it did all sound like Babylon, but he couldn't just take Rastaman's word for it, although Allen couldn't see why he would make it all up. Either way he kept quiet.

Maroon-T stormed off, as if he had said it anyway.

'Nuh tek notice. I knew im back home. He come from a rich family in a Maroon area. Him come bitter at his reception hya an tek dem reasoning. Dat's why he talk wrong,' said Rastaman, feeling guilty as he knew the same description applied to him.

'Is it possible to be a Maroon Rasta and vice versa?' asked Allen.

'Yuh mus be born a Maroon, but yuh can become a Rasta. But every islander love Nanny now. Anyway, it one time everybody have a Nanny. Ya-Ya. Livin in a country parish on a family plot holdin everyting togedda,' said Rastaman.

'Yes, here too,' said Allen, wondering what Lizzie was doing.

'Ever livin love,' said Rastaman, before making a formal speech rather like the Maroon had, in Standard English:

We must become members of a new race, overcoming prejudice, owing our ultimate allegiance not to nations but to our fellow men within the human community.'

At the look of surprise on Allen's face, Rastaman felt obliged to explain his change in style: 'If we wanna spread de message, it no good people nuh understandin wi.'

Allen thought that, on the basis of Rastaman's speech, everybody from the Rookery was Rasta without knowing it.

'Man, come and smoke de herb,' said Rastaman, warming to this earnest but strange white man.

'Which one?' asked Allen.

Rastaman looked at him quizzically. To his surprise, he thought he had seen 'the herb' growing in the fields and even wild in England, which he took to be bush weed.

'I mean, there are too many to count. Is it in *Mrs Seacole's Wonderful Adventures in Many Lands*?' asked Allen.

'Me nunno, but me sure she did use it. How yuh know bout her?' asked Rastaman with surprise.

'My Nanny has a copy and told me how she came from Jamaica and helped care for British soldiers in the Crimean War at the time of Florence Nightingale.'

'She did come from where mi family live, Black River in Jamaica.'

'Isn't that where the slave ship Zong was sailing when many slaves – men, women and children – were thrown overboard for the insurance money?' asked Allen, squirming at the thought.

'Yes, mon. How yuh know bout dat wickedness?' asked Rastaman in astonishment.

'From the caption of a picture – The Slave Ship – in a book.'

'Raatid,' exclaimed Rastaman with a sharp look at Allen.

Allen bit his lip and refrained from asking what colour the water was in the Black River.

III

Allen hadn't liked the squalid room Denzil had found him in a packed tenement house, nor had the tenants taken to having a solitary, weird-looking white man in their midst. So he had slipped away at the first opportunity and found a better room in one of the bombed-out blocks next to another huge bombsite, well away from Denzil's club. His living conditions didn't differ that much from those in Hadleyrow and he had reconnected with his beloved nature, which was sweeping into the bombsites across London. London had not been so green since before the Industrial Revolution.

He found a casual portering job at a local fruit and vegetable market, where he felt at home with all the produce. He was paid cash in hand, had virtually no expenses and even began to save money. As usual, he worked as hard as he could to exhaust himself and the longer he was there the less he felt like taking any initiative with regard to his future. However, the other porters at the market were becoming increasingly resentful of Allen's prodigious work output, which was putting them to shame and threatening their jobs.

In any spare time he had from work, Allen sat in the corner of the local pub, nursing one pint of beer all evening and working on his cards, which he had been accumulating since he had discovered his friends in the old books.

He knew many of the quotes by heart, but he found some, like other memories, didn't stick for unknown reasons that seemed unrelated to their significance. When he had read that his Celtic ancestors had scratched their legends on wands of hazel and aspen with their spare script of Ogma, and the ancient Greeks noted down maxims that they carried with them and read repeatedly, he had started to write down his favourite quotes on a set of index cards.

The first was one of his own based on this practice itself, not because he couldn't remember it but as a perpetual reminder to practise the habit:

Repetition is treatment. Repeating the right advice again and again is essential.

Allen had been astonished by how many of the ancient Greek writings were relevant to him. Aristotle, whose messages had reached Allen more than two thousand years after his death aged sixty-two, might as well have been in the room with him when Allen had read:

It is the mark of an educated mind to be able to entertain a thought without accepting it.

This was precisely what Allen aspired to, but failed to achieve, always feeling tainted by having what he considered to be inappropriate thoughts. But the quotation implied that it was possible with a sufficiently educated mind, which at least he was always striving to achieve. However, he had had mixed feelings when he had read another of Aristotle's thoughts:

No excellent soul is exempt from a mixture of madness.

Allen's second oldest friend in the books, Plutarch, who was a slightly less ancient Greek, had described Allen's state succinctly:

Nowhere can he find an escape from his imaginary terrors. Every little evil is magnified by the scaring spectres of his anxiety.

The revelation that the symptoms of his condition had been recognised nearly two thousand years earlier comforted him greatly. But such relief was always temporary and trailed in the wake of relentless fear without limits, never diminishing, ever replenishing from an infinite source of anxious nervous energy. The more he tried to argue himself better, the cleverer the self-doubting enemy within became. Struggle defined it.

Allen worked on his cards continuously, memorising them, rearranging them, trying to understand them better and to revise them in light of his experience. He was careful not to leave them around for prying eyes to see, but once he had been caught working on them during a break at work and mocked by those he showed up as lazy.

After this, he recorded notes on nature as boldly and colourfully as he could on one side of each card to distract attention from the faint, pencil scribble of his personal notes on the other. This gave him a little more leeway should he be caught again writing or reading them, or, heaven forbid, if he ever left them lying around. Not much leeway, though, as there were plenty who considered an interest in the wonders of nature weird enough, let alone keeping a set of notes about them. It would certainly be enough evidence for them to question his sexual orientation, even without seeing the other sides of the cards.

It was a long, dull summer and Allen had no idea how

long he had been at the market when he bumped into Radish wandering about one day.

'Wha appen, man? Chaka chaka doti hows,' said Radish, looking at the bombsites and slum dwellings.

'What?'

'Look like duppy live dere,' said Radish.

'Duppy?' queried Allen.

'Restless spirit dem dat haunt old building dem, specially graveyard a night-time. Dem love de night. Dem love de scent a basil an jasmine, so nuh plant dem near your yard.'

'We did, but we had no trouble,' said Allen.

'Duppy know who a frighten. But if duppy do trouble yuh, throw salt, wear your clothes inside out, put your cap on back-way, walk back-way an swear,' said Radish.

It seemed to Allen as though it took less to deter duppies than most of the living evil souls he had met.

'Dem like red but not blue, but some seh is odda way around.'

Allen thought it wasn't worth bothering with that one. He had noticed blue flowers losing their colour in the gloom before red ones, so he wondered at what level of light a duppy could still see him if he wore blue.

'Run for wata.'

That was very familiar. Allen knew that water was pure and holy and would reject the unholy. Ghosts, fairies, demons and vampires were unable to cross running water, despite their other powers. Witches dissolved in water and around Hadleyrow it was said that the black hound without a single white hair would do the same. But non-swimmers near the Pits needed to balance the odds before risking running for water, like those Briscoe had told him about who had run from lizards.

'Trow tings down for dem to stop an count since them cyaan count pass nine.'

Compulsive counting! Allen realised he was lucky his obsessions hadn't triggered any overt compulsions to counteract them, such as endless repetitive washing, cleaning, checking, hoarding or symmetrical arranging.

Although he did not suffer compulsive counting – which could divide people's attention, multiply their anxiety, add to their stress and subtract from their lives – once, when returning home at the end of a run of more than fifty miles, Allen had lost all energy and had spent the last ten miles trying to calculate how long they would take him. He had still been calculating by the time he got to Hadleyrow about two hours later. Allen started to feel that he understood some of these duppies better than he understood most of the other people he had met. He grinned at the thought.

'Nuh mock,' said Radish.

'I'm not,' said Allen, mortified that Radish had thought that he would do so.

'Dem a part a life inna de islands. Anyway, me hear seh your country de most haunted inna de worl.'

'That's right,' said Allen surprised that Radish should know this. Allen had read that when Henry VIII had broken away from the Roman Catholic Church, he had effectively shut down 'purgatory', so restless souls of the dead were left to haunt the country instead.

In Hadleyrow, people still feared the ghosts of Hallowe'en, which some villagers knew as the Celtic Samhain. It marked the end of the harvest and the beginning of winter on the last day of October, falling halfway between the autumn equinox and the shortest day at the winter solstice, when the gate between the worlds was open and spirits passed freely.

'If duppy wearin black him harmless. But if he wearin white him dangerous. Coolie duppy de worst.'

Allen remembered Lizzie's explanation as to why ghosts always wore clothes and sometimes even carried a briefcase and a rolled umbrella: 'Because when youm see a ghost you see 'em in their time.'

'An if all else fail, expose yourself,' said Radish.

'What?' exclaimed Allen.

Allen loved most of Radish's ideas for dealing with duppies, but the last one jarred. In his case, not only was he too shy to do such a thing, but he didn't think it would be very effective either.

'If di dutty duppy man dweet den must mek come mekiman,' said Radish, getting carried away a bit.

Allen couldn't make any sense of that one, and Radish didn't bother to translate.

Either way, Allen didn't have to worry about ghosts or duppies. There was no work for them with Allen; he did the damage all by himself.

Duppy know who a frighten.

IV

Without Briscoe's presence bridging the gap between them, Allen and Radish made an unlikely pair, but they had a lonely life in common and, although communication between them was limited, whenever they met up they were pleased enough for the company.

'Me a starve, mek wi a go MaMa's yard,' said Radish one day.

When they arrived, the coming together of MaMa and Radish was like two sumo wrestlers crashing into each other, except thankfully both were fully dressed.

'Raatid, Radish man, where yuh been? Come, yuh big vegetable, yuh,' she said.

The extended hug that followed had the appearance of a sumo bout, with both trying to lift and throw the other out of the yard. MaMa held her own and the bout stopped through mutual exhaustion, giving Radish further pause for reflection with regard to his waning powers.

'Radish, man, yuh need some nourishment, yuh losing yuh strength, man,' said MaMa, as if reading his mind.

Radish was a bit subdued after that retort. *Why did everybody relish telling somebody what they already knew about their failings? He knew only too well that he was losing his strength.*

Allen sat quietly in the yard, sad once again at the sight of such warm emotion between friends. However, having often observed the fragility of friendship, he supposed he was still better off without it. He had taken the direct route to the embittered, estranged state without having to fall out with any friends.

MaMa showed them her famous menu. There was ackee – deadly poisonous unless picked when ripe and cooked correctly – with salt fish, onions and peppers; rice 'n' peas – really red kidney beans – cooked in coconut milk, with small pieces of salt pork and hot peppers; sweet potato, yet another failed aphrodisiac; slices of melon-like pawpaw drizzled with lime juice and sugar; naseberries, like toffee apples; and cocoa tea, a sweet hot chocolate with condensed milk, cinnamon, nutmeg and bay leaves, a cup of which – with a corn starch flour dumpling floating in it – would make a complete meal by itself.

Radish didn't even look. He knew that MaMa could never get these things during the post-war ration book austerity, except for the rare occasions when immigrants or sailors from the islands brought in supplies. Most customers came just to read the menu and to be reminded of the good old days back home, and were satisfied with whatever MaMa managed to pile on their plates. Nobody ever complained; not that they would have dared to, anyway.

'Might as well just nyam de whole damn thing,' said Radish.

Allen settled for the cocoa tea, which tasted and looked just like cocoa to him, which it was.

Having eaten everything on offer and virtually cleaning MaMa out of all her stock, Radish felt more like his old self. He even thought about taking Allen on at arm-wrestling again but thought better of it, just in case.

'How can you eat so much?' asked Allen in amazement.

'Lef mi nuh,' said Radish.

'Why did you leave these, though?' he asked, reaching for what MaMa had called bonbon de terres, which were still piled on a side plate.

'Dem nuttin but dried dirt-mud mix wid salt and sugar from when de slave them inna the fields did starve,' said Radish.

Allen wondered how many bonbon de terres would make a peck. He had been told he had to eat a 'peck of dirt' before he died. He had taken this literally, thinking it was because eating dirt could ease hunger pangs, cure mineral deficiencies and absorb poisons. But he knew from the peck baskets the field girls used to gather crops that it was a large amount and he didn't think he would make it in time, even if he did eat all these bonbon de terres.

Allen had also heard that the mysterious scratch marks on the wall near the entrance to the parish church across the road were where scrapings had been taken to cure fever and impotence. The ability to cure such an unlikely combination of maladies was typical of many folk remedies. The first, without stigma, allowed attempts to relieve the other without shame. Others said the scratch marks were made by the black hound without a single white hair, but people didn't want to hear that.

'Oh well, pass dem over ya,' said Radish, interrupting Allen's reverie.

MaMa had let slip that a sailor had just brought in some red snapper fish and plantain, the perfect combination. Radish liked the girl who worked for MaMa, so he went into the kitchen to see her and to ask her to cook up the new stock. When she refused, he tried to convince her instead that they would be a perfect combination, but to no avail.

'Yuh can stuff yu plantain someweh else. Yuh renk an outa order, bwoy. No palm me up, yuh dutty brute. Galang bout yuh business,' the kitchen snapper snapped.

Seeing a cage of pet rabbits in the yard, Allen asked why there hadn't been any in MaMa's mountain of food, as rabbit would have been the first choice, wild or tame, for those at the Rookery.

'No, man, we cyaan nyam up Br'er Rabbit,' said Radish.

Allen was shaken. *How could Radish know about his favourite childhood stories?*

'What did you say?' asked Allen.

'No, man, we can't eat Br'er Rabbit,' said Radish, translating for him.

'Brer Rabbit?'

'Yes, mon. Br'er Rabbit – Kalulu – de trickster from Africa, though him a hare dere. Me like de story about him begging not to be thrown him inna de maccathorn bush, as if dat was de worse ting, knowin it do im no harm,' said Radish.

First Brer Rabbit and a hare, and now his favourite story! Allen didn't know what a maccathorn bush was, but obviously it was thorny. He recalled Briscoe complaining that everywhere he turned 'macca juked him' and now realised what he had meant.

'I know that one. It's my favourite!' said Allen.

Allen loved this idea, but he hadn't yet been able to use it against his enemies. Unlike Radish, though, the stories had not stopped them eating rabbit back home. Rabbit was the main meat they had eaten, wild and hutch.

The orchards teemed with rabbits and hares, which could strip the bark from the trees. Every winter, the fruit trees were painted with a thick soup of clay and carbolic solution, which hares and rabbits wouldn't touch. During one shoot of five guns in forty acres of top and bottom fruit, four hundred rabbits and thirty-seven hares were shot in three hours; needless to say by a shooting party of incomers from the airport who couldn't tell the difference between rabbits and hares, and were ignorant of the consequences.

Now, for the first time, Allen made the connection between the hero of his favourite stories to the guts on the kitchen table and the delicious stew in the pot. His brain was usually quicker when it came to making such disturbing connections.

They were not skilled at killing things. They had bred rabbits, which they killed inhumanely by holding them by the ears and repeatedly bashing them on the back of the neck with a poker, as their ignorant variant of the mythical 'rabbit punch'. They had also hatched and raised an Easter cockerel chick for Christmas dinner, which, when the time came, they had killed by slamming its head in a door. He had no idea how their neighbour had killed and prepared their pigs for the pork they always brought around just before Christmas, although he had heard of pig-sticking. Allen always wondered why Christmas came so close to the shortest day, the Winter Solstice, on December 21, which Lizzie still celebrated.

As usual, Allen completely lost track of time as his life settled down into a steady routine. He met up with Radish at MaMa's yard whenever he could. When he was there he eavesdropped on stories about his own exploits, which had piled up like duppies at a crossroads.

There were rumours relating to Allen's status as either a hero or a coward. On the basis of his fear of spiders, he was a coward. On the basis of his lack of fear of lizards, he was a hero. Nobody, including Allen himself, realised that on the basis of how he dealt with his anxiety state – when he was practically on the floor with suffering and had almost nothing left with which to tackle it – he was a hero who fought his breakdown with formidable but misguided courage. If those who had no experience of an anxiety state were to experience his symptoms, they would think that they were dying. Neither did he realise that, as the long-term causes of his problems lay in his innate predisposition and accumulated stress, he wasn't responsible for his condition, and could have taken credit for having to deal with it.

Allen certainly didn't recognise that the symptoms were real and that there was nothing illogical about his fear, nor that bearing all this uncomplainingly should be a source of pride rather than of shame. Neither did he realise that his mental struggles enhanced his understanding, appreciation and compassion for others.

But the events on the bomb site, when he had spewed out a lizard and flown, had shifted people's perception of Allen into the realm of the supernatural. Normal rules didn't apply if he was a 'science man', 'buh man', 'duppy catcher', 'professor', 'meki man', 'jumbi man' or even a duppy.

That he couldn't drive; that he didn't go with girls in the bars; that he had tried to kiss a man at Denzil's club and was interested in plants proved, to those who did not know Denzil, that Allen must be a batty man. Whether a duppy could be a batty man, was a totally new concept that had never been posited before, ever, anywhere in the whole wide world.

He wondered what Gill was doing.

V

Gill was trying to convince her mother that it was not irresponsible madness to get engaged to Piotr, who had proposed the previous evening.

They were sitting in the front room of the farmhouse with the last boxes of their belongings, waiting for the van to arrive and watching the demolition and excavations getting nearer. They felt they would have to carry the boxes out themselves if the van didn't arrive soon. The old ship's beams that had been used in the building of the house were creaking with the vibrations, as if it was about to sink in a storm, which it was in effect, albeit in a sea of mud. The beams had survived one sinking centuries ago, and perhaps they would survive another as flotsam to be useful once again.

'I know I've only known Piotr for a short time! I don't need to be told that, Mother,' said Gill.

Even without the extra tension, Gill's mother could disturb her normal good nature more than anyone else. Gill was getting close to subscribing to the old saying: 'You may forgive your enemies but never your parents.'

'What's the rush?'

'We love each other, so what's the point in waiting?'

'There's every point in waiting. So as to be sure that it's not just a passing fancy. You've had no previous experience with boys.'

'You always told me not to, Mother. You can't have it both ways!'

'Look at all the wartime marriages that have gone wrong already.'

'There are a lot that are going right as well.'

'Are you sure you can separate him from his story?'

'Can you separate anyone from their story?' asked Gill.

'You can't, I suppose, but if a couple have similar stories they cancel each other out, and it's easier to judge their compatibility,' said Gill's mother.

Gill kept quiet as she realised her mother had a point.

'Are you sure you don't just feel sorry for him?' asked Gill's mother.

Gill was getting uncomfortable, as she couldn't dismiss her mother's position as easily as she had thought. *Perhaps she should give her mother a little more credit.*

'Are you sure he doesn't want to marry you just so he can stay in the country?'

'Mother! That's a terrible thing to say. I trust him completely.'

'How many young brides-to-be have said that, do you think, only to be let down?'

'I don't care. This is different. It's my choice and I trust my judgement. He loves me too. I know he does. It would be impossible to fake the emotion he shows.'

'Why did you cry when you saw that *Brief Encounter* film, then?' asked Gill's mother.

'Because it was so sad.'

'Well, those actors were faking their emotions and you

were taken in by them,' said Gill's mother, giving Gill pause for thought yet again.

'What passport has he got?' Gill's mother continued, considering it her duty to protect her precious daughter.

Gill became agitated as her mother's relentless questioning touched on a sensitive subject for Piotr.

'He hasn't got one. He's classified as a "stateless allied alien".'

'What happens if he wants to go home to see his family?'

'He hasn't got any family there any more. The communists are calling Poles to return, but he doesn't trust them. His experiences have made him never trust anybody in authority.'

'What happens to you if he's deported?'

'He won't be,' said Gill a little less confidently. Piotr had confided in her that he was worried he would be sent back if he got into trouble with the police. This was a possibility working at the airport, where he could easily become innocently mixed up in major crime, or even be framed.

'What was Piotr doing at the police station the other day?'

'He's left his place in Fletham and moved into the village across the road to be closer to me and his job. He has to tell the police every time he changes address for longer than two weeks.'

'Hmm. That doesn't sound very good. Will he have to do that for the rest of his life?'

'No. Only till he's a British citizen,' said Gill, her heart sinking as she realised her mother had finally forced her to admit that Piotr might have an ulterior motive for marrying her.

The bulldozers were moving perilously close. A rat scuttled out of the cellar.

'I thought you said you liked him,' said Gill, switching

tactics.

'I do, but all confidence tricksters are likeable. That's how they get away with it. You couldn't be an unlikeable confidence trickster.'

'But you know he's a devout Catholic,' said Gill.

Her mother considered countering this point by referring to the amoral priests and even popes she had heard about, not to mention what they said was happening at the children's orphanage near the Green Man. But realising it undermined her own faith, she fell into a confused silence.

'Mother?' said Gill, puzzled by her silence.

'Why not just wait until he gets a British passport and then you'll know he's not marrying you to get one.'

Although still completely confident of Piotr's integrity, Gill agreed in order to placate her mother and to clear the way for her marriage.

Piotr had no problem with this as he had already started the process of applying for his British passport, which he had been keeping from Gill as a surprise.

His passport came through on a snowy December day just after Christmas, in time for a spring wedding.

VI

Gill's parents arranged for the wedding to take place at the Catholic Church in Fletham, with the official reception at the church hall next door. It was a picturesque spot on the green, right by the pond.

Subsequent discussions with Gill about the details, however, were not so straightforward.

'But Mother, everybody's supposed to be able to attend the service.'

'I know, but I'm not having any Tom, Dick and Harry wandering into the service,' said Gill's mother.

'They're very nice people,' said Gill, trying to lighten the mood a little.

'Who are?'

'Tom, Dick and Harry. They work up at the airport.'

'I'm definitely not having anybody from the airport at the service or at our reception.'

'Why not? They're the only friends Piotr has. They won't cause any trouble,' said Gill, crossing her fingers under the table.

'They can have a separate reception at the airport. We'll hire that marquee in the public enclosure for them. It'll be good enough for that lot,' she replied.

Gill's mother resented spending any money at all on the airport people, but paying to keep them away from the official proceedings in Fletham would be worth every penny. She was still uncomfortable with the whole idea of the marriage. It had all been so quick. She still hoped Gill would meet a nice, well-spoken English boy from outside their troubled area.

But although Piotr had a funny name and looked a bit foreign, at least he didn't have any trace of an accent, except when he pronounced 'rations' as 'Russians'. Consequently, she had been confused when Piotr had said he was looking forward to seeing the end of them. Gill had told her that Polish people hated the Russians, but even Gill's mother thought that was a bit extreme. *Thankfully he was Catholic and not Church of England or non-conformist*, she thought. *Anyway, she had to be grateful that Allen had disappeared completely from Gill's life and had stayed disappeared.*

As a devout Catholic, Piotr believed in free will. He considered that he was captain of his ship and, with God's guidance, had steered his own course to dock in his haven. He couldn't believe that he had been jealous of Gill's friendship with Allen. *How could he have been so insecure as to imagine the miserable, deformed pagan had a chance when faced with such purity of purpose? The differences in their lives demonstrated that he, Piotr, had chosen the right course, while Allen had chosen another and would have to suffer the consequences.*

If the 'miserable, deformed pagan' had been involved in the discussion, he would have liked to see Piotr trying to steer the coracle in which he had ended up through no choice of his own. He was sure Piotr would have gone round and round in circles, just as he did.

Whatever Gill's mother thought, at least they both met the requirements of the rules governing a Catholic marriage, particularly that they had reserved for marriage the expressions of affection that belong to married love. These rules were otherwise so complex that many Catholics, let alone non-Catholics, in the village couldn't understand them. Not that they needed to. In fact, until a few years earlier, the traditional pagan independence from the Church relating to marriage had endured in the village, where besom weddings – in which the consenting couple jumped over a birch broom held across the doorway of the house – had been perfectly legal, with everyone regarding such couples as married.

As for the selection process, some brides-to-be would have chosen their husbands – if they had had a choice, which was very unlikely in the village – by scratching the initials of potential husbands onto hazel nuts and throwing them into the fire at Hallowe'en, or Nut-Crack Night as it was known locally by those who still observed the Celtic Samhain. The loudest pop and brightest flame indicated the prospective bride's true love. One poor girl had been devastated when her nut exploded, hit her in the eye and set fire to her dress. Those who did get married were met by an old woman, usually Lizzie, and given a basket of hazelnuts to encourage fertility. The locals also believed that a good nut year meant many babies were on the horizon.

Those that did not share these beliefs called it Nutcase Night and considered the participants to be complete nutters.

CHAPTER TWO

I

According to the locals, Lizzie knew everything that happened in the area and much that didn't. She gathered a good deal of her information when she was tending her skeps, as people came to tell the bees their news, particularly births and deaths. They didn't really do this as friends, but out of fear of dire consequences if they did not; the motive for most superstitions and religions. So, despite Gill's mother's efforts to keep the wedding plans a secret for as long as possible – just in case it got cancelled for any reason she hadn't been able to think up yet – Lizzie soon found out.

On discovering the story, Lizzie scuttled to Kate's place with the news, her bare ankles getting stung by a pile of freshly pulled nettles outside Kate's door.

Kate had been huddled over the dying embers of an open fire, using strands of her own hair to darn an old pair of stockings. She hadn't understood a word when people told her that airhostesses returning on overseas flights brought fully-fashioned silk stockings back from shops abroad.

Like Lizzie, she found it difficult to keep a fire going now that all the trees and hedges were being cleared and burnt in huge bonfires in the fields. As she stood up to greet Lizzie, she steadied herself with a hand on the low ceiling. Lizzie would have had to stand on a stool to touch it, despite some villagers believing she could levitate.

"Ave youm 'eard about Gill and Piotr?' asked Lizzie, scratching her ankles.

'Oh, Lizzie! You startled me. No, I haven't. What's up with your ankles? And look at your laces again. Here, sit down and let me have a look.'

While Lizzie told her about Gill and Piotr getting married, Kate rubbed the baking soda and dock leaves she always kept handy for such occasions over Lizzie's stinging ankles. She tied Lizzie's bootlaces and tended to her hair, which wasn't easy as, like a mole's, it had no compliance and grew in all directions.

When she was done, they sat on the bench staring into the remains of the fire. Kate put her arm around Lizzie's thin shoulders to comfort her as she thought Lizzie might be sad for Allen.

The flickering firelight accentuated the ravages wreaked on Lizzie's face by the weather through years of long hours in the fields. The same firelight enhanced Kate's pallid complexion with a soft glow. There was nothing remarkable about her appearance except that, unusually for one born in the village, she had good teeth, which she cleaned with nothing more than salt, a bit of cloth and by chewing on pieces of alder bark.

Kate especially watched over Lizzie at work. She would put her shawl around Lizzie's shoulders when it rained and would slip across and help Lizzie get her money up during piecework. During the breaks she would tie Lizzie's kerchief and bootlaces, which would inevitably have come undone. As a result, Lizzie had quite regularly lost her old, ill-fitting boots in the quagmire. She and Kate had often laughed as she hopped around trying to retrieve a boot without putting her bare foot down in the mud. This she never managed, mainly because they were laughing so much, so she would have to endure the rest of the shift with her foot sliding around the muddy insides of the rescued boot.

'Least I won't get no blisters on that un,' she would to say.

Lizzie would have loved a pair of Wellington boots with no laces to confuse her, and which could be found more easily in the mud. Kate had been saving up to buy her a pair. Woe betides anyone who tried to put upon Lizzie if Kate was near. Kate always looked out for Lizzie.

Depending on the weather, they were inevitably covered in dust, soil or mud, and were considered dirty by those with cleaner jobs. Nothing could have been further from the truth as, without exception, the field girls practised the highest standards of personal hygiene, notwithstanding the lack of running, let alone hot, water at home. Lizzie even drank a cupful of frothing soapwort extract every Sunday morning. 'Them cleans the outards, stands to reason them must clean the innards,' she would say.

Every day was hard out in the fields, but that day had been especially tough. They had been set to weed stinging nettles by hand from a field of second-year mint that couldn't be hoed for fear of damaging its runners, and Lizzie's gloves had been stolen by one of the itinerant Gypsy workers. When she had asked the new overseer, a young man, if she could run across the fields to get another pair from home, he had retorted: 'What do you think this is, a benevolent society?'

So Kate had lent Lizzie her gloves and had pulled stinging nettles all day with her bare hands. There had been more nettles than mint in that field and the superstitious were surprised not to find elves living there. Kate comforted herself with the belief that the stinging would at least relieve her already rheumatoid-arthritic hands and keep sorcery at bay. Some thought her mad when she took a bunch of nettles home, but the leaves would make a nice cup of tea when she had a cold, as well as increasing her hens' laying and repelling flies.

'Look on the bright side, could be worse,' was Kate's favourite phrase, which, seeing Allen's struggles, she had taught him at an early age. But despite her optimistic nature, she was becoming increasingly nervous about their state of isolation down at the Rookery.

Once an area had been encircled by the developers, the ruthless 'peace terms' were easily enforced by the occupying forces. Resistance was futile and short-lived, as the occupants were left with no bargaining position other than becoming martyrs to their cause, which nobody did. Some even considered it their patriotic duty not to make a fuss, as they were still united by the wartime spirit.

The airport had started under Prime Minister Winston 'Winnie' Churchill, and they were sure he would never let anything bad happen to them. But even Winnie – great wartime leader, noted orator, historian, writer and artist, despite suffering a deep mental anguish, which he called 'Black Dog' – had been duped by the civil aviation lobby to believe that the airfield was necessary for the wartime needs of the RAF. Nevertheless, he had still objected to the diversion of manpower and resources from the invasion of Normandy in 1944 when the war was still far from won. When a delay had been suggested, the civil air lobby had panicked and pressed on with even greater urgency.

The Rookery had been the last area to come under siege.

In the times when maps were rare and the ancient pagan ceremony of beating the bounds had still been practised each year, the villagers of Hadleyrow had never bothered to do so around the Rookery. They hoped the Rookery might be forgotten as part of the parish and that it would quietly detach itself and disappear into the Pits. Nobody in their right mind wanted to go poking around down there; despite the fact that violets, primroses, and celandines lit the scene in springtime and the hedge nightingales' powerful song lent an air of enchantment for those who were brave enough to penetrate its maze.

Given the isolation and uncertainty, the cottages down at the Rookery were quickly falling into disrepair. When the neglected and damaged thatch let the rain in, damp penetrated everywhere and the wattle-and-daub walls soaked the water up like a sponge.

'These cottages'll only stand with them 'ats on,' Lizzie used to say.

Thatch and wattle-and-daub had been used since before the building of Caesar's Camp. The cottages were made from straw, sticks and mud, and now the wolf was at the door, huffing, puffing and about to blow them all down. If they were to find refuge in a house of bricks it would have to be in Fletham.

Some of the villagers had been more than happy to escape their rural backwater and be moved to the new housing in Fletham, where there were shops, pubs, social clubs, a small cinema, schools, public baths and a railway station. But Lizzie wouldn't move and Kate would never desert her.

II

As he banked the light aircraft, Melville got a clear view of the developing airport below. As a senior staff member of the Ministry of Civil Aviation, he felt proud to be involved in such an important project. He had been sent down from Whitehall to check on the situation. There had been rumours of trouble as the destruction of the village neared completion. The conditions on the ground were such a mess that, with a newfound companion, he had taken up a light aircraft to obtain an overview of the location.

From the air, the devastation of the village was heightened by the contrast with the remaining unspoiled countryside surrounding it, which would soon suffer the same fate. The smaller fields looked like a patchwork quilt of every conceivable shade of green, yellow and brown, bound together by the stitch-work of the hedges; while the larger arable fields with their rows of germinating crops looked like corduroy.

Only the orchards gave the scene a bolder texture. There were acres and acres of plum, pear, apple and cherry orchards, within which he could make out the pig shelters and baths, but not the pigs themselves. The apple orchards, famous for a variety developed in the area by a Richard Cox in the early 1800s, were speckled with the colour of wallflowers grown as an under-crop, which also supposedly encouraged the fruiting of the trees.

Most of the residents had been evicted by now, but some were still hanging on, which threatened to delay the project. With the war over, emergency wartime legislation could no longer be enforced, and more and more opposition was emerging now that the deception was being increasingly exposed. The airport management team feared that, before long, even those they had already managed to dispossess might start lobbying for the return of their land or for the proper financial compensation they had been denied.

Melville didn't have much time for the villagers. With few exceptions they had been exempted from military service, as farming was a reserved occupation. Meanwhile, he and his RAF mates had been in the thick of it over Europe, with many of them dead or terribly injured as a result. Apart from the small number of rich farmers, he considered the villagers to be uneducated peasants steeped in ignorance and superstition, especially those from the Rookery.

Melville couldn't understand why the remaining villagers hadn't already been dealt with. During the war he had taken part in massive bombing raids on civilian targets for the greater good, and, despite himself, the thought flashed through his mind that the same principles could be applied here, albeit on a much smaller scale. A wave of guilt surged through him at the thought, and he redoubled his efforts to concentrate on the scene below.

The civil aviation lobby had gone to extraordinary lengths to disguise its intentions to establish a commercial airport. Runways had been laid in the typical triangular RAF pattern, which allowed landing on any runway in any light wind directions even though, considering the reality of the prevailing winds, only two could be used for commercial operations. Five RAF officers and a hundred men had been posted there, and even Melville's selection for his delicate role had been influenced by the fact that he was an ex-RAF pilot who had survived the war in Bomber Command with distinction.

They had initially named the airport RAF Hadley Row,

using the old name for the village, last used on a map of 1754, in a ruse to imply that it was still nothing more than a row of dwellings on the western edge of the ancient and once notorious Honeslowe Heath. This origin was reflected in the fact that, when travelling south down Hadleyrow Road from The Three Magpies on the main road, the old farmhouses and buildings had been mainly on the right-hand or western side before it continued round as part of a loop of roads, about three miles long, which re-joined the main road about a mile further west of The Three Magpies.

It had been against the civil aviation lobby's interests to admit that the village had developed into a vibrant, productive, agricultural community on Grade One agricultural land in the heart of the great Thames Valley Market Gardening Plain, which had made a huge contribution to food production during and after the war, when food imports were severely restricted and starvation threatened.

The efforts of the German Air Force in the area during the war had been as nothing compared to the more accurately targeted and deadly onslaught from the civil aviation lobby. The Germans, who had been watching the campaign of destruction since it began, had been impressed by the ruthless efficiency of it all, but were puzzled at the delay in starting the project. Berlin's Tempelhof Airport terminal had been built in 1927 and was massively reconstructed in the mid-1930s by the Nazis to become one of the largest building complexes in the world.

When control of the developing airport had finally passed to the new Ministry of Civil Aviation on January 1, 1946, Melville had attended the 'official opening' of the soon to be renamed London Airport. This had been organised in a hurry to silence any critics as the extent of the deception was becoming clear. It had been a wet day and the runways had glistened in the rain. The water draining from them had clouded the once gin-clear water of local rivers with washed-out cement, destroying a balance of nature that had endured for millennia.

Members of the press and every conceivable dignitary had been driven in buses down the one-hundred-yard wide, three-thousand-yard length of Runway One – which had taken enough concrete to have built a road to Scotland – to observe the departure of the first commercial flight from the airport: an Avro Lancastrian 'Star Light' airliner, based on a wartime Lancaster heavy bomber, destined for South America.

From his plane, Melville could see that a massive trench was already being cut from the centre of the triangle or runways, north across the main east-west runway. In the trench he could see a long, box-like concrete construction, partially roofed over and waiting to be covered with earth. It was the first section of a road and pedestrian tunnel to allow access to the new central terminals from the main road.

The original control tower and passenger terminals of tents and asbestos-panelled prefabs awaited the end of their short existence like rabbits as the maw of the tunnel approached like a snake's to swallow them up.

The whole site looked as though the war in the air had continued unabated for the past five years, which in effect, it had for the villagers, albeit against a different enemy. It was a scene of chaos and desolation, all brown mud, yellow sand and gravel, with barely a trace of greenery. As Melville looked down it was impossible to reconcile what he saw below with a passage he had read during his research for the posting:

If you turn down from the main road by The Three Magpies

you will come upon a road that is as peaceful as anywhere in England. There is a calmness and serenity about it that is soothing in a mad, rushing world. Its pure sweet air is scented with the fragrance of green, untainted country.

Just to the edge of the destruction he could see the specially prepared grass runway of the original airfield from which he had just taken off, like the baize of a billiard table. Two small, man-made rivers flowed side by side from northwest to southeast, like silvery threads across the tapestry of the remaining fields. At the time of digging, these rivers would have had a considerable local impact as they cut across ancient fields, redefining boundaries and patterns of irrigation. Centuries later, the arrival of the railway, which could be seen further south running as straight as the nearby Roman Road to the south-west, must have had an even greater impact, as indeed the Roman Road itself would have had centuries earlier.

About a mile south east of the airport he could see the massive network of rails of the freight-shunting yards and the nearby tall spire of the main church of Fletham.

Fletham had been yet another major farming and horticulture centre, which at first had benefitted from a transport revolution, with the arrival of the railway and the opening of the station in 1848. As a consequence, it had developed into a commuter town, with huge housing estates spreading over the once-fertile soil. However, unlike Hadleyrow, at least the original village had survived with its parish church, vicarage and manor house isolated in a crick in the road to the west.

In a playing field on one of the estates he could see the outline of what was once the largest area of horticultural glass in the world, under which the greatest known concentration of tomato plants had been cultivated. Despite him being dubbed The Cabbage King, these had been the best-paying crop of A.W Smith, whose fruit and vegetable empire had supplied a large proportion of London's food before, throughout and just after the war.

Two tiny figures could be seen playing tennis on new courts laid over the foundations of one of the glasshouses, oblivious of what had been there before; a new generation that knew it all, but nothing at all. They certainly weren't aware that at the time of Domesday there were two slaves in Fletham, hundreds of years before Europe's trade in African slaves.

The Roman Road, the new rivers and the railway, had by now been accepted, even to the point of securing a place in people's affections. Melville was confident that the same would eventually happen with the airport. He would do all he could to help push it through. Nothing should be allowed to stop it now they had come so far; such great benefit to so many would follow. He had no time for those selfish, short-sighted villagers.

Close by, to the south, he could see the massive reservoirs storing water for London, which had been suggested as an alternative when the idea of a canal alongside Runway One for Flying Boats to alight was abandoned. As a pilot, he could understand how the reflective surfaces of the reservoirs, the acres of glasshouses and the nearby sewage-settling lagoons had confused German pilots on their moonlit flights searching for the London docks and had diverted their bombing to this unlikely spot.

Only about fifteen per cent of the German bombs fell within five miles of the target and Melville could see the craters left by high-explosive bombs, scattered in the fields. However, he knew that many unexploded bombs remained buried, especially in the beds of sand and gravel around the Pits, waiting to wreak their destruction. He had heard from the bomb disposal units working in the area that sometimes when defusing unexploded bombs they found notes written by Jewish women, working undetected in the German munitions factories, explaining that they had sabotaged them.

Further away to the south and east he could see three previous airfields, which had been superseded by the new developments at Hadleyrow. Melville felt gratified that this area had been a hotbed of transport innovation, especially aviation, confirming that this was definitely the right place for the development of the latest and largest international airport in the world, with plenty of flat surrounding fields to allow for expansion.

By this time it was getting dark, but Melville decided to make another circuit, as he had been so engrossed in the overall scene that he still needed to pay special attention to the area where the most recent trouble had been centred.

'Is that the area you were telling me about, Burian?' he asked his companion in the cockpit.

He had met Burian on one of the regular shooting parties organised by the deputy commander of the airport, a keen field sportsman. Rabbits and hares had been attracted to the area by the remnants of the abandoned crops. In turn, they had attracted the hunters: foxes, feral cats and men with guns and dogs. Although the locals benefited from the game that was shot, they wouldn't take the hares; not out of distaste, but of fear, believing that they generated melancholy or worse in those who ate them.

Local legends of a wounded hare being followed into a

thicket, leading to the discovery of a beautiful young woman bleeding from a wound in her leg, inspired many a lad to follow the hunt; it being as likely as any other way to meet a beautiful young woman in the area.

The shooting parties were not bound by the normal seasonal restrictions and shot anything that moved at any time, including a few feral sheep left over from the flock that had been put out to feed on the fields of sprout stalks and to manure the soil. Sheep had also been used inside the glasshouses to improve the soil, but they had jumped out through the glass and had had to be replaced by poultry.

Hadleyrow must have been the only place where a hunting party returned with dead sheep, at least intentionally. They didn't notice that one of their number, an ex-serviceman who had fought with the infantry from the D-Day beaches to the heart of Germany, always shot high or wide, scattering the game in the process and never killing or wounding anything.

On one occasion, someone had suggested taking potshots at Lizzie. Everybody had laughed, some more uneasily than others, but they all believed it would take a silver bullet or a crooked sixpence to bring her down.

In those days it wasn't unusual to see a hunting party with guns wandering across one runway while a plane landed on another, but then all the airliners were converted ex-World War Two bombers and their ex-RAF pilots had experienced men with much bigger guns firing directly at them.

His companion in the cockpit seemed a decent fellow and Melville, trusting his own judgement and considering the urgency of the situation, had unofficially accepted his offer of help in clearing the remaining villagers from the site in a humane way.

'Yes. That's it,' said Burian, staring intently at the few old cottages below with flat, cold, grey eyes. Burian was short and thickset, with a deeply lined face and thick, dark hair flecked with grey, which was combed straight back without a parting.

They were flying over the Rookery. Close by, the Pits could be seen as large, dark, foreboding, ragged patches lined with yellow sandy banks and the pale green of willow and alder. Even from this height it was clear why they were surrounded by an aura of dread and mystery, and were largely avoided by the villagers.

Wary of the close proximity of the Pits and of the fading light, Melville decided not to risk landing on the grass airfield from which they had taken off, but to land on the main concrete runway of the new airport. He had no instrument landing system aboard the plane to pick up the radio beam that extended upwards towards them from the airport, but in this light aircraft he had plenty of leeway on the massive runway.

With regard to the landing lights at the end of the runway – which at night could be seen more than twenty miles away, confusing night-flying birds on their migrations – he had no need for the pilot's mantra:

Red over white, you're all right.
White over white, too much height.
Red over red, you're dead.

He would negotiate the approach and landing by the seat of his pants, as he had done all over Europe during the war.

But without warning, he was struck with fear. His mouth became dry, his heart pounded, and his breathing quickened and became shallow. Sweat ran down his back and his palms became wet. He gripped the controls and adjusted the ailerons to keep the wings level. A gust of wind took him sideways and he pressed the rudder to keep the nose straight and on line. He hated flying in a light aircraft in gusting winds, but his feeling of terror had preceded the buffeting.

He remembered some advice he had overheard during the war for those who panicked in the cockpit. He forced a bizarre smile onto his face and drove his nails into the palm of his free hand. He was suffering 'the twitch'; pilot slang for a sudden loss of self-confidence akin to a premonition of disaster; a panic attack.

He had survived five years of war in Bomber Command with the enemy trying to shoot him out of the air; he had pulled out of a graveyard spiral with only a few hundred feet to spare; he had bounced a plane to destruction on landing; and he had landed a plane with the undercarriage up, the latter incident, to his amusement, being reported in the papers as 'plane lands upside down'. All of these incidents had reinforced his devil-may-care reputation. But now, in peacetime, on a local flight in a light aircraft, he was paralysed with fear.

He had lost his nerve in a split second. Every certainty in his being had drained away. He was drenched in guilt as he recalled the pilots he had silently mocked for feigning sickness to avoid missions; for being afraid of heights when climbing on board the big bombers, sometimes even having to be blindfolded and led up the steps; for being claustrophobic inside their cockpits or gun turrets; or for fainting at the sight of blood.

Almost immediately, they were flying over the old Green Man pub, built in 1627, which had somehow survived the destruction. The vibration shook soot down the highwayman's hideaway behind the fireplace, just as a red-necked tourist from the USA peered in, turning him – to his horror – black.

At fifty feet they were just above the last remaining house before the airfield perimeter. As it had originally been to one side of the developing airport, the authorities hadn't targeted this house with the same determination they had shown in clearing the rest of Hadleyrow. It was the home of a hardworking farming family. Like their ancestors before them, they had lived in a peaceful, rural idyll in balance with nature until, without warning or compensation, the sky had fallen in on them.

Once over the threshold of the runway, Melville could ignore the touchdown zone marked by white lines, which also neatly marked the site of Caesar's Camp. He wondered what its original inhabitants would have made of him arriving in such a fashion. Perhaps they would have accepted it as yet another screaming banshee, with which the air would have then been as thick as it was today with flying planes. He caught a glimpse of the reflective green eyes of a fox and the amber eyes of a hare, which completed the set with the red landing lights.

Although he made a textbook landing, Melville didn't stop shaking until he shut the plane's engine down.

III

Awoken by the sound of a light aircraft landing on the main runway, borne on the gusting wind, Kate lay shivering feverishly in her damp bed. It was damp from her uncontrolled sweating and damp from the rain dripping through the thatch that had been deliberately damaged while she was out in the fields.

Kate had always been a fine worker. She never grumbled or complained about any work she was asked to do, however rough or unpleasant. Nor did she boast about what she was capable of doing. On occasion, the foreman tried to match the work the girls did, which improved his knowledge of their hard lives and increased his standing amongst them. Kate was the fastest and most efficient, especially at the more difficult gathering of red, white and blackcurrants, and on no occasion could he match her for speed and excellence of work. She would flash her smile and say that her bushes were better cropped than his, but they all knew she was too good for him, or anybody else come to that.

Despite the hardships, the field girls enjoyed a bond of camaraderie born of shared 'troubulations' and 'sufferations', as Kate used to say in her inventive way. A froth of banter, laughter and song effervesced from them all day long, protecting them from the harsh realities of their work, like cuckoo spit. Kate usually laughed as she spoke, and trying to read meaning of an accustomed sort into her speech was about as effective as trying to make a translation from a rippling brook. She never cried, especially not for craft or prettiness. Kate was as beautiful on the inside as she was on the outside, contradicting Lizzie's advice to: 'Never judge somebody's insides from their outsides.'

Despite the harsh realities, the scene looked like something out of a musical film on sunny days, with birds singing, bees humming and the girls in their colourful kerchiefs moving among the laden fruit trees. Kate, her voice like the migrant nightingales in the hawthorn thickets, led the singing, with the gang joining in for the chorus to keep their spirits up. Kate had always been enchanted by the distant world of the Hollywood musicals she had seen at the Fletham Playhouse. 'Bewitched, Bothered and Bewildered' was her favourite song, although Lizzie didn't like it for obvious reasons.

Kate had never missed a day's work before, but failed to see how she could get to work that day due to her illness. *But if she didn't, who would look after Lizzie in the mud?* She forced herself up before falling back into a stupor from which she would never awake.

Not yet thirty, Kate had been destroyed by an insidious infection that not even Lizzie's concoctions of garlic and ox bile, or of feverfew, lungwort and ground ivy, could cure. Like the beautiful and graceful swifts whose dominion was the skies, Kate, once caught in the mud, had been unable to struggle free. She had become so frail that Lizzie had said: 'Youm couldn't see 'er body for 'er soul.'

It was widely accepted by everyone with any knowledge of Kate's hard life that her illness had been brought on by exposure to the severe conditions in which she worked. She was 'only a field girl', and it was by mere time and chance that she died in a damp bed rather than in the mud of the fields. She had lived and died like her Celtic ancestors, and thousands of years of herbal lore had failed her, as it had failed them and millions more. Modern medicine hadn't helped either. It could have done, but it hadn't reached her down at the Rookery.

She was disowned by officialdom in death, and in the confusion of the developments she was hurriedly buried outside the deserted Methodist chapel. Her grave was marked with a wooden cross on which somebody had scratched: 'Blessed are the meek.' Nobody knew what would happen to the grave when the bulldozers finally arrived.

All the field girls were devastated by Kate's death. Lizzie, who had found Kate's body cold, waxen-yellow and stiff in the damp, stained sheets, lost her mind, lost her soul and was herself no more. She was one of the living dead; a zombie, as

Radish would have said.

IV

After a long, cold, wet winter, Briscoe drove back up to London from Hadleyrow to see some relatives. He was in a complete quandary with regard to meeting up with Allen again. Although he was bringing the good news that the police at the airport had closed their investigation into the attempted robbery, he dreaded bringing news of Kate's death and Gill's engagement and now imminent marriage to Piotr, if Allen hadn't already heard.

Allen hadn't already heard. He hadn't seen Radish for ages and had been completely isolated from the West Indian network. The local networks had no connection with the airport, nor did they ever talk to him.

When Briscoe found Allen, he told him the news that the investigation into the robbery had been abandoned, but he couldn't bring himself to tell him about Kate and Gill. On hearing the news about the robbery, Allen was surprised at the pull he felt to return to Hadleyrow. He decided to return with Briscoe, but had no idea who took the decision, or why.

Briscoe could hardly refuse, but he realised he would have an even greater responsibility to tell Allen the bad news during the journey. He realised how bad it would be if Allen found out from someone else after the journey, but the longer he left it the more difficult it became.

As Allen prepared to travel back with Briscoe, he desperately hoped that his London adventures might have had a beneficial effect on him. His old friend William Cowper, who would have been two hundred and twenty if he hadn't died aged sixty-nine, duly turned up to reinforce Allen's hope with the observation that:

How much a dunce that has been sent to roam
Excels a dunce that has been kept at home.

Allen felt particularly close to Cowper, as, like him, Cowper was a desperate outsider who had found new pleasures every day just looking at a hedge; not to mention that he had raised three orphaned baby hares. However, despite these humble pursuits, he had been the most popular poet of his day and his verses were the war cry of abolitionists.

Cowper's reassurance, however, was short-lived, as Socrates, an ancient Greek, pushed in to observe that a certain man had grown no better by his travels as 'he took himself along with him'.

Allen couldn't understand why Socrates, aged seventy, had been forced to kill himself by consuming hemlock for concluding exactly what Allen had more than two thousand years later: that he didn't know anything and nor did anyone else, and, if they thought they did, they were wrong. Allen wondered whether the hemlock Socrates had used was the same as the one he knew in the hedgerows, growing up to ten feet in height and leaving its dry dead stalks standing over winter.

While he was there, Socrates pushed in again, giving Allen a split second of rare pride in his state of mind with his view that: 'The unexamined life is not worth living.'

But this time Allen immediately contradicted the great man. He longed for the peace of an unexamined life. He felt it was his examining that had opened up the floodgates that would have been far better left firmly closed, not that he really had a choice in the matter.

On the other hand, he hated the arrogance and ignorance

of those who said: 'If it works, don't worry about it', and took no interest in anything. He couldn't help but feel that thinking and worrying – if that meant becoming more conscious of the awesome nature of things – was the way the universe became aware of itself, even if it was only to realise that it was a pitiless waste of time and space.

Allen's heart sank. His abstract thoughts were gathering momentum; a sign that his old patterns of thinking persisted and were beginning to resurface despite all his adventures. He wasn't surprised. *How could they not? It was the way his brain worked. It was just cranking up again.* As he well knew, no allowances were made for it malfunctioning, as if the brain wasn't part of the physical body and any malfunction was one's personal responsibility. But it crossed Allen's now manic mind that if the brain – the most complex structure in the known universe – were simple enough for him to understand, he wouldn't be able to understand it.

Searching through his cards he found some lines by a chap he only knew as Horace, who lived some four hundred years after Socrates:

*Why should we move to find
Countries and climates of another kind?
What exile leaves himself behind?*

By some miracle of random organisation, the next card contained lines from Milton, who wrote more than a millennium later:

A mind is not to be changed by place or time.

He didn't need a card to remind him Lizzie had summed it all up for them by saying: 'Wherever youm go, there youm be.'

However, his main concern as he contemplated returning to Hadleyrow was that the last time he had seen Gill she had run away in horror.

Millions – especially the Eastern Europeans – had endured and survived the unimaginable terrors of the Second World War and had still successfully created new lives in totally foreign lands. Allen's genetic load and resultant social isolation, on the other hand, had proved more powerful than any environmental advantages the Eastern Europeans or those from the Caribbean assumed he enjoyed. Even a war criminal from Europe or a 'rude-boy' from Jamaica with a ratchet and a big white smile had a much better chance of making a life for himself than Allen ever would.

Either way, he knew he was done for. The pressures had accumulated until any sensuous reflexes had broken down completely. Despite thinking nothing of putting a bumblebee in his mouth, he still wasn't prepared to eat a ladybird. He could have tried bedstraw boiled in oil, but he didn't know which bedstraw or oil to use. He assumed it would be the lady's bedstraw, its sweet, sun-drenched scent appropriately redolent of medieval bedrooms, but he suspected that in his case it might be the less aromatic hedge bedstraw, although he knew neither would work anyway.

He had tried a potato, once valued as an aphrodisiac, although he hadn't known what to do with it. Some boys in the village stuffed them down the front of their pants, settling for the illusion. Many village men claimed to carry a potato against rheumatism, which everybody knew was a cover.

On the day they were to leave for Hadleyrow, Briscoe winced for his tyres and suspension when he saw Big Radish leaning against the bonnet.

'You gwan live long! I was just thinkin about you,' said

Briscoe in an attempt to put Radish at ease, just in case he had detected his initial reaction.

'Any chance me can come wid unnu? Me need a break from dis ya city life,' said Radish resignedly.

Briscoe instantly dismissed concerns about wear and tear on the suspension and tyres, but was paranoid about Radish letting slip the news about Kate and Gill. He knew it had to come out sooner or later, but he just couldn't face up to it. Still, Radish was a good man and might be useful if they got into any tight corners, despite his waning strength.

'What d'you think?' Briscoe asked Allen.

'Good idea. He can get a job at the airport.'

'Sure thing, Radish. We a go weh now,' said Briscoe.

So off they went, with Allen in the front seat and Big Radish filling the back.

They made slow progress out of the city. Even under these mundane circumstances, one of Allen's more troublesome friend's arrived to observe that:

The facilities which now exist of moving human bodies from place to place are amongst the curses of the country, the destroyers of industry and of morals and, of course, of happiness.

Nobody from Hadleyrow would have argued over that with radical politician and political journalist, William Cobbett, who would have been one hundred and eighty-seven if he hadn't died in 1835. A tireless campaigner on behalf of the common labourer and for the reform of parliament and the Church of England, Allen admired Cobbett's concern for: 'the hard-pinched, ill-treated, the beaten down labouring classes of England, Scotland and Ireland'.

However, Allen didn't count Cobbett among his closest

friends, as he disagreed with him over many other things, especially when he had read that Cobbett considered those fighting for the abolition of slavery were guilty of:

> *All the mischief that it is in your power to do to the labouring classes; because you describe their situation as good, and because you do, in some degree, at any rate, draw the public attention away from their sufferings.*

The traffic stuttered along.

'If the road block up for some reason, back home them have parties. That really block them up, so them have one next party,' said Briscoe.

'Me a starve,' said Radish, testing his grip on the front seat and barely seeming to compress the soft upholstery.

Nobody responded.

Radish gripped the back of the seat again. There was no doubt he was losing his strength. He listened to Allen and Briscoe as they reasoned with each other on every subject under the sun.

'Raatid, man. How yuh know all dis stuff?' asked Radish.

'Just cos me did haffi leff school, nuh mean seh me did stop learn,' Briscoe replied.

In Allen's case, Radish assumed it was a result of the usual white man's privilege, not knowing that Allen had left school at a younger age than he had. Radish couldn't read or write, but had always taken comfort in the compensation of his great strength. Now that this was waning, Radish was worried. Very worried. Panic stricken, in fact. Neither did Radish have any known family, a regular woman to look after him, or now even a job.

Radish couldn't have known that Allen was in a worse position because, apart from being able to get a job, his position in life was irredeemable.

V

They hadn't gone far when they were stopped by what was obviously a road accident ahead.

'We better check it out. Radish, you stay with the van,' said Briscoe.

Allen followed Briscoe through the thickening crowd. To his shock, as soon as he caught the first whiff of abdominal contents – a smell he knew so well from the kitchen table in Hadleyrow – he froze in his steps. It was as if he had walked into a plate glass window.

Briscoe went on ahead and disappeared into the screaming crowd. Allen would have done the same if he had been someone else, but he wasn't and he couldn't move. It was as simple as that. His subjective experience of anxiety wasn't a great deal more than it normally was in his so-called resting state, he just couldn't move. If somebody had come up and threatened to shoot him on the spot he would have appeared brave in his indifference to the threat.

In contrast to his physical paralysis, there was no stopping his mind, which raced on at an even more manic pace than usual. He had known a lady in the village whose son had lied about his age to join the army during the First World War. He had frozen in action and subsequently faced a firing squad, despite still being officially too young to be in the army. He hadn't been killed outright, so the officer in charge had finished him off with a revolver.

The two of them quite possibly had similar childhoods playing in beautiful, sunlit pastures and woodlands. Yet it had still been considered acceptable for one to shoot the other in the head, even though the executioner hadn't been exposed to the same trauma as the victim.

Anonymous villagers had sent the mother a white feather every Armistice Day since, and her son's name had not appeared on the war memorial at the parish church. After several years of abuse and grief, she had drowned herself in the Pits. A lot of people in the village had said 'good riddance'.

Allen's mind raced on while his body was rooted to the spot. *Who were these people who were so detached from the suffering of others and sure in their personal convictions that they could put a revolver to the head of a mortally wounded man, blow his brains out in cold blood and feel proud of themselves? Who could emerge unscathed from the carnage of the battlefield and continue their previous existence as though nothing had happened? Who could observe the suffering of others with detachment; as something separate from their own? Didn't they realise, like Allen's friend John Donne had said centuries ago, that the same bell tolls for them?*

Could slavery have been perpetuated with such moral vigour for so long if people had frozen at the smell of a slave ship on the Middle Passage? One ship might have sailed, but more than eleven million slaves wouldn't have been transported from Africa across the Atlantic. In any battle, hand-to-hand combat would have stopped after the first penetrated abdomen, and even if the authorities had begun to shoot those who refused to fight, each firing squad would only have followed orders once, all of which would still have been once too often.

It took Allen's mind but a split second to compute all these associations as he desperately attempted to move forwards and rationalise his inability to do so.

But he still couldn't move. He couldn't understand it. He wasn't supposed to have a future or care about anything. He had never flinched from the torture exacted on his mouth over the years, whereas he had heard of war heroes who were unable to face the dentist. He had eviscerated countless rabbits and a few chickens on the kitchen table at Christmas, whereas he knew a brave pilot who fainted at the sight of blood. He had never flinched from a physical fight. He had broken bones and suffered massive blows to his head, but he had always just got on with it.

But recently he had heard of a new book called *1984*, in which the forces of evil knew that everyone had at least one overwhelming fear that could be exploited by exposing the victim to it in a special room: Room 101. Allen realised he was in his Room 101, even though he was standing in the open, and that his fearful thoughts and his hard-learned quotes had deserted him in the face of this stark, cold, paralysing fear.

When Briscoe returned from the scene of the accident he made no reference to the fact that Allen hadn't followed him.

'Him dead all right. Him spread all over the road.'

Notwithstanding the hurricane of thoughts that had stormed through his mind in justification of his own paralysis, including the thought that being unaffected by suffering in others was a prerequisite for being able to perpetrate it, Allen was filled with respect for Briscoe's actions. He just couldn't win.

As if reading his thoughts, Briscoe said: 'No mind, man. I couldn't have touched that lizard, never mind put it in mi mout.'

Allen was stunned by Briscoe's insight and lack of braggardly swagger. He had more in common with Briscoe than he did with the villagers in Hadleyrow.

But this totally unexpected support was not enough to shut his mind down. Not having seen the body himself, he was obsessed with preventing other people from seeing it. Not, he hoped, from a need to recruit accomplices to his dilemma, but from a desire to prevent other people being exposed to the horror.

Allen gradually became able to move again and followed Briscoe back to the car. He had lost any remaining self-esteem and had been surprised by how much he still had to lose. It was clear that there was no point in all his thought and conjecture. His reaction to the accident had demonstrated the futility of thought. Nevertheless, his mind would roll on regardless, with the screeching squall of nightmares behind it, like gulls behind the plough.

The delayed shock of the accident was such that both Briscoe and Radish forgot any thoughts about Gill and Kate.

VI

Allen's generalised anxiety ramped up even further after the accident. He didn't know what had happened to Gill, although he was sure he had done the right thing by leaving her, for her sake at least. On the other hand he knew he should never have left Lizzie and Kate as their world was being destroyed around them.

Allen didn't know how he had ended up being looked after by Lizzie, whom, consequently, he had always thought of as his nanny. Whatever the reason, they had lived in a pool of love in what outsiders perceived as the dark end of the village. But that pool was quiet and still, its deep waters unstirred by overt emotion.

As a result, Allen had become increasingly watchful lest he transgressed unspoken expectations of purity in thought and deed. The relentless scan for potential sin within himself had inevitably involved him imagining such sins, so the continuous intrusive fear of him committing those sins had arisen from the very checking process that attempted to ensure they were absent. *Oh, it was all so clever!*

Despite the temporary relief from unbearable tension that the reassurances from his friends gave him, he had read that they enabled him to avoid facing his fears, thus reinforcing them by according them significance and inspiring the contrary mind to automatically scan for exceptions. *Oh, it was all so very clever!*

Even so, Allen knew he couldn't do without his friends and their reassurances. He particularly valued their reassurances that he wasn't going mad, whatever that might mean; that he wasn't losing his mind; that he wasn't evil in having the thoughts, images and ideas that crowded in on him.

He realised it was more effective for survival that anxiety would always outrank reassurances. Perhaps his direct Celtic ancestors' eternal watchfulness and the limitless ingenuity of their catastrophising imagination had ensured the survival of the tribe. In return, perhaps its less anxious members had been wise enough to recognise the damage wreaked by the burden the watchful ones carried on their behalf, and treated those that suffered in this way with compassion rather than the disdain and rejection they experienced today.

Sometimes when a particularly bad intrusive thought or image was triggered Allen would let out an expletive, and his face would distort even more with the effort of suppressing the unthinkable. But, as he understood it, even this tiny relief was denied him. Not that he had any control over the reaction.

He had lost count of the times that he had read the card on which he had copied the anonymous advice:

Do not make the mistake of supposing there are certain thoughts you shouldn't think. Shrink from none of it. It must be repeated again and again that recovery lies in accepting such thoughts as part of ordinary thinking. Trying to discard thoughts at will, especially when the thought is distressing and the mind tired, reinforces them as they strengthen in the face of resistance.

He found confirmation of this advice in Montaigne's observation:

Nothing fixes a thing so intensely in the memory as the wish to forget it.

This also confirmed, to Allen's fleeting satisfaction, his own observation that it was logically impossible to consciously not think of something.

Typically, Lizzie had come up with her own saying that had cut to the heart of the problem, when he had overheard her advising a villager who was distressed as she had had a bad thought about a neighbour: 'Thoughts only be thoughts. Just thoughts.'

Allen's rational self could see that fearful thoughts, which could be so profoundly shocking, were just like any other worrisome thought: the exact opposite of what one hoped for. But he realised that at the heart of his disorder was the fear that thoughts had great meaning and power; that they were premonitions or even the seeds of the events themselves that might come true just because he had them; that just having the thoughts meant that he was a wicked person who could cause harm.

This fear was only slightly lessened by Montaigne's observation that:

Thoughts can run into a thousand extravagances…in which mild agitation there is no folly nor idle fancy they do not light upon.

Living with Lizzie and with Kate next door, it had never occurred to Allen that females could be considered weak or inferior in anyway. They were field girls, who worked long hours in all weathers. Their favourite virtue was endurance and their ideal was not to flinch from hardship or pain, which they didn't.

Loss of young men in the two world wars and the relentless nature of their work meant that many, including Kate, never found love. For them, as with Allen, the only romance associated with St Valentine's Day was that it was the day on which grey partridges traditionally paired up after spending the winter in coveys out in the fields. Otherwise, its only significance for them was that it was the correct date for sowing seeds to get good seedlings for planting in cold greenhouses a month later.

From September to March, the field girls harvested cabbages and Brussels sprouts. When it rained, the leaves were full of water and the mud was like thick brown soup. They would wrap sacks around their heads and shoulders, use the large sprout leaves as rain hats, and tie their skirts around and between their legs.

In the summer, they could work from three in the morning until nine at night picking and preparing loganberries, blackberries and raspberries as well as bunching cut flowers, mint and parsley.

Only the 'digger men' in the glasshouses worked harder. They prepared the flowerbeds in the glasshouses for planting. The best could turn more than forty rods or a furlong in a long day from four in the morning until eight at night. If the soil was infested with woodlice the beds had to be blowtorched, which was a backbreaking job. But as Lizzie always said: 'At least them never get rained on, or 'ave to squelch around in the mud.'

However, the field girls had no concept of themselves as dispossessed victims. They were kind and generous to a fault; not that they had much to give except their love and understanding. They were meek and didn't expect anything in return, least of all to inherit the world as the Bible promised.

The Gypsy workers who had found Lizzie in the fields as a baby had initially named her 'Ciara'. It meant black and mysterious, which described her dark complexion and unknown origins. However, people struggled with the pronunciation and she soon became known as 'Lizzie'. This was not a diminutive of Elizabeth, as she liked to think, but due to her perceived resemblance to a lizard, a symbol of age in old paintings: small, spare, quick, sharp-eyed, with a weather-beaten, scaly complexion and the ability to slip away unnoticed.

Lizzie had no mirrors at home and never looked at her reflection in any surface, except by accident, when she always wondered who it was. She never went out in the daytime without a kerchief tied around her head like a highwayman's mask. As Lizzie couldn't tie a bow properly it frequently came undone, at which times people would avert their eyes. This had led to Allen's idea that the surfeit of highwaymen in the area in earlier days could have been related not only to the dire poverty, the heavy coach traffic on the main road and the wildness of the heath, but also to the large number of facially disfigured people, who had taken to a life of crime in which they could experience a sort of freedom behind their masks, albeit short-lived. He thought it a curious coincidence that many local birds also had masklike eye markings.

With regard to the ongoing insults Lizzie endured, it drove Allen mad when Lizzie used to say: 'Sticks and stones will break me bones but words will never 'urt me.' Words cut him to the quick and engendered a burning anger in him that never faded.

Despite her rejection, Lizzie was respected and feared for her knowledge of folklore and ancient plant medicines. She had learned much from the old villagers, whose experience reached back into the previous century, but also from old battered copies of Culpepper's *The English Physician* and *The Complete Herbal,* published in 1652 and 1653, both of which had been given to her by one of the farmers she cleaned for. Lizzie had developed a special empathy with Culpepper when she discovered that he too had been accused of witchcraft.

Although herbal remedies were largely ineffective, they were at least open to all. Religion, the only other source of solace and hope for those who were sick in those times required faith. Allen certainly didn't have sufficient faith to believe that he would ever have a perfect smile. He considered the tenet of the faithful just as arrogant and heartless as the secular equivalent of positive thinking in fighting and beating disease. Both beliefs were cruelly insulting to those denied their hopes through no fault of their own.

CHAPTER THREE

I

Looking out of the van window as they sped along, Allen caught the first glimpse of a green field between the ribbon development along the main road west. Although his anxiety levels were rising in anticipation of his return to Hadleyrow, each glimpse of greenery helped to calm him and the signs of spring lifted his spirits further.

No matter how bitter the winter, spring always pushed forward, driven by hidden forces. It might be delayed, but it wouldn't be denied. It was a season of gleams and moments of sunshine glittering between storms. Once launched, the wonder of the English spring defied the worst, no matter how delicate its first heralds – the snowdrops – which Allen had once made into posies wrapped in ivy leaves for Gill.

Primroses tufted on sunny banks, crocuses tooted through lengthening grass and daffodils took the wind with beauty. There were reminders of Gill everywhere: the 'day's-eyes' he had made into daisy chains for her to hang around her neck; the buttercups he would hold under her chin to see whether she liked butter. She always had, but he had still liked to check.

The van scooped up a whiff of wild garlic through an open window, along with some airborne seeds, which, having caught a lift, drifted out of the window further down the road. Tall strands of cow parsley filled the ditches with their white umbrellas. Swathes of white flowers emerged on the blackthorn, which often heralded a cold snap – the 'blackthorn winter' – when frosts would blend with a profusion of white flowers, the blown petals of which could fill the air like a blizzard.

Galaxies of what he called dandelions peppered the verges with yellow and gold. Allen's limited knowledge of these exasperated Lizzie, as throughout the year there were more dandelion-like flowers than dandelions. The true dandelion was one of the few flowers for which she preferred the Norman name, as did Cowper, to the Anglo-Saxon 'witch gowan'. Allen's misuse of dandelion for all the others, which had perfectly acceptable Anglo-Saxon names, compounded her annoyance at his ignorance.

Ragwort was shooting but not yet flowering. It provided a feast for the caterpillars of red and black moths, which concentrated the plant's toxins for their own defence. Allen wished he could concentrate the vitriol aimed at him and return it to his tormentors in a concentrated form.

Allen had no idea how long he had been away from Hadleyrow. He was always puzzled by other people's certainty about time. To him, as a more recent friend of his – Albert Einstein, who was actually still alive – had said: 'The distinction between past, present and future is nothing but a stubbornly persistent illusion.'

This perfectly reflected a strange feeling he had once had while reading in the failing light of a winter's afternoon in a secluded part of an old farmhouse in Hadleyrow. As he glanced out of the window at the great black shape of a yew tree, and the rose by the window tapped on the glass in the wind he had felt lost in a pattern of timeless moments.

Allen knew the Celtic concept of time was circular rather than linear, and one of the Mauritian Chinese at the airport had told him that the ancient Chinese believed time was but a ladder into the past. Allen had formulated his own vague concept that there was no future as such and that the present was the front edge of the past, which it created and which left a permanent trail. As a boy he had tried spinning around quickly to see it. Luckily for him he had never succeeded.

Despite Allen's fascination with time, his upbringing with Lizzie had not helped his appreciation of the everyday matter of measuring it. Timepieces were not widely available to the villagers, so other than at dawn and dusk, they placed too much trust in nature's signs on cloudy days, just as they did with nature's medicines.

The small red flowers of the scarlet pimpernel were supposed to close at three in the afternoon. But it was also known as shepherd's weather glass, as its flowers closed up when bad weather was coming, so you couldn't tell the time from it then, nor make weather predictions after three in the afternoon.

Jack-go-to-bed-at-noon, which grew in the rough grass like a large dandelion, did the same. After flowering, all dandelion-like flowers produced 'fairy clocks' – globe-like seed heads of tiny parachutes – which could also be used to tell the time by counting the number of puffs needed to blow off all the parachuted seeds. Based on this method, the less fit thought it was later than the fitter among them did, and the very fit thought it was always one o'clock.

The songs and calls of resident birds that had somehow survived the winter defiantly filled the air, although the sad wheezing of the greenfinches suggested perhaps they should also have flown south for the winter. Skylarks on flickering wings poured their liquid song from the vast skies. Great tits – a name the boys found hilarious to shout out when girls were around – punctuated it all with their monotonous call, like squeaky bicycle pumps. Rooks cawed, whirled and swirled around the real rookeries, like torn black rags caught in the wind, squabbling over their crude nests of sticks high up in the swaying elm trees.

Migratory birds arrived after incredible journeys across continents, deserts and oceans, following the tide of emerging leaves, flowers and insects in the wake of the sun's increasing arc north after the shortest day, at which time some villagers still breathed a sigh of relief. The journey was reversed, sooner or later, as the sun moved south again, although some had learned to stay. Allen wondered whether, on their return, those that still migrated mixed freely with the stop-at-homes or whether they found them too dull. Despite following the sun, many navigated by the stars on clear nights, silhouetted against the moon, their passage announced by the ghostly rustling of wings and eerie disembodied calls in the dark air. Lizzie stayed indoors at these times.

Young salmon and adult eels swam downstream to the ocean, while adult salmon and young eels swam upstream, having navigated thousands of miles in the ocean and survived natural hazards, as well as the villagers' nets, traps and garden forks. But some 'sneaker' salmon males learned to stay the year round and await the return of the females. Allen thought Denzil would have been impressed by this strategy.

All these epic migrations were fraught with dangers but were impossible to resist for the migrants. Human migration, also fraught with danger but impossible to resist for many, followed in the wake of the development of the new airport.

The displaced from Eastern Europe considered Britain their 'paradise found', while those from the Caribbean – most of whose great expectations of the mother country would be thwarted – came to see the Caribbean as their 'paradise lost'.

Many in Britain were looking to emigrate, while those who stayed and settled accused them of deserting a sinking ship. The same ship that had saved so many from the shipwreck of Europe was now seen as a shipwreck itself, even by some of those it had rescued.

But none of this was Lizzie's fault, even though she had fallen or been thrown out of a balloon and seemed a little too familiar with hares. Nor was it Allen's. They couldn't have known what was coming.

Allen was awoken from his reverie by the sound of an aircraft overhead. They were nearing airport country.

II

When Briscoe, Allen and Radish finally reached the airport, they parked outside the corrugated iron Nissen hut that served as the kitchen for El Al Israel Airlines. Briscoe knew they were often looking for kitchen hands and that, although they only prepared kosher food, they were still ready – like all restaurants – to employ almost anybody who applied to do the menial kitchen work.

Briscoe pushed an apprehensive Radish through the door and it wasn't long before he re-emerged, beaming, to announce that he had been offered a job washing up and preparing vegetables, and that he was to start the next day. He had been surprised to see the kosher kitchen being overseen by a rabbi who was sitting on the draining board. Sitting on any food-related surface was totally taboo in the West Indies on the grounds of hygiene.

El Al didn't fly on the Sabbath or religious holidays, had very few operational aircraft, and its few scheduled flights often broke down and didn't make it through to Hadleyrow. Much of the food prepared for the scheduled flights, had to be thrown away on news of their non-arrival. With Radish working there, however, the pig bins remained mysteriously empty. The same would have occurred if he had worked for British Overseas Airways Corporation with seventeen times the passenger miles.

'Let's check the public enclosure,' said Briscoe.

'You go ahead. I've got to find Lizzie and Kate. I'll catch up with you later,' Allen said unconvincingly. He had no intention of trying to reconnect with anybody other than Lizzie and Kate.

Briscoe realised it was his last chance to tell Allen the news, but before he could compose himself Allen had gone. Briscoe wanted to run after him but knew he would never catch him. He would just have to face the consequences when they occurred.

As Briscoe and Radish approached the public enclosure they were surprised to find the large, brown, canvas army bell tent outside the public enclosure café packed with people. They entered tentatively and looked around at an untidy array of cream-painted, tea-stained, rusty, metal tables with folding legs that wobbled.

It dawned on Briscoe that – as if to compound his guilt – they had stumbled upon Gill and Piotr's wedding reception, or at least the overflow part of it, which he had heard people talking about. Now he was relieved that Allen had gone off to look for Lizzie, as he assumed she wouldn't be at the reception.

Nearly all those present were smoking cigarettes. Red and white packets of four littered the tables and propped up the wobbly ones on the uneven ground. There were many people Briscoe had not seen before, some of whom he assumed were Gill's less respectable relatives, as he knew some of them were Irish and had arrived to work as navvies on the tunnel.

The group of workers from the airport and adjacent industrial estate would have been distinguishable even to a stranger. Women were noticeable by their absence as most of the men had such broken lives and a clear buffer zone had been left around them due to their misleadingly intimidating appearance.

Many of the locals took measures not to sit next to any of the group in a public place, deliberately timing their bus journeys so as to avoid them as they travelled to and from work. If the bus was late and they were still queuing when a shift ended, many would simply walk away, leaving puzzled workers much nearer, if not actually at, the head of the queue.

There were those from the Caribbean, a few Mauritian Chinese, individuals from various other parts of the British Commonwealth and refugees from all parts of Central and Eastern Europe: heroes, cowards, victims and perpetrators of atrocities alike. There were also refugees of a sort from other parts of the UK. Some were escaping localised, nominally religious conflicts: Catholic 'Norman Conks' and Protestant 'Billy Boys' from Glasgow, along with Catholic Irish Republicans and Protestant Northern Irish Loyalists.

On the outside of the group sat Burian, his son Luka, Big Raditch, known behind his back as the 'Mad Russian', and Maurice – a Chinese Mauritian known as 'Morris Seven' as there were six older Chinese Mauritians of the same name working in the area – and Prof, who had come back down when he had heard that the robbery fiasco was all forgotten.

Burian's son Luka was a pleasant-looking lad of around the same age as Piotr, with whom he had become friends. He had been taken from Ukraine to Italy by his Uncle Vasyl, a famous actor in Ukraine, along with his English nanny, to escape the Ukrainian starvation of the early 1930s.

Luka and his nanny were inseparable, mainly because she had always frantically tried to avoid his uncle's unwanted attentions. Therefore, Luka spoke good English and a little Italian, but no Ukrainian. Consequently, he had been virtually incapable of communicating with Burian after he had escaped from Austria after the war to join them in Italy. Luka's mother had disappeared without a trace and was never spoken of. Luka, Burian and Vasyl had subsequently gained entry to England in 1945 without any vetting whatsoever.

Despite being known as 'The Mad Russian', Big Raditch came from Latvia and hated the Russians, having been subjected to forced labour in the coalmines under the Russian occupation. The 'Mad' part referred to the stupendous stamping rages he suffered periodically, which resulted in the immediate emptying of the area around him. It was a disconcerting sight on the factory floor, let alone in the pub or on the top deck of the number 117 bus at a time when there was virtually no vandalism, swearing in public places was an offence and gentlemen still gave up their seats to ladies on buses and trams.

Like Piotr, Big Raditch knew only too well that the Russian slave labour camps still operated in Siberia. He also knew that serfdom, which was little better than slavery, had lasted for centuries in Russia, right up to the turn of the twentieth century.

Big Raditch and Morris Seven made the most unlikely

pair. They worked together in the bacon factory next to the airport, sweeping pork and bacon up from the floor before weighing and boxing it up for the pork pie section. Any difference between the weights of pork going into the bacon factory, the bacon produced and the boxes sent to the pork pie section could be accounted for by the difference between the weight of the women's bras and their contents going into the factory and the weight of their bras and contents on the way out.

The inner group consisted of Dick, a young English merchant seaman who was nursing a swollen, throbbing hand, having tried to burn an anchor tattoo off with bleach; Mick from Northern Ireland; Pat from the Republic of Ireland; and a distinguished-looking chap – inventively known as 'Gent' – who had farmed sheep in Australia.

Briscoe sat next to Prof and swapped stories of what had happened since they had lost touch at Spot's club. Radish felt excluded, so he slipped outside to test his grip.

III

So different were the backgrounds of those in the group of workers from the airport and adjacent industrial estate, that they largely lived within their own disrupted worlds. It was hard to believe that they were all guests at the same wedding reception. It was a small miracle that they could even exchange the time of day, let alone converse about anything meaningful. Here, the opposite of talking wasn't listening, but waiting. Most couldn't even be bothered to do that and they simply talked over each other in a maze of overlapping monologues, with a few occasionally lapsing into their native languages.

'Man, dis lika chat ina tongues round de table a Babel,' said one of the West Indians.

'Yes, babble around the table,' said Dick, missing the biblical allusion.

'Complete waste of time,' said Mick.

'I'm dying for a cheese sandwich,' said Pat, apropos of absolutely nothing.

'Ach, fat chance now the ration's been cut back,' said Mick.

There was a lull in the conversation as the group appeared to contemplate Mick's observation.

At this point, Gill and Piotr arrived from the official reception, which had been held in front of a select congregation at the Roman Catholic Church Hall in Fletham. They were on their way to their honeymoon and only intended to stay a short while, more to be polite than anything else.

Despite themselves, everyone stared at Gill. They didn't mean to be rude or disrespectful; it was just a biological reflex.

'Look how him walk sweet,' Briscoe whispered to Gent, who was trying not to notice. Gender counted for little in patois, in direct contradiction to the full-blown sexism of the societies in which it had developed.

'Is dat me call rydim,' continued Briscoe, relieved that Allen hadn't come with them.

Gill and Piotr wandered among the guests, with Gill shyly avoiding the admiring glances. She had the impression that Piotr wanted to show her off to the assembled company. She hated the idea, but given Piotr's terrible story she could understand his pride in the marriage.

'Did you know that Allen's back?' asked Mick innocently when they approached.

'No!' Gill exclaimed. She flushed and dragged Piotr away. She still felt terrible about the way her friendship with Allen had come to such an irreconcilable end.

'Who's that creepy-looking man who keeps staring at me? He looks like the dreaded Leech-Gatherer on the lonely heath Lizzie told me about,' said Gill with a shudder, albeit relieved to have been able to escape the subject of Allen so quickly.

'Funny you should pick him out right away and say that. That's Burian, the man I was telling you about. His name means 'dwells near weeds,' said Piotr.

'The one you said was your enemy?'

'Yes.'

'Why's he your enemy? Did you do something to him?'

'No.'

'Why then?'

'It's to do with our histories. When you come from an island, it's difficult to understand the problems countries like Poland and Ukraine have.'

At that point, the noise of a taxiing Viscount turboprop aircraft prevented any further conversation. The screaming whine of its engines matched the intensity of Burian's hatred for all things Polish.

Despite his need to remain calm and observe, Burian was on the edge. He was fed up with the Poles' popularity among the British for their role in the war and, despite it suiting his purposes, with the British ignorance about Ukraine. He had never met anybody in England who had even heard of Ukraine, let alone knew where it was, or what its role in the war had been. He couldn't believe their ignorance in not having heard of a land with an area five times greater than the British Isles, which had lost at least five million of its population of thirty-two million during the war, as opposed to around six hundred thousand of Britain's forty-seven million population.

Burian had listened to the Irish talking of their famine or 'starvation', but nobody seemed to have heard of the much more recent Ukrainian 'starvation', in which millions had starved to death and further millions had been deported to camps in Siberia.

The Viscount had taken off and was whining away in the distance, and the raised voices of Piotr and Burian could be heard during the temporary lull.

'Shut your popish Polish propaganda,' hissed Burian.

Mick and Pat exchanged concerned glances at Burian's reference to the pope.

'Write to me in Berdychiv, *khokhol*!' retorted Piotr, using the Russian slang for a Ukrainian.

There was an almighty crash as the table collapsed under Burian's flying assault on Piotr. He didn't get very far, as Raditch – who had been watching over the group through his rimless glasses with an impassive stare – grabbed his collar and slammed him back into his seat.

'Get off, you mad Russian,' shouted Burian.

Big Raditch paused momentarily in complete shock.

'Get off, you black bastard!' Burian shouted, to everybody's total incomprehension.

The West Indians sat transfixed. They could not believe that a white man had called another white man a black bastard. In fact, they had never seen white men going at each other except in the films. They had always seen whites as a unified block against blacks like themselves.

Quite unbelievably, it was not the first time Raditch had been called black, as the Russians had called the Latvian slave labour miners that as their skin was ingrained with coal dust. It was, however, the first time anybody had called Raditch a Russian, let alone a mad one, to his face.

Another screaming Viscount added to the tension. Although technically safe, everybody cowered at the threat of a blast of debris from the runway and of Raditch's wrath. Raditch looked as if he was going to explode and stamped after Burian, scattering tables and chairs in his wake.

Acting as if the difference between past, present and future was indeed nothing but a stubbornly persistent illusion, the Catholic 'Norman Conks' and Protestant 'Billy Boys' from Glasgow decided to take the opportunity to settle old scores from several hundred years back; as did the Irish Republicans and the Northern Irish Loyalists. In the ensuing mayhem, the usually clear demarcations between the opposing factions broke down and people simply fought whoever happened to be nearby.

Attempting to rally the Protestants under a banner, one of the 'Billy Boys' pulled a tablecloth off one of the tables, inadvertently revealing Prof and Mick cowering under the table in earnest conversation amid the mayhem.

'I was never afraid,' said Prof.

'What are you doing under here, then?' asked Mick, who hated fighting and being expected to feel otherwise because he was Irish.

'If everybody had got stuck into the Nazis before the war like me, Hitler wouldn't have got nowhere,' Prof said, comforted by recollecting how, before the war, he had fought Moseley's Blackshirts in the East End.

'But when I hit some bloke he turned out to be a plain-clothes copper. I was fitted up with a brick and sent down for the only time in me life.'

Somebody crashed into the table and Mick only just caught a bottle of whiskey before it hit the ground. He took a swig and passed it to Prof.

'I also sorted out the blackout gangs,' Prof continued.

'West Indians?' asked Mick.

'Nah, you nutcase. There weren't any then.'

'Who then?'

'Teenagers too young for call-up, deserters and even neighbours who looted bombed-out premises during the blackouts.'

The battle raged around them, but it was relatively quiet under the table in the eye of the storm, and Mick and Prof were happy enough to stay where they were and continue their conversation.

'How did you get all those?' asked Mick, pointing to Prof's scars.

'After the war. I got this one when a bloke slashed me with a razor,' he said, pointing to a scar that ploughed vertically down across his left eye, miraculously not blinding him. 'And this one when a bloke hit me with an axe,' he continued, fingering a deep groove across his forehead.

'Nearly scalped me and the flap of skin fell over me eyes so I couldn't see. I should've got a gun and shot 'em. I was never afraid. Nobody loves yer like yer mother.'

A giant Pan American World Airways Lockheed Constellation revved up its four mighty engines for take-off, causing them both to put their hands over their ears. Luckily for Mick, this interrupted Prof, who had begun to ease his shirt down over his shoulder like a Soho stripper to reveal more scars among the mounds of flab.

Somebody on the fringes of the action shouted: 'We've got to stop this before the coppers get here.'

'The landlord once stopped a fight in The Three Magpies by heaving a beehive into the middle of the bar,' shouted another.

The regulars of the four local pubs never mixed except on race days, when there was always trouble. The bitter rancour between them, based as it was on identification with a particular group, and guardianship of territory and status, was no different from expressions of human nature the world over. Yet the locals around Hadleyrow were expected to absorb and accommodate the greatest wave of immigration from the most diverse origins the area had ever known while recovering from the efforts, dangers and privations of the war, and faced with the destruction of their village and ancient way of life; for which they received nothing but criticism.

'I know where I can get a beehive,' shouted another, rushing away.

He soon returned with an old skep in his arms and chucked it expectantly into the middle of the tent.

When the battle continued unabated he looked questioningly at the chap whose suggestion it had been.

'There's no bloody bees in it, you lunatic,' mouthed the other.

At that point, the Lockheed Constellation swung round in preparation for take-off. It was the most powerful aircraft of its time and its blast caught the tent like a hurricane hitting a sail, lifting the massive central pole clean out of the ground. Fortunately, Raditch collided with it at that moment and grabbed the pole as though it were a giant caber at the Highland Games.

Having witnessed the mayhem from outside, Radish rushed in, forgetting any fears regarding his failing strength. Seeing Raditch struggling to keep the pole upright, he grabbed it from the opposite side. They tottered around, holding what looked like a giant maypole between them, with people dancing round it as they held on for as long as they could before being thrown off. During their titanic struggle, Raditch and Radish eyed each other warily with the vague feeling they had seen each other somewhere before, even that they knew each other.

Raditch got his foot stuck in a fire bucket, which – when he finally managed to kick it free – flew low to the ground and ricocheted off Prof's head onto Mick's, knocking them both clean out.

The pilot of the Constellation revved up the engines to a crescendo before releasing the brakes. The aircraft, its wingspan greater than the distance of Orville Wright's historic first flight, surged down the runway and roared away faster than any wartime fighter plane to continue its scheduled round-the-world flight.

The final blast from the propellers lifted the marquee clean off the ground. The counterbalancing weight of Radish and Raditch still clinging to the central pole led to the tent filling like an umbrella in a storm and sailing across the public enclosure, scattering everyone in its path until it crashed into the VIP Departure Lounge. Luckily, the lounge was empty.

The incoming passengers had dispersed. The outgoing passengers were aboard the Pan American Constellation flight, already nearing the cruising speed of three hundred and forty miles per hour at twenty-three thousand feet, and the staff had gone outside to wave them off. Onlookers screamed in terror as they assumed an aircraft had overshot a runway, as they couldn't imagine anything else crashing with such impact at an airport.

Raditch and Radish crawled around under the pile of collapsed canvas, looking like two giant tortoises before they finally emerged. They slapped each other on the back and went off to find something to eat as they were both starving.

Introducing themselves would be a confusing process.

Prof and Mick slowly regained consciousness, looking up at the clear blue sky with no idea of what had happened and both vowing never to drink whiskey again.

When the news of the fracas reached Gill's mother she felt a huge wave of self-satisfied relief that her prejudices against all those airport immigrants, other than Piotr, had proved correct. Others suspected Lizzie's involvement but doubted that even Lizzie would have been able to come up with enough flying ointment to lift that lot off the ground.

'What were you thinking?' Gill asked Piotr as they made their honeymoon-bound escape. 'Thank goodness my parents didn't come.'

'I'm sorry, but at least you've seen it for yourself,' said Piotr.

'If that man hates you so much, why did you ask him to write to you in Berdychiv? Is that where we're going for our honeymoon?' asked Gill, thinking perhaps that Piotr had only said they were going to Eastbourne for two days to hide a surprise.

'No,' said Piotr, who couldn't suppress a grin. 'It's a saying, like "Leave me alone".'

'I've never seen such hatred in a man's face.'

'The whole history of that area is a terrible story, that continues today. The population of the Siberian labour camps, like the one my mother and I were released from, has risen by more than two million since what you call the end of the war.'

Gill sat in silence, overcome by the thought of the evil people in places she had never heard of before she met Piotr. She realised many of them were now in Britain, including Burian, and that there must also be British people just like them, awaiting their opportunity. She wished she wasn't learning all this on her wedding day.

IV

Piotr was walking over the fields for the first time since the honeymoon. He was still in a trance. Nothing could have prepared him for the experience. The truth that God sanctified the marriage bond in such a way that once entered into and consummated between baptised persons it could never be dissolved, was evident to him in the ecstatic union they had experienced.

The contrast with his previously deprived existence was so overwhelming he couldn't believe that not only did it have the blessing of the Church, but also that it was legal. They had both been very nervous, but despite their mutual innocence, or even because of it, they had experienced an ecstasy neither could now imagine ever being without. Everything new they discovered about each other reinforced their love. Piotr was now even more terrified of losing Gill, which experience had taught him could happen at any moment.

He had not gone far when Luka rushed up to him. 'Piotr! I'm so sorry my father ruined the reception,' he said.

'It's not your fault. I did provoke him.'

'Why does my father hate Poles so much?'

'History, as usual,' said Piotr.

'Tell me. I need to understand my father better.'

'OK, but you'll have to walk along with me as I have to get back to work.'

'What are you doing?' asked Luka.

'Er, just a bit of surveying.'

To his dismay, Piotr had been asked to begin a survey

in preparation for the expansion of the airport over to the north side of the main road. It was another easy job, as the pan-flat fertile plain continued for miles around, but he felt even guiltier about his association with the airport as he knew that the plan was to obliterate the village and farms there, just as they had done in Hadleyrow. This included the Norman church, the grand vicarage, the magnificent tithe barn and the houses, including the one to which Gill's parents had moved to work.

This time, however, to his deeply felt shame, he had not yet leaked any information. He had even kept it from Gill. Previously, Gill had reacted well when he had told her about his involvement with the airport developments, but he had lost his nerve this time. He knew he would have to come clean and resign from his job, but he needed the money until he could find something else. The longer it went on the harder it became to put straight.

'Where are you going to start?' asked Luka.

'Er, down towards the Pits,' lied Piotr, compounding his sense of guilt.

'So, why does my father hate Poles so much?' repeated Luka.

'Well, there have been endless disputes over borders between Poland and Ukraine, and both were invaded by the Germans from the West and the Russians from the East, before and during the war. I guess your father would have been in his twenties at that time.

'In Ukraine, millions were conscripted into the Russian army, but in Western Ukraine thousands became "Hiwis", willing helpers of the Nazis, including those recruited into a new Nazi SS Division, which committed terrible atrocities.

'On the other hand, many Ukrainians joined the Ukrainian

insurgent army and fought Germans, Russians and Poles, while a heroic minority paid a terrible price trying to protect their Polish and Jewish neighbours. Your father could have been involved in any of these ways, or none at all,' said Piotr, realising he had given a far from perfect account.

By this time, Piotr and Luka had wandered over the remains of the fields. They could see the low, dark shapes of the remaining cottages of the Rookery across the desolate fields, which were criss-crossed with straggling hedges and ditches. Huge, blue-black clouds billowed up and there was a chill in the air. The harsh call of a green woodpecker warned of an approaching storm.

'That's where Allen used to live with his grandmother, isn't it? I heard he's back,' said Luka.

'Yes. Have you seen him?' asked Piotr.

'No.'

There's a storm coming in, so I won't be able to do much more out here. Let's go back to the public enclosure,' said Piotr.

They reached the public enclosure by a circuitous route through various chain-link fences and across new concrete slip roads.

When they were settled in the public enclosure café, Luka took a battered-looking book from his pocket and handed it to Piotr.

'I wanted to show you this,' said Luka.

'I wondered what you were carrying so furtively,' replied Piotr.

'When my uncle left for Australia he gave it to my father. He kept it hidden and doesn't know I've got it. Apparently it's written in Ukrainian and I wondered whether you could translate it for me,' said Luka.

'Can't you read Ukrainian?' asked Piotr in surprise.
'No. I never learned to read or write it when I was young.'
'How come?'
'I had an English nanny, who I spent all my time with.'
'What happened to her?'
'Being English she got to England long before me and I never saw her again.'

Piotr resisted asking Luka for any further details of his life, especially as he was Burian's son, and turned his attention to the book. It had a cardboard cover and was printed on poor-quality paper.

'I'll need a bit of time,' said Piotr taking a quick look inside.

'I've got to get it back before my father finds it's missing, as he obviously doesn't want me to know what's in it. He said it was about Uncle Vasyl's acting career in Ukraine before the war and that I wouldn't be interested. But I think it might give me some clues about what my father did during the war,' said Luka.

When Piotr got back to his room, he settled down to have a good look. Ukrainian was different from Russian, no matter what he had said to Burian when he was trying to stir him up.

Scanning through, he saw that some of the pages had been carefully cut out. Piotr concentrated his translation efforts on the pages just before the missing chapter, where he read:

> *In 1943, aged 28, my brother Burian joined the ranks of the new Nazi SS Galicia Division 'Galatchina'. As a grammar school graduate he was sent to SS-Unterführerschule, Lauenburg, the Sergeant Major's School, founded there in 1940. The military unit to which he was attached wasn't sent to the dreadful battle near Brody (13-22 July, 1944), which saved him from death or the Soviet Gulag camps.*

Burian made his thorny, post-war way to the West, suffered in internment camps and lived under the constant threat of being given up to Stalin's stooges. Having realised that returning to Ukraine would be impossible, my brother made his way through Italy, where Luka and I were reunited with him in a transit camp. From there, completely unvetted, we, along with 7,100 fellow Ukrainian men from the 14th Waffen SS Galicia Division, were allowed to enter England.

With sweat running down his back, Piotr checked and double-checked that he had translated correctly, realising with a jolt that Burian was almost certainly a Nazi war criminal. Not everyone had volunteered for the SS Divisions – many had been conscripted against their will and many had deserted – but the fact that Burian was an anti-Russian, anti-Polish, Ukrainian nationalist at a Nazi SS sergeant major's school was incriminating. Piotr didn't bother with the rest of the book.

Piotr had heard rumours that the 14th Waffen SS Galicia Division had been involved in some of the worst Nazi atrocities during the war. He also knew that innocent Polish civilians from the Russian camps, and Polish troops who had fought so heroically in Italy under General Anders and had chosen not to return to a Poland under Stalin, couldn't believe that Nazi war criminals were mixing freely with them after the war in the reception camps, receiving the same treatment and subsequently being allowed entry into Britain without any screening.

So Burian was free as a bird, planning to emigrate with his son to his brother's place in Australia while thousands of other survivors of the atrocities were refused entry to Britain and continued to suffer with shattered bodies and minds that would never mend.

Piotr had to work out the balance between tipping somebody off that there was a Nazi SS refugee planning to emigrate to Australia on the one hand and protecting Luka's innocence on the other. A new life in Australia would be a wonderful opportunity for Luka. Piotr didn't know what Burian had done personally. Besides, if the British authorities had, without any vetting, let in tens of thousands of Eastern Europeans who had fought with the Nazis and committed war crimes – while excluding most of their victims and even forcibly giving thousands over to the Russians to face further persecution and even execution – he realised they wouldn't want to be reminded about it.

He also suspected, that his voice would not be heard by an establishment that allowed British fascist leader Mosley, after a comfortable imprisonment during the war, to run training camps in the New Forest; not to mention the Duke and Duchess of Windsor – the ex-king and his American divorcee wife, both Hitler admirers – who were allowed to live in luxury in Paris.

Certain he would get it wrong, Piotr decided to protect Luka's innocence by pretending that he couldn't do the translation. The only action he did take was to respond to Luka's queries about why people had been so cruel during the war by telling him to ask his father.

Once home, Luka tried to return the book unnoticed, but having already discovered that it was missing, the ever-watchful Burian, challenged him as soon as he came through the door.

'You did *what?*' shouted his father, his face twisted with rage. 'You stupid, stupid, bloody *hivno*.'

Luka, who had initially coloured up with a shocked expression, became increasingly horrified and angry as the tirade went on. He had never seen this side of his father before; only the tightly repressed look. He decided he would never like his father and couldn't suppress the fantasy that Burian wasn't his real father. Piotr, on the other hand, would mourn the loss of his father, whom he had never known, all of his life.

V

Allen had gone to Lizzie's place straight away. He thought he was returning to where he had started, but he had left one place and returned to another. Piles of earth, sand and gravel towered over everything. Every road, path and open area was thick with mud. However, he was comforted by the thought that the airport would last but for the blink of an eye compared to the length of time the Rookery's cottages of mud, sticks and straw had survived. The only trace of the airport the force of nature would eventually leave would be its footprint marked out by the pattern of gorse – with its dense, untidy, spiny dark green foliage and bright yellow flowers – which thrived on disturbed ground and could reveal evidence of man's activities for centuries.

Lizzie's old cottage appeared out of the surrounding desolation and chaos like a mirage. Leading up to the front door were two short hedges of sweet-smelling myrtle, planted to ensure marital bliss; to no avail in Lizzie's case. In the small garden, marked off with a rickety, wooden fence, there was a tangle of undergrowth that strangled and swamped everything except for the large, gnarled, woody bushes of sage and rosemary, the blue flowers of which would soon hum with clouds of honey bees from the cottagers' abandoned skeps and the wild colonies.

Sweet briar and brambles with scarlet and yellow leaves beside the green scrambled into the thatch and dotted it with colour. Ivy, a symbol of love, embraced the walls. The villagers had loved Lizzie's ivy flower honey and ivy berry vinegar.

A holly tree had been planted near the cottage to draw lightning away, and a rowan tree – the picken or quicken tree – closer to the door to keep witches away. Villagers still used its branches for their cattle goads with an old verse in mind:

Had it not been for your quicken-tree goad
And your yew tree pin
You and your cattle had all been drawn in.

Throughout the village, people had had so much anti-witch stuff positioned around external doorways it was difficult for anything or anybody to get in or out, natural or supernatural.

Allen would have taken all the defences down for a witch called Nannie he had read about in an old Scottish poem. She was described as a beautiful, young, erotic figure dressed only in a short linen nightshirt, a 'cutty sark'. But the curious coincidence of her name was enough to cause Allen to suppress that line of thinking, so that even his imaginary pleasures were thwarted.

Three hazel pins stuck into the walls and sprigs of rowan in the thatch were there to protect inhabitants from fire, an ever-present risk given the open spitting hearths, oil lamps and dripping candles. Water in the small borrow ponds in the gardens, created when clay was dug for daub for the walls, should have been more effective in quenching any flames, but they were now choked with vegetation and the water was thick with algae, like pea soup, the name given to the fogs that increasingly reached down from the coal-burning factories and homes in London.

Years earlier, when the water was clear, Lizzie had noticed that on still days the pond skaters, which detected tremors in the surface tension of the water, trembled in response to the flying machines landing at the three new airfields in the locality, acting as nature's seismographs. In this way, counting the pond skaters as one unit, Lizzie had been a close second to them in becoming aware of the gathering threat from the air.

There was no pure water left in the wells either. The decline in the use of farm horses and the loss of their manure and that from London on the returning carts – which also brought vegetable waste from the markets for composting or to feed hens and hutch rabbits – heralded the end of the proper care of the land.

Previously, horse ploughing, manuring, crop rotation and the application by hand of matured soot by benighted 'soot gangs' – members of which were black with ingrained soot – had deterred pests and conditioned the soil to the extent that even the containers of pests the Germans had dropped on the fields during the war had failed to become established.

The exhaust trails of aircraft taking off settled on the soil below and contaminated crops, as did the exhaust from the increased motor traffic that was passing along the main road. These days, fewer villagers went blackberrying along the hedgerows or to Berry Hill, which the heavier laden aircraft barely cleared.

The cocktail of toxic chemicals washed into ponds, the Pits and the rivers, poisoning their ecosystems and draining down to the water table, poisoning all the wells and returning to the food chain via irrigated crops and contaminated grazing. However, Allen had already stopped drinking water from the wells, having read that not so long ago shiploads of mummified Egyptian cats and perhaps worse had been ground down for bone meal fertiliser.

The vegetable patch at the back of the cottage was cultivated to obscure the fact that the field girls could help themselves to whatever they liked from the vast array of crops on which they worked. The one exception was the produce from within the greenhouses, from where a single tomato would earn them the sack if they were caught red-handed by The Cabbage King.

The rotting thatch of the cottages leaked, letting in all manner of wildlife, including birds, rats and squirrels. A variety of wildlife had shared Allen's bed from time to time: bedbugs, itch mites, fleas and even a rat on one occasion. He had felt a presence in the bed and, as he sat up, a dark shape had shot across his pillow. Lighting his lamp, he had seen a large rat looking at him as bold as brass before scuttling up into the thatch. There was no Niamh of the golden hair or witch in a cutty sark for him.

After the rat incident, he had dug up the valerian bush outside the door – the small white flowers of which the Pied Piper had used to attract rats – and dissuaded Lizzie from using its dried root to keep her linen fresh. This, of course, had no effect on the rats whatsoever.

Although the villagers' gardens backed onto open fields, there was a short, fenced alley behind them that led to the shared outside privy. The privy was little more than a movable shed with a hole in a board over a hole in the ground; a system that had remained unchanged since Saxon times. There was always a foul stench there and stinging nettles grew up around the board. When the hole in the ground was full, a new hole was dug in a fresh patch of soil and the shed was moved along the alley accordingly, like a sedan chair, hopefully without anyone in it.

Red Goosefoot, with its red-tinged leaves, stalk and tiny flowers, flourished in the filled holes, conveniently marking their positions. When there were no fresh patches along the alley, soil collectors came with a horse and cart, dug the whole lot out and composted it with large amounts of straw that would later be used on the fields, thus conforming to Lizzie's edict that: 'Youm must go where yer crops do grow.'

Tomato seeds survived the whole passage to provide generations of natural tomato crops in the fields and sunny hedgerows, which villagers made the most of without reflecting on their origin, except for Allen of course.

Despite the supposed hardships, Allen had loved his life growing up in a rural idyll. Although he had had nothing as a child, he had also wanted for nothing. His best companions had been innocence and health, and the best riches ignorance of wealth; a thought that sounded as if it had come from a poem written by one of his old friends.

'We be born with nothin' and we still got most of it left,' Lizzie used to say, adding more somberly: 'Them rich men's joys encrease the poors' decay.'

Allen's happy memories had sustained him since his breakdown, preventing it from becoming total, and had highlighted the plight of the children robbed of their childhood years at the children's home located within a few miles of his paradise.

He looked up at the chimney and saw the tip of a besom broom, a sign that Lizzie was out. But even though he knew she could forget and leave it up there when she was at home, he took it as an excuse – much to his sense of shame – for not going in, afraid of what he might find. Nor did he go into Kate's when he saw the damaged thatch and the door swinging on its hinges. *Something was wrong and he had been found wanting once again.* He guessed that they had finally been evicted and hoped that they were still together, as he couldn't see Lizzie surviving without Kate.

To the north he could see the yellow blaze of the airport lighting the darkening sky like a weary dawn roused too early. In the old days, the village would have been dark after nightfall, with the gentle glow of a few oil lamps and candles like glow-worms, but the airport lights blazed all night. In their immediate vicinity there was no night and day, and no change in day length with the seasons. When he was a boy he had known about twenty types of early flowering plants, many of which now flowered throughout the year, even primroses – prima rosa – the first flower, the queen of spring. He couldn't have known Hadleyrow would become such an unnatural place.

With nowhere else to go he decided to camp out near the Pits, where he had an emergency base, while deciding on his next move.

PART THREE

CHAPTER ONE

I

The unofficial meeting was held in the new, but temporary, control tower. In keeping with the deception that had been maintained since the origin of the airport, the tower was of standard RAF design, consisting of a three-storey building with a construction that looked like a small glasshouse on its flat roof, which gave the air traffic controllers an all-round view of the airport and its surroundings. The tower looked misleadingly permanent as it stood over the passenger terminal area: a clutter of prefabs, caravans and canvas tents that, even on still days, flapped and billowed in the turbulence created by the aircraft.

In addition to the air traffic controllers, those with access to the tower were afforded a sweeping panorama of the developments. These included the airport hierarchy and anybody they cared to invite up to observe the scene of the future of international civil aviation. Those who saw it as the devastation of the countryside and the Thames Valley market garden industry by placing an airport in the wrong place were not invited.

Gill's catering job involved serving the air traffic

controllers while they were on duty. As she was young and athletic, she had been given the task of carrying everything up and down the steep, cast-iron stairs on the outside of the control tower. She was uncomfortably aware of the leering looks she attracted, especially as, since the honeymoon, she now knew what was on their minds. She had been shocked and disgusted to discover that some men would loiter at the bottom of the stairs for the sole reason of getting a glimpse up her frock. She still had a lot to learn about the opposite sex, and her own come to that.

She would have resigned on the spot if she hadn't been dissuaded by some of the locals. She was the only local with daily access to what was, to them, operating as enemy HQ. She had even sacrificed herself to the point that, whenever she wanted to get a glance at any plans and papers on the table, she steeled herself to bend over more than was necessary when setting down the tray, safe in the knowledge that all eyes would be on her body rather than on what she was looking at. Most of those present were so keen to chat to her that they didn't mind her hanging around the place longer than necessary. She hated herself for this subterfuge, but balanced it against the fact that the locals needed to know what was going on more frequently than Piotr could leak from the occasional official meetings.

On this occasion, Gill had been told to take refreshments up to a special meeting that had been convened by the deputy commander to coincide with a flight-free period when the air traffic controllers were downstairs on a training course. As she set the tray down, she was shocked to hear Burian's voice as he mounted the stairs. She busied herself in a corner to avoid catching his attention and to try to pick up a clue as to what he was doing there. However, as soon as he entered the

They Couldn't Have Known

room, Burian locked his gaze on her and scanned her up and down in a lascivious way that made her shiver. Even as she hurriedly made her exit she could feel his gaze on her back as if he were touching her.

'Gentlemen, gentlemen,' said the deputy commander. 'Let's get started. We all know each other except for Burian here, who Melville co-opted for his specialist knowledge of the problem we're facing. He works on the industrial estate. Melville was very impressed by his wartime experience in Russia with regard to relocating peasants. You all know the problem we have on our southern borders, and he's been on a flight with Melville to get an overview of the area.

'Since the war has ended, we can't continue to operate under the cover of the Defence of the Realm Act. Although nobody has been organised enough to challenge us yet, Melville tells me he's getting whispers from Whitehall that a number of people are curious about what we're doing down here and how we're doing it. Also, some of the larger farmers and landowners across the main road are starting to worry that they'll be next in line and are beginning to get organised. So we need to shift that mad old woman from down there before she can make any more trouble for us.'

'Isn't there somebody else down there with her?' asked one of the group.

'No, her mad grandson, or whatever he was, has disappeared. And the only other one down there was some field girl who luckily for us died recently,' said the deputy commander with a grin.

'I hope you're not advocating violence,' said one of the younger men.

The deputy commander bristled. He was getting fed up with all this namby-pamby liberal stuff, mainly from those who hadn't seen any action during the war. He wasn't going to have this beautiful airport stopped in its tracks by the last of those mud-hut-dwelling peasants down there.

'Where will she go once you get her out?' asked another young man.

'We've got a Nissen hut up here on the north side. She could be held there with the others until they can rehouse them in Fletham, even though they'll most likely chop up the doors for firewood when they get there. There's a lot of council building going on over there and somebody owes me a favour,'

'Others? Held?' queried the second youngster.

'What?' replied the deputy commander.

'You said "others" and "held".'

'Slip of the tongue,' said the deputy commander, rivulets of sweat running down the centre of his back. This wasn't going as smoothly as he had hoped. Considering what was at stake, he was amazed that anybody would care about such people.

'So it's agreed. We hand the eviction problem over to Burian and then we can all get on with completing the finest civil airport in the world.'

People murmured and shuffled their papers in embarrassed silence as it began to dawn on them what they might have become party to. Only the deputy commander, Melville and Burian were satisfied, as they had managed to get the others to share responsibility for their proposed crime.

Burian felt a surge of nostalgia. Once again, he was to be involved in the eviction and relocation of subhuman peasants, or at least one, for a greater good. He was proud of his work during the war and had never felt any guilt or remorse for his actions. He had been working for a better future, and he had

had the courage and guts to do the work that others wouldn't for various cowardly reasons, but from which they certainly benefited.

Now for that mad old witch, he thought. To his surprise, the thought caused him a degree of unfamiliar discomfort. He had meant to think: *Now for that mad old woman.* He didn't want to give Lizzie any credence for being a witch now that the hunt was on. He didn't like witches.

He had grown up listening to stories about witches with pendulous breasts flung back over their shoulders, flying in the night on their besom brooms; stories of Baba Yaga, Old Bony Legs, the Arch-Crone, the Goddess of Death, with her iron teeth; accompanied everywhere by the 'creaking and groaning of trees, by leaves whirling in the wind, and by a host of wailing and shrieking spirits'. Admittedly, Baba Yaga had no power over the pure in heart, but that was of no help to Burian.

He had suffered night terrors ever since he was a boy, during which he would awake in the night frozen with fear, with the vision of an old hag or a hobgoblin sitting on his chest, slowly suffocating him.

He also remembered the very real 'Night Witches' in the war: female Soviet pilots whose nocturnal bombing raids in primitive biplanes had struck terror into him and his men while hunting partisans in the forests. The Night Witches used the smallness, slowness and manoeuvrability of their old wood and canvas biplanes to glide silently into the attack with their engines cut, restarting them only after they had dropped their bombs. His men had likened the whispering of the air through the wire stays of the wings to the whoosh of a passing witch's broomstick. One winter in Hadleyrow he had been startled when he had heard a similar sound as incoming winter thrushes from Scandinavia – redwings and fieldfares – dropped down from the night sky.

Burian tried to clear his mind of witches by concentrating on less disturbing prey. *He would take the first opportunity to fix that dammed Piotr once and for all. That moaning Polack had discovered his Nazi past and that was a matter of life and death: his life and Piotr's death.* He barely understood why the deputy commander didn't want any killing during his mission. But Piotr wasn't part of the contract, so he had a free hand with him. *He would finish that snobby Polack off for good, leaving that beautiful new wife of his for another type of hunt. It was almost too good to be true.*

Burian thought the British were mad with their concern for people and their rights. They had even started letting blacks in from their colonies, along with their families! OK, so they had let him and his SS comrades in, but they were at least bringing money into the country that some anonymous source was paying into their English bank accounts. And anyway, they were white and civilised.

As everybody moved towards the door, the deputy commander drew Burian to one side. 'Be careful. We don't want any fuss. I've heard that Lizzie's a bit strange. She may be more trouble than you've bargained for.'

Burian smirked. 'You English have no idea what went on in Russia. I think we can handle one little old lady.'

'Steady on, old chap. I flew fighter cover at Dunkirk and from D-Day to VE Day. I know what's what.'

'Yes, but what happened in the West was nothing. We, I mean the Germans, suffered over ninety per cent of our, I mean their, losses in the East.'

Although Gill had been forced to abandon her eavesdropping on the meeting when Burian had recognised her, one of the young officers who was besotted with her told her what he had heard as soon as she smiled at him. At the end of her shift she sped off over the remains of the fields to warn Lizzie of the heightened danger. Gill felt guilty that she had neglected Lizzie since Kate had died, but all her time and emotions had been taken up by her marriage to Piotr.

II

It was dusk by the time Gill reached Lizzie's cottage, but there was no light showing and it was with some trepidation that she pushed at the half-open door in fear of what she might find inside. She stood on the threshold and called Lizzie's name several times. The place was so small and the walls and floors so flimsy that anybody inside would have heard a mouse squeak, which indeed she did in the recess of the wall that acted as Lizzie's pantry.

Although she would rather have assumed that Lizzie wasn't in, she knew she had to check. A terrifying alternative had become a distinct possibility since the death of Kate, who hadn't been much older than Gill herself. Gill was frightened by the thought, despite her devout faith. Nevertheless, she forced herself to cross the threshold into the dark interior.

She found some matches and lit the stub of a candle, but the looming shadows it cast created more apprehension than it dispelled. It looked as though there hadn't been an intruder as Lizzie's much-loved, white china mug inscribed with 'A Present from Eastbourne' in gilt lettering still stood precariously on the narrow window ledge. Lizzie had never been on holiday or seen the sea, but she had been given the mug for curing a lady's warts with juice from the stems of greater celandine. A half-finished basket made from honeysuckle stems with the bark peeled off mirrored the basket-like nests of the dormice in the fields made from the bark they had peeled from honeysuckle stems.

It was clear that there was nobody downstairs, but she could hear scratching noises on the floorboards above, there being no ceiling. She felt her way up the ladder with her heart in her mouth. When she got to the top, she was startled by cockroaches scuttling away from the light. She smelt the dried, aromatic flowers and leaves of common wormwood that Lizzie had scattered to deter fleas, and the musty smell of old newspapers with which Lizzie had vainly tried to paper the damp walls.

Gill kicked something that rolled away under the bed. It was one of the horse chestnut conkers, which Lizzie persisted in scattering to deter spiders in the autumn, to absolutely no effect.

The iron bedstead, looking larger than it was in the tiny front bedroom, was heaped with a quilt made from squares of old rags. Lizzie would have awakened by now if she had been asleep and Gill couldn't face rummaging with her hands to see if Lizzie was in there, for fear of what she might find.

In the tiny fireplace she found a birch besom covered in soot and used the handle of it to gingerly poke the pile of rags on the bed. To her great relief, she felt no solid object and was doubly reassured when she realised that the old-fashioned broom must have slipped back down after Lizzie had pushed it up the chimney to indicate – to those who knew such things – that she was out.

Gill and Kate had tried to convince Lizzie not to do this on many occasions. They didn't say so, but they were worried about Lizzie exposing herself to even more superstitious prejudices than she already was. The ancient belief that if a witch was inside a house she would rise on her broom through the chimney had been reinforced whenever the villagers had seen Lizzie's broom poking out of the chimney, despite the fact that she wasn't on it. Whenever this subject arose in conversation, Gill and Kate would tell everyone that Lizzie was sweeping the chimney, which inadvertently she was, often ending up as black as Dick Turpin in his secret hideaway at The Green Man.

Lizzie did have a recipe for a flying ointment, which was to be rubbed on broomsticks to facilitate flight. It was made from aconite, petty spurge and nightshade, but which of the four local nightshades wasn't specified and Lizzie had never dared to experiment for fear of one actually working.

Anyway, a witch flying around Hadleyrow at this time would get mixed up with the flight paths, be confused by the Visual Approach Slope Indicator lights, be picked up on the Flight Control radar, and talked down onto a runway.

The belief that ringing church bells would knock witches off their broomsticks persisted. Some old villagers had claimed to hear the church bells ringing when Lizzie had purportedly fallen from the balloon. The fact that she had been a baby at the time was disregarded. It was also believed that church bells warded off lightning, which had resulted in hundreds of bell-ringers being struck and killed over the centuries.

Ignorant of Gill's prior arrival, Burian arrived outside the cottage to gather some intelligence for his planned campaign. Seeing flickering candlelight inside Lizzie's hovel, he had crouched in a hedgerow to see what he could learn about her movements in the evenings. When he saw the silhouette of a surprisingly sensuous form stirring what looked like a giant cauldron in the upstairs front room, he began to lose some of his earlier confidence. Burian had grown up with stories of shape-shifting in Ukraine and they were deeply ingrained within him.

He was tempted to set fire to the thatch there and then, but desisted because he needed his hunting party and his dogs to ensure that she stayed in there while he was doing so. He was well practised in the technique.

The light was extinguished and a shadowy figure flitted out of the doorway and disappeared into the gathering night with surprising speed. He knew that Lizzie was still mobile, but this was different. A barn owl swooped from the eaves on silent wings. The trees creaked and groaned, and leaves whirled in the wind. In the distance, the eerie screeches and wails of tawny owls and the chatter of the sedge warblers sounded like a host of spirits accompanying the flitting figure.

Gill returned in a thoughtful mood. She hadn't been to Lizzie's since sometime before her wedding and she had been shocked at the desolate scene. She was convinced by the state of the cottage that Lizzie was no longer living there. No matter how desperate her situation, Lizzie would have kept the place as neat and tidy as she could. Glowing embers would have been awaiting revival in the hearth, but the place was cold and damp, and the wattle-and-daub walls were soft to the touch. It wouldn't be long before the whole place slumped back into the mud from whence it came.

CHAPTER TWO

I

Allen had settled easily into his makeshift camp near the Pits. It was centred on an old Gypsy caravan – now completely hidden in an alder thicket – which, decades earlier, had become stuck in a gravel beach of a fast-flowing brook. The conditions here were better than at Lizzie's cottage as there was running water nearby. It brought Allen even closer to nature than ever; the only situation in which he felt the slightest relief from his anxiety. He realised Lizzie must know of his camp and hoped she would soon find him, as he was sure William Cowper would.

He loved the openness of the surrounding landscape, laid down millions of years earlier as beds of sediment in a prehistoric estuary, flat as a pancake; perfect for agriculture, but also for gravel pits and airfields.

Of the fertility of the soil, Lizzie used to say: 'Youm can smell it in the May blossom, and feel it in yer rheumatism.' When farmers, horticulturists or gardeners moved to a less fertile area – as they were now being forced to do – they were puzzled, at least at first, as to why the crops they planted didn't grow perfectly and sometimes not at all. The resultant landscape, according to Lizzie was like: 'A paintin' in oils well rubbed in the canvas. As rich as a plum cake.'

At night he would sit on the steps of the caravan and look at the clouds, or the moon and the stars. He recalled walking in the dark with Gill and putting glow-worms in the band of her straw hat to add their soft light – foxfire – to her face.

The thought lingered and Allen began to feel a pull from across the main road. Over the days of solitude the pull strengthened. He had never felt such a pull before. He thought of Talbot, the stray dog that had adopted him and Gill, who had been drawn irresistibly to the Pits.

They had named him Talbot as he was a large black-and-white hound that looked like a breed that had been known locally in the old days. They didn't know where he came from or went to, but whenever they were in the fields Talbot would turn up. He was always a welcome companion, in spite of his annoying habit of trying to bite the lucky rabbit's foot they each wore on their belts in unwitting remembrance of the Celtic goddess of dawn: the hare. Allen had a natural control over Talbot, unless Talbot caught a whiff of the Pits, when nothing and no one could stop him taking off and plunging into their threatening depths.

Allen couldn't remember the last time he had crossed the main road, but it suddenly dawned on him that when Gill's parents were evicted, they had been offered the posts of head gardener and housekeeper at the Great House over there, along with accommodation in the tied bothy cottage. With this realisation, he knew he needed to resist the pull towards the house with all his strength. But, like his inner demons, the power of the force grew in proportion to his resistance.

Although the streets were empty of pedestrians, he became tense as he crossed the main road. He turned his collar up as far as it would go and fluffed up the makeshift scarf he had made by tying his socks together, trusting that his bare ankles would attract less attention than his face.

As he entered the main square with its village green, fine houses, magnificent timber medieval tithe barn, grand parish church and even grander vicarage, he marvelled at the picturesque scene. He hated to admit it, but, compared to this, Hadleyrow had indeed been nothing but a row on the heath.

Allen had been to the church once before to deliver produce for the harvest festival. But even then his reputation had suffered further in the minds of the superstitious, when, shortly after he left, a ball of lightning out of a clear blue sky entered the open front door of the church, smashing pews and windows, and filling the church with a foul, sulphurous odour and thick black smoke. The ball had then divided into two, one part smashing out through another door and the other mysteriously disappearing inside the church.

The pious in the congregation saw it either as the 'work of the devil' or as 'God's wrath'; each view held with equal conviction. Two men playing cards at the back of the congregation couldn't help thinking it was a bit of an overreaction on God's part; whereas the vicar who had been trying to look up the skirt of the attractive young widow in the front pew had expected worse and was amazed he had got away with it.

They had all suspected Allen of being involved in some way.

Allen wasn't religious in an orthodox way. He didn't believe in 'Churchianity', so he never suffered forbidden thoughts on the subject.

He hadn't been surprised to read that these were the main

obsessions reported by religious people, particularly nuns, on whom the burden of purity of thought was even greater with regard to sexual feelings and the consequent fears even more terrifying as they were blasphemous. In this way, the innocent and the blameless took huge burdens of guilt on themselves, while the true offenders against humanity proceeded full of self-justification and free of guilt.

It was a good illustration of the principle that if you were not repulsed by a thought, you wouldn't fear having it, and it wouldn't develop into an obsession even if, by chance, you did have it.

He would repeat one of his favourite cards over and over again: 'They depend on your dislike of them for their very existence.'

The religious attributed blasphemous thoughts to the devil, who tormented the pure in heart. There was nothing laughable about that. *What's in a name?* The condition certainly made people feel as if they were possessed by the devil, hobgoblins or whatever other evil troublemakers were lurking around; imps of the mind. The truly devout even thanked God for providing a test of their faith.

In his better moments, Allen could see clearly that obsessive intrusions flourished in sensitive and kind people who hated and feared violence and suffering. That is why good, kind, caring, optimistic thoughts never developed in that way. He wondered if anybody who had been brought up to consider cruelty acceptable – as must have occurred during the centuries of slavery and more recently in Nazi Germany and Communist Russia – had intrusive thoughts of love and kindness and were racked with fear and guilt for having them as they were forbidden.

Allen couldn't resist the inevitable now. He felt like an

iron filing under the pull of a powerful magnet. On reaching the bothy he couldn't stop himself walking up to the front door and ringing the bell. At first he hoped nobody would be in, which would have given him time to come to his senses. But after what seemed like an interminable silence, he heard somebody approaching the door.

Gill's mother couldn't suppress her sense of surprise and dismay when she made out who was at the door. *Good God! Old socks around his neck! That's a new one even for him!*

She gathered herself at once and, with some relish, said: 'You're too late. Gill and Piotr are married.'

Gill's mother had barely been able to believe her luck when Allen had disappeared. It compensated in large measure for her beloved, precious Gill marrying a foreigner. She had never imagined that she would be rid of that funny-looking pagan so easily. Despite the wedding, she had been dismayed to hear of his return and had feared him reappearing in this way.

With Allen still standing in the doorway, she reached for the phone that was just inside the door, and slowly and deliberately dialled a number. Allen hadn't realised they might have a phone and couldn't imagine who she was phoning. Only a few of the large farmhouses in Hadleyrow had ever had one. When he heard Gill's voice at the other end of the line he stood frozen to the spot. If he hadn't been, he was sure he would have collapsed to the ground.

'Guess who's here,' Gill's mother said.

Allen could hear no more. He felt as though he was underwater, with powerful ocean currents in his ears. He had done the right thing in the first place by getting out of Gill's life, leaving her free to find the love he couldn't give her; a life free from the burden of knowing him. But now he had done the wrong thing and returned.

He could never have anticipated the power of the pull he had experienced, which was as powerful as the block that had paralysed him at the scene of the accident. He couldn't see any free will operating in either case. It was obvious that, as a result of the overwhelming changes in his life, the balance of his mind was even more disturbed than he had realised.

As Gill's mother continued speaking on the phone while grinning at Allen, he finally managed to wrench himself free and run away, as he always did. Despite his apparent rudeness, Gill's mother was greatly relieved.

II

Allen missed a turn and found himself loping along a network of alleyways, allotments, bomb sites, railway embankments and the long back gardens of a new housing estate, which dated from just before the war. The network formed a connecting web of nature across the growing urban sprawl, which was destroying farmsteads, smallholdings and acres of horticultural glasshouses. The crash of broken glass punctuated the increasing background noise from the road and airport.

However, despite the damage to the countryside, it was a different type of paradise for the new residents, where they tended their new houses and long gardens with the attention and respect they deserved. The gardens resembled a suburban version of the old strip farming that had existed before the hedge-bound enclosures of the rich and powerful 'stole the commons from the goose'.

Overall, the produce grown in these gardens wasn't much less substantial than when it had been farmland. Those who owned rabbits and chickens, as most people still did, could fill their hessian sacks with sweet-smelling herbs to feed them just as easily on these new estates as they once had done in the fields of Hadleyrow.

Their pigs sometimes escaped to roam free, but there was never a great panic as they could find their way home from miles away. The bolder children even rode the more docile ones to the awe of the less adventurous, who had to settle for giving each other piggybacks. The pigs were remarkably intelligent and the children enjoyed teaching them tricks, which the pigs learned rapidly, even without reward.

Allen had long realised that the intelligence and emotional sophistication of animals was poorly appreciated. He had heard the intricacies of communications between unhatched chicks and their mother, and her grief-stricken wail when she was eventually separated from the chicks. The more Allen had learned about the behaviour of farm animals, the more he had understood Lizzie's phrase: 'It be only a wall 'tween farm and farmyard', and the more he lost his appetite for farmed meat.

Lengths of old field hedges survived along some of the back alleys. Like the new privet hedges, they had been planted as single-species 'quickset' hedges of hawthorn or hedgethorn, but over the centuries they had become enriched with other hedge-forming species, which illustrated their age.

Destroying hawthorn was supposed to court disaster, but the bulldozers were tearing up miles of hawthorn hedge with no apparent retribution. The machines still started first time, never broke down and the drivers thrived on their work.

Lizzie had used hawthorn leaves against heart disease and other circulatory problems. She also used dew from its leaves for the complexion of others, but not for herself or Kate. She was beyond it and Kate had no need for it. Lizzie would never show Kate the other aid to beauty to be found in the hedgerow, the juice of which dilated the pupils when dropped in the eyes.

'Youm don't want folk lookin' in yer windows,' Lizzie had said.

Although the elm and ash had shaded the crops and robbed them of water and nutrients, they had originally been left to grow because of the elm's association with the 'elven' and the ash's reputation as one of the most magical of trees. But because of the airport, the last of these magnificent old trees only survived along some of the alleys of the urban sprawl, with polished hand and footholds created by the daily climbing of the local children.

For the most part the privet hedges were neatly clipped, but in places they were neglected and had grown straggly and wild, defying their suburban taming. Privet was a plant of love and youth, with sweetly pungent ivory flowers. But, as if as a warning to young lovers, their black berries were a violent purgative.

As dusk gathered, Allen became aware that he wasn't alone in his restricted wilderness. Rats and cats slunk through the longer grass, foxes emerged from dens in unlikely places at the ends of overgrown gardens, bats flitted overhead, hedgehogs snuffled and grass snakes and slow-worms slithered through the undergrowth. The glow and scream of the airport grew by the second, so he had no need for the leaves of compass plants to point the way to the spreading monster.

Allen arrived at the perimeter fence unobserved. It was getting dark as he emerged from his suburban nature trail and he was almost blinded by the lights and deafened by the noise of the airport.

When he saw The Three Magpies – now the only remaining

building in the old village to have survived the final onslaught – sadness and a sense of loss burst to the surface. Allen felt vulnerable and exposed, and he didn't like it. He decided he preferred his familiar, frozen, locked state of generalised anxiety. *Some choice*, he thought.

Although Allen had never been welcome at The Three Magpies, it now appeared like an oasis in the desert. Even if people wouldn't talk to him, perhaps he would be able to eavesdrop and catch up on what had happened while he had been away.

He waited outside the pub in the drizzling rain until somebody came out. Then, burying his face in his socks, he slipped in through the open door. Just inside, in a dark nook, there was a table with an empty beer glass on it. He sat down and settled back into the shadows, nursing the glass in his right hand. He looked around the bar and started to isolate individual conversations from the surrounding chatter in the same way he had identified exchanges within the dawn chorus while sitting in the hedgerows just a few hundred yards away.

III

'Allen! What are you doing here?'

Allen was stunned to hear his name.

'It's me, Harry. What are you doing here?'

'Er nothing really. How about yourself?' Allen replied weakly.

Harry always got the job of driving the motorised Kia-Ora orange around the public enclosure, singing: 'We all adore a Kia-Ora!' Ever since childhood he had always been the loudest in bandying insults and jokes about him.'

Harry looked tanned and fit, with sun-bleached yellow

hair as if he had just stepped out of a railway poster for a seaside holiday. He had always attracted the best-looking girls. Except for Gill, that is, which was something Harry had never understood, especially seeing as she was so friendly with Allen. In fact, being friends with Gill had saved Allen from even worse treatment at the hands of the local lads, not that Allen had ever noticed, as it had always been bad enough.

'I was shipped back from Korea, funnily enough on the boat I'd heard the West Indians talking about, the *Empire Windrush*.'

'Korea?' Allen was amazed that he reacted to anything any more, but despite himself he was surprised by this revelation.

'Yes, I got called up, but I wasn't worried about Korea as conscripts weren't supposed to be sent out there, at least not if they were under nineteen. But before I knew it, I was on my way. I think most of the battalion were national servicemen. What about you?'

'I was exempted.'

'Was that because of the way you...?' Harry's question petered out in his embarrassment.

'No,' Allen answered tersely, too embarrassed to confess to it being on account of him still being listed as an agricultural worker, one of the essential services, which exempted him for a period of eight years unless he left farming.

The fact that the airport development had forced Allen from agricultural work into the bacon factory, from where he had moved to the airport in quick succession, hadn't been picked up by the authorities and Allen wasn't going to draw their attention to it. Whether his disfigurement would have exempted him, he didn't know. It shouldn't have done, as he was so fit and strong, but he had never seen a soldier who looked the way he did.

Originally, Allen had dreaded the idea of going into the army. It had been nothing to do with the fear of being a soldier; in fact, he could imagine situations in which he would excel with his stamina and strength. But he knew that he wouldn't have been able to face the prospect of living in close proximity to lads like those in the village, who would have taunted him endlessly. Now, since witnessing the accident, he also knew he would have frozen at the first bad wound he saw; in others not himself.

'Were you wounded?' asked Allen, following his own train of thought.

'Not physically. I cracked up and was sent back in disgrace.'

Allen was dumbfounded, not only by the news, but by the chap's candour. Harry had been the confident, happy-go-lucky lad Allen had always longed to be, and yet here he was admitting to the same so-called cowardice Allen had accused himself of at the accident. It was worse for this chap, though, as his was a public humiliation in the military sphere and would be on record. Allen's mental block, on the other hand, hadn't been witnessed by anybody who knew him, except Briscoe, perhaps, and was an internalised personal shame that he would admit to no one. He certainly hadn't realised at the time of the accident that things could have been a lot worse.

'Like you, I'd lived through the war and been brought up on war stories and films, but it was nothing like that. I was terrified all the time. No one mocked; we were all in it together. Just lads from the plough tail,' said Harry.

'One night we were defending a hill position, when we heard screams and bugle calls as the enemy attacked. We fired blind down the hillside, but they still reached our trenches. A mate of mine, also a national serviceman who wanted to be a PE teacher, was hit by a burst from a submachine gun and dropped dead right in front of me. Another mate was splattered all over the place by a grenade. I froze until the smells made me vomit.

'The blast from a shell collapsed the trench wall on top of me. Luckily, my head was lodged in an air pocket underneath a duckboard so I could still breathe. I must have passed out and been left for dead. The next thing I knew our lads were dragging me to the field hospital on a groundsheet.

'Behind our lines I saw tanks coming back with bodies mangled in their tracks. They put canvas screens around them to try to hide the mess before they hosed them down. I don't know how they got anybody to do it.'

He broke off.

Allen looked on in alarm as he saw the Harry's face turn pale as he started to wretch, gagging for breath. He didn't look as though he had been on holiday now. Allen could barely control a violent contortion of his own face at the thought of it all. He hated this world and couldn't see how anybody could find any joy in the burden of existence. He was beginning to take comfort in his alienation from just about everybody and everything.

Harry regained some of his composure and continued. 'The Chinese and North Korean soldiers were just poverty-stricken peasants, sometimes only armed with sticks. For every pound of supplies they received, the Americans shipped in two tons to their troops.

'Under fire, you couldn't get to a latrine, but no one said anything because everyone smelt bad. Perhaps the smells were the worst thing of all.'

Allen's perverse mind immediately took flight. *Would such horrors be rendered less revolting if they were accompanied by sweet-smelling perfumes? Or would they in turn be experienced as foul-smelling by association? Perhaps people who were less struck by the horror simply had a less sensitive sense of smell, or even no sense of smell at all. Had that ever been researched?* Allen had to pull himself back to the conversation before he spiralled even further into his manic internal world.

'Eventually, some just gave up and resigned themselves to being killed, but I couldn't do that and the longer it went on the worse I got. All we cared about was staying alive to lead normal lives again. The funny thing is, although we talked about women, sex was scarcely mentioned. It was simple home comforts we wanted. I fantasised about wearing pyjamas again,' said Harry, with a hint of a rueful grin revealing a tiny spark of his old self.

The little grin pierced Allen to the heart. Harry was continuing to astound him with his sensibilities.

'We just wanted to live. Nothing else mattered.'

In its contrariness, Allen's brain immediately thought of those in perfect physical health, with loving families, money and all they could want materially, who committed suicide in what would seem like paradise to most. Often they showed relentless persistence after several failed attempts.

At that moment, his old friend Milton turned up again to explain:

The mind is its own place, and in itself
Can make a heaven of hell, a hell of heaven.

Harry's account broke back through Allen's mental diversions. 'We didn't have any time for those who hadn't been through what we had: those at the rear, especially anybody who outranked us and could still order us about; let alone those back home who didn't even know where Korea was.'

Allen shifted uneasily, although the comment hadn't been

aimed at him.

'Two weeks after I won a medal for that action defending the hilltop, I lost all my confidence. I got up from a chair and suffered a massive anxiety attack. The world fell away. I felt worthless, terrified of the future with no hope; just depression, terror and misery.

'I wasn't the only one and they knew it, even though they tried to make out I was. They could have threatened to shoot me, like they would have done a few years earlier, but it wouldn't have made any difference.'

Allen had a jolt of déja vu, recalling how he had had the same thoughts when he was frozen to the spot at the scene of the accident.

'And ever since, I can't get the images out of my head, or the new ones that creep in,' said Harry.

He leant forward and gripped Allen's arm. 'I think I'm going mad. I have these terrifying intrusive and persistent unwanted ideas, thoughts and images.'

The words electrified Allen.

'All sorts of horrible images crowd in and I imagine myself, or rather try not to imagine myself, committing atrocities, but the images keep coming. The harder I try to stop them the more they come.'

Allen was thunderstruck, both by Harry's continued openness and by the exact parallels with his own condition. The only difference between them was that his own breakdown had developed after years of chronic stress, whereas Harry's had been precipitated by acute dramatic trauma.

'Streams of unacceptable ideas, thoughts and images that I can't ignore drain me. I don't know where they come from. I can go for days trying to convince myself that I'm not cruel and violent for having them, but they just get more and more frightening. The worse they get, the more I feel forced to follow them through to find out how bad they can be. The more I try to stop them, the more they come. They strike with such force they take my breath away. They turn my stomach, sour my mouth. It's like being kicked in the chest by a horse. My heart thumps and stutters. My legs and feet throb and burn.'

Allen was overcome with empathy for Harry. Even though in all other respects Harry appeared to be his polar opposite, he had experienced everything Harry was describing. He felt he should share his own suffering with Harry, but he couldn't open up. He tried to convince himself that it would be disrespectful considering everything Harry had endured. Instead he tried to help him with his hard-earned insights.

'Try not to fight them. Be prepared to think and feel anything. Try to see that even the most shocking are only generated by fear,' said Allen, quoting one of his cards.

Harry looked at him quizzically. 'That doesn't seem possible to me. I'm suffocating.'

'No, it won't seem possible now. But try to see that you're in this state through no fault of your own. Be prepared to think and feel anything. Stop fighting. Float past, don't stop and listen in. Accept that there's no quick and easy cure. Be patient. Let time pass. Try to develop a detached acceptance of intrusive thoughts as irrelevant.'

Harry stared at him blankly. 'I don't know what you're talking about.'

'When you lost confidence in yourself it was bound to lead to fears that you weren't a good person, resulting in endless self-accusation and a fear of what might be within you. If the feared thoughts were part of your true character you wouldn't be so revolted by them. The part of you suffering the revulsion must be your true self.'

For a moment, Allen felt pleased with his little speech, until he realised that Harry hadn't even been listening. Not that that mattered, as he had in fact been telling himself.

'And it's getting worse,' said Harry.

'Worse?' queried Allen, dreading the revelation of a development that even his exhausted mind had not yet envisaged.

'Yes. They're entering my dreams.'

Allen felt a surge of relief that this was all it was. This had happened to him, but eventually he had been able to accept that given the seamless nature of the brain it was inevitable, and also that the dreaming or half-waking state was the most removed from the waking responsible self. Or at least he hoped he had. In fact, he knew he hadn't and the next dream would be just as shattering.

Allen recalled one of his cards:

Our restless minds
Too quickly conjure fearful images
Like bad dreams we mistake as real.

'Anyway there's a lot worse than me in here,' said Harry.

'That chap sat over there by the fire, just a bit older than me, was shipped out as a national serviceman to fight the communists during the Malayan Emergency of 1948. He was in a patrol made up mostly of conscripts who, under orders from two regular NCOs, killed villagers. Apparently, he froze and didn't wound or kill anyone, but he lost his mind over the sight of it all.

'And that old boy over there's a Major General from the First World War who was accused of cowardice as not enough soldiers under his command were killed. He was relieved of his duties in disgrace. He spent the rest of his life trying to clear his name until he broke down and ended up an alcoholic,' said Harry.

There it was. One of Allen's mantras: *Could be a lot worse.* But, given that his condition sought out every worst motive in himself, Allen was wary of gaining comfort from someone else's greater misfortune. *That was no good, but he couldn't stop himself from trying to quantify and compare suffering. Still, everybody did and now he had heard it from Harry.*

Whatever someone suffered, the first thing people would tell them was how lucky they were and how much worse it could have been. 'Lost a leg? You were lucky! Could have been both.' Allen couldn't work out what people had to suffer before they were considered unlucky enough not to be lucky.

Allen could see that mental suffering was even more difficult to quantify. As Allen saw it, the subjective impact could only be quantified by the reaction. If people recovered mentally from a trauma relatively unscathed, with no long-term subconscious damage, then that trauma, by definition, couldn't have scathed them that much. Not because they were 'strong', but because they were not as sensitive or perceptive as others.

Allen was startled when another of his old friends, Samuel Johnson – who would have been two hundred and forty-odd if he hadn't died aged seventy-five – bustled in. Allen was a bit worried as Johnson and Milton knew each other and had different political opinions. Allen couldn't believe no one else in the bar noticed Johnson arrive, riddled as he was with facial tics and involuntary bodily contortions. His arrival reminded Allen that he was indeed lucky and that things could have been a lot worse, as Allen had not suffered such physical symptoms, at least not yet. Allen took to him not only as someone worse off than himself but also because of his generous and humane nature. He had read how Johnson accommodated a strange group of misfits and losers and that his man servant and main heir was Jamaican.

Allen nearly asked Harry whether he had sought help, but had choked on the words, as it was the last thing he would do himself. In his experience nobody cared, which he had noted on one of his cards:

Let it be
They don't care to know about it
You must manage by yourself.

Johnson reminded Allen that he too had avoided the asylum by keeping the true extent of his disturbances largely to himself. Allen had felt as though he was writing his own diary when he had copied out a description of Johnson entering adult life:

In such a state of intense anxiety, bewilderment and despair that it seemed to him like the onset of madness. Overwhelmed by a horrible melancholia, with perpetual irritation, fretfulness and impatience. With a dejection, gloom and despair, which made existence a misery by what he called his 'Black Dog' barking from breakfast to dinner.

In relation to which, Allen had also copied an observation of Johnson's that had virtually saved his life:

Disorders of the intellect happen much more often than superficial observers will easily believe. Perhaps if we speak with rigorous exactness, no human mind is in its right state.

This struck him as a more erudite version of the phrase that he heard commonly around the village, where it was thought to have been coined by some chap called George: 'Never judge a book by its cover.'

This, of course, was the exact opposite of what people did to Allen on a daily basis. And although he only read old books with plain leather covers himself, even he judged others in this superficial way. He realised it was a symptom of the way the brain worked. *What else did it have to form first impressions from, other than appearance?*

He shouldn't have been surprised at Johnson's arrival as he realised his old friends inevitably arrived by association with his thoughts. *How could they not?*

Harry interpreted Allen's preoccupied silence as a lack of interest in his story and wandered away to clear tables. Harry was learning to accept people's lack of interest; they couldn't know what it was like. *How could they?*

IV

Allen stayed in the bar until eventually even his old friends left him. Luckily, despite Dr Johnson' antics, no one else in the bar had been aware of Allen's exalted company. But even if they had been, they would have simply dismissed them as another bunch of weirdos displaced from the Rookery.

As he looked at the lonely figure of Harry clearing the tables, Allen realised it was only circumstances that had kept him from the horror Harry had experienced. His heart also went out to the millions around the world who had been exposed to such trauma through no fault of their own and had had to live with the consequences, while others were never tested in such a way. Given the way his mind worked, this wave of grief extended not only back into the past, but also into the future to unborn generations.

The landlord, an incomer he didn't recognise, was holding forth at the bar. Allen didn't have to wait long before his attention was riveted, as if he had heard the harsh crek-crek of a corncrake in the middle of the room.

'Whenever a big plane lands during opening time and a group is travelling on west, passengers end up at the bus stop outside so the queue blocks my front door and that mad old woman goes up and down selling them posies of herbs like some Gypsy,' said one customer.

'It's about time they shifted her away altogether. She's a bloody nuisance,' said another.

'Well she isn't doing any harm,' replied a burly-looking man dressed in a way that identified him as a local.

'She gives me the creeps,' said the landlord.

'Well I heard she does a lot of good helping passengers if they're frightened of flying or aren't feeling well,' said the burly local.

'Bloody witchcraft if you ask me,' retorted the landlord.

'She's not natural, for sure. Some do say she's an old witch left over from the village,' said one of the men.

'Leave it out. Who believes in all that mumbo-jumbo in this day and age?' said the burly local.

'Just about everybody under a wolf moon on a stormy night on the heath,' said another local, unconscious of the fact that no incomer would have the faintest idea what a wolf moon was.

'Give us a break. You don't know Lizzie if you think that,' countered the burly local.

Allen had hardly breathed up until that point, as it was obvious whom they were talking about, but on actually hearing Lizzie's name he couldn't suppress an involuntary twitch, causing him to knock his glass over on the table. The group at the bar turned their heads and peered in his direction.

'You all right, mate?' said one.

'Mmmm,' mumbled Allen as he shrank further back into the shadows, furious at having drawn attention to himself.

The group turned back and resumed the conversation, relieved that at least somebody had been sitting there on this occasion. Glasses had an odd habit of falling off that table when no one was sitting there.

'They keep trying to get rid of her, but she just slips away and disappears,' said another.

'Well at least they flushed her out of her cottage when they damaged the thatch again a few weeks ago.

'No, I heard she left when that friend of hers died.'

Allen froze. He knew Kate was Lizzie's only friend, but he couldn't make sense of it.

'What, that Kate?' said another.

Allen was mortified by his reaction to this thunderbolt, which was so far beyond his comprehension it had been like hearing a news bulletin on the wireless. Only anxiety and guilt had the power to overwhelm him, which it duly did over his reaction.

The only thing he did know was that he must find Lizzie, as without Kate her situation would be more perilous than he had thought. But considering the steady rain that now fell and the nature and state of his clothing, he decided to find shelter nearby for the night and resume his search for Lizzie in the morning.

He opted in the end for a large, empty pig bin around the back of the kitchens of the airport's still tented arrivals and departures area. At least it would be dry and safe from rats.

He gathered up some dry paper and cardboard from another bin, lined the pig bin with it and settled down every bit as comfortable as any wild bird in its nest, listening to the sweet drumming of the rain on the lid.

Allen wondered what Gill was doing.

Luckily, it was outside his experience to imagine. She certainly wasn't wondering what he was doing.

Allen wondered what Piotr was doing.

Piotr was sharing an exquisite experience with Gill and he certainly wasn't wondering what Allen was doing either.

Perversely, Allen even wondered what the Big Fat White Toad was doing. Luckily, he wasn't able to imagine that he was heaving his hanging belly-folds off the pretty young bar girl, who lay quietly sobbing on the soiled mattress. The Big Fat White Toad felt pleased with himself. *If he didn't visit these girls, what would they do for a living? He was doing them a favour. He was spreading his wealth and stimulating the economy. He was a real man.*

The bar girl knew things could be worse and that girls who were prettier, richer and of higher colour than she seemed to enjoy this lifestyle, but she didn't and she was determined to break free and reclaim her true self. She didn't know how yet, but that strange looking white man had treated her like a human being and given her hope.

Allen wondered what Lizzie was doing. *Perhaps she had managed to get out of fieldwork. Without Kate to help her he couldn't see how she could have carried on.*

CHAPTER THREE

I

As it happened, it was Lizzie who found Allen. He had woken with a start when the lid of the bin was lifted. He hadn't expected anybody to be dumping anything in it before he was up and away. He tensed himself for a shower of kitchen waste, but it didn't come. He could only see the silhouette of the head of the person who had lifted the lid, but there was no mistaking who it was.

Lizzie was more shocked than he was. She always began her morning rummage through the bins there, where the best food from the night shift was usually to be found. If she hadn't already lost her mind she would have done so on finding Allen in the bin. She hadn't known where he had disappeared to and now he had turned up in a pig bin. She didn't even try to make sense of it.

In fact, Lizzie hadn't tried to make sense of anything since Kate's death, and she had become increasingly fearful. After Kate died, Lizzie had felt the ancient impulse to burn Kate's cottage and her few possessions, as the Gypsies did to cleanse the taint of death. When her own thatch had mysteriously caught fire – which she feared might have happened as a result of her thoughts – she had subsequently spent an increasing amount of time in the stables of a demolished farmhouse, which still awaited their fate.

However, such was the sprawl of the airport, which had obliterated nearly seven square miles of countryside, that it was impossible even for Lizzie to avoid interacting with it. As a result, her life had become a confused mix of the Stone Age and the Golden Age of Aviation. Like the urban fox, she had become an opportunist and took every opportunity for survival that the airport presented, while avoiding it as much as she could.

Before Allen could recover from his surprise and reassure her, Lizzie had taken off running. It was what she did.

By the time he had clambered out of the bin, Lizzie was gone. However, he knew that she had nowhere to go except the Pits. The ghostly shape of a robin flitted about in the early light, its sporadic song heralding the dawn. A vixen screamed invitingly but unseasonably in the distance. The dry bark of an equally disoriented dog fox coughed out. They might get lucky, but offspring born during the wrong season would suffer. Natural rhythms could only be distorted so far; there were always consequences.

Allen froze as, in the distance, outside the old Nissen hut that served as the deputy commander's kennels, he could just make out a shadowy figure. *Burian! Why was he up to so early in the morning on his own with the dogs?*

For the first time in his life, Burian had decided to act on his own. As Lizzie seemed to have an uncanny knack of knowing just about everything that was going on around her, he had to assume that she knew it was him who had tried to burn her out. Although it seemed unlikely that such a mad old witch would ever be taken seriously, he had to assume the worst.

He was determined to get Lizzie and, while he was at it, that snobby Pole, Piotr, who he was sure knew about his war crimes. He could wait no longer. He knew Lizzie and Piotr would soon both be out in the fields somewhere, whatever the weather, and he was going to deal with them once and for all. He couldn't risk being returned to the communists to face a war crimes trial.

He couldn't have known that there wasn't the slightest risk of this happening even if he was exposed. He couldn't have known that his new country would guarantee him the rights and protection he had denied his victims, or that his new country would deny his victims the rights and protection they had given him. He knew the English were mad, but not that mad.

Sponsored by his brother, he was on the brink of a new life in Australia. There they would raise their happy, healthy families together without a thought for the families he had destroyed in Ukraine in the most terrible ways imaginable; neither for the lives he had blighted, nor the future generations he had denied existence. He was proud to have done his duty.

Burian's Australian paradise beckoned and it couldn't be lost at any cost. His brother had found him a job at one of the farm schools to which thousands of children from institutions had been sent after the war under the British government's child migrant scheme. The farm school to which he had been allocated was sponsored by the grace and favour of British royalty and was held up as a shining beacon of the scheme. Like a fox, he couldn't wait to get among the pigeons again. Other cunning foxes were already there.

Those who Burian had co-opted to burn Lizzie out, or worse, had left him as soon as they had realised the extent of the awful affair into which they had been drawn. Burian couldn't believe these English people were so sentimental. *He would have shown them a thing or two in Ukraine.*

Realising trouble was ahead, Allen was totally confident in his physical powers. As real danger increased, his internal fears decreased proportionally, conferring on him a rare sense of calm, which even his damaged mind could not disturb.

He had a card for it:

People who experience excessive anxiety are almost always very courageous. Any fear they experience is fear of their symptoms, not fear of a situation. There is all the difference in the world between the two.

Allen should have been worried, but his own problems seemed to have granted him a certain resistance to those of the world, up to a point, at least, as he had discovered at the time of the accident.

He realised he wouldn't need his cards while searching for Lizzie, so he decided to hide them somewhere safe, despite the fact that he found comfort in simply touching them, like a rosary. He wrapped them in some greaseproof paper that he found around the remains of a chicken carcass in a bin and wedged them into the first old hedgerow he came across.

II

As Allen edged out of the encampment of temporary buildings and tents, piles of earth from the tunnel excavations obscured his view over what had once been a flat landscape. His only point of reference was the stub of Hadleyrow Road next to The Three Magpies. From there, he faced south and tried to retrace its original route. At one point, Allen came across what he thought could be the slightest trace of a triangular pattern next to a runway. With a pang, it occurred to him that it could be what had been Reaper's Corner, 'where once the signpost caught the passing eye'.

This line finally brought to mind the name of his old friend Oliver Goldsmith – writer and poet, who would have been two hundred and twenty-odd if he hadn't died aged forty-four – who had chronicled in verse the destruction of a village by the landscaping of a large estate for a rich landowner, and whose lines had haunted Allen throughout. At least the development Goldsmith described still respected nature, if not the displaced villagers. Allen couldn't imagine what he would have made of the airport.

In Goldsmith's words, Allen 'scanned along the straggling fence that skirted the way' towards the Pits in search of a suitable vantage point from which to observe developments. Crusty orange lichens on the branches of hawthorn and blackthorn gave the appearance of autumnal foliage, as if spring and autumn were colliding in the illusion of past, present and future.

Allen sheltered under a gnarled hedge oak on a mossy cushion, his back against the ivy-clad trunk. He checked his orientation from the green powdery algae and spiderwebs on the side of the trunk, where they were protected from the predominant south-westerlies, and awaited for Burian and the dogs to emerge out in the open.

Although he was in his beloved wilderness, he felt strangely uneasy for some reason. The leaves began to drip as the red sun burnt through the mist. A breeze was rising up from the south. Allen shivered. His eardrums told him the air pressure was dropping, as did the bubbles on the stream as the loach, the weather fish, became agitated and air escaped from their swim bladders. He caught the sharp, peculiar smell of an approaching thunderstorm; the air musty with bacterial spores and gas from ditches, ponds and bogs released by the low pressure and the first raindrops.

A cold front was moving through. Towering clouds were rising and swelling up on powerful currents of moisture-laden air, their tops growing larger and rounder as the bases grew darker, threatening the arrival of a violent thunderstorm. In the remains of Lizzie's cottage, the man with the brolly swung out of the weather house and the lady in her summer dress swung in, even though there was nobody there to observe them, despite what the philosophers said.

He saw a rabbit in the pollarded top of a willow along the ditch and heard the calls of a rain bird and a storm cock heralding the change, which made him wonder whether the chance of a heavy rainstorm was, in fact, no more than even.

He watched plucky little ringed plovers scuttling around the edge of the advancing excavations. He hadn't seen any before the war, but they seemed to have been attracted by the chaos of the transient landscapes of bomb sites, gravel pits and now the airport, which had driven people away. Sometimes the plovers seemed to be barely one step ahead of the bulldozers, but even if their nests and broods were destroyed they simply started over again. They could raise three broods in a season among the mayhem. Their spirit was indomitable.

As the rain swept in, the site of the devastated landscape deepened Allen's unease. Lines from Goldsmith echoed in his mind again:

Even now the devastation is begun,
And half the business of destruction done.

He picked some chicory leaves and nibbled them to ease his melancholy. The wind veered clockwise to a northerly, wafting the ominous smell of the airport towards him. There was a lightning flash in the distance and he counted the interval to the thunder: five for every mile, as Lizzie had always done to know when to 'put the cutlery away wet so as not to draw it in, 'specially before noon when it be stronger'.

Out of the corner of his eye, he spotted a hare crouching in its seat under a bramble bush a little further along the hedge. Like Allen, the hares had been behaving more and more abnormally as their habitat disappeared. They had been driven into the marshy margins of the Pits. 'As mad as a marsh hare,' people said at these times, even in March. Allen wondered whether the hare was also suffering a rising tide of anxiety that generated fearful spectres. It was nibbling something, but he couldn't make out whether it was chicory leaves or not.

The hares' remoteness, watchfulness and cleverness in hiding away, even in flat, open country, made it difficult to get near them, contributing to the mystery that surrounded them. But when the storm passed Allen saw three hares lope onto the edge of a runway and start grooming the mud from their fur, especially from the bottoms of their powerful hind feet. They lay in a circle, reminding Allen of the mystical symbol of the lunar cycle and fertility, a carving of which – despite it being a pagan image – could be found juxtaposed with the Green Man inside the Norman church across the main road.

Allen knew the foxes would also be watching. It was the only time a fox had a chance of catching a hare, with or without foxgloves, or 'foxsocks' as he called them, to soften their step. But even then they didn't have much of a chance, other than by ambush, as the hares were fifty miles per hour steeplechasers and so agile it was virtually impossible for a dog of any breed to run them down in open country. This was also even true when they worked in pairs in the enclosed fields of the baying hare coursers, the surrounding hedges of which Gill and Allen had unblocked at every opportunity.

The hares' large amber eyes were set to see more of what was behind them than in front as, once on the run, that was where any predator would always be. In combination with their eyes, their large, swivelling ears – the black tips of which signalled to potential predators that they might as well give up the chase before they started – left no gaps for predators to sneak through.

The more Allen saw of the hares, the less he feared them. He had a card for it:

Anxiety and irrational fears arise out of separation from what is real and are themselves ultimately unreal. Involvement with what is real exposes unrealistic fears as the illusions they are.

Allen knew he had to keep in touch with reality and stop ruminating – stop picking at the scab, stop scratching the itch – as it maintained his preoccupation with thinking. This increased the conscious accessibility of intrusions so that the overall effect was a failure to revise dysfunctional beliefs about intrusive thoughts in a favourable way.

But Allen didn't know any so-called normal people who could stop simple, everyday compulsions such as picking and scratching, let alone the ones that had him in their grip. *So what chance did he have, and why should anyone ever imagine that anybody could 'pull themselves together' when the ability that was needed to do the pulling together was the very thing that needed pulling together?*

Allen struggled with the contradictions and paradoxes of

his endless analyses, but had to admit that they could be quite elegant, particularly the realisation that the fearful need to control thoughts led to the development of uncontrollable intrusive thoughts and the failure to control them.

A stab from a blackthorn twig brought him back to reality. Everywhere he went macca juked him.

III

Allen's attention was alerted when something caught his eye in a distant field. It could have been a bit of old black rag blowing in the wind, but the odd glimpse of the flapping black shape revealed that it was heading against the wind. *Bits of old black rag couldn't head against the wind, but Lizzie could. Yes, he was sure it was her out there.*

At the same time, he heard the barking and yelping of the pack of dogs. They were not proper hunting hounds, but a motley collection of strays that had been lost or abandoned during the destruction of the village. As a result, they were unpredictable in nature and hard to control. Burian emerged into view, desperately hanging onto the long rope he had threaded through their collars.

It dawned on Allen that Burian might also be on Lizzie's trail. *Otherwise, why were the others not with him, especially the usual dog handler?* On his own, out here, Burian wouldn't have been too much of a concern to Allen, but the dogs introduced another dimension, as did the shotgun Burian was carrying.

Burian hadn't been out with the dogs by himself before and it was a more difficult task than their regular handler had made it appear. Once the dogs caught the scent and eventually the sight of a hare, he couldn't hold them and they were off across the runways. He knew he would be under observation from the control tower, so he acted as if he had loosed the dogs on purpose.

Those in the control tower did indeed have him under observation and, despite him being on his own, they did assume he was out clearing the runways of game, as it was an unusually quiet period as far as arrivals and departures were concerned. However, they were puzzled to see the dogs veering away from the hare on the runway towards a black shape; possibly a tumbling lapwing that was flapping about towards the Pits further south. They didn't notice the hare making its escape in the opposite direction.

Allen could see that it was no tumbling lapwing and guessed that Lizzie was acting as a decoy to draw the dogs' attention away from the hare. *There was no other explanation. She would never have shown herself like that otherwise.* He dismissed the bizarre idea that the hare might have been doing the same for Lizzie's sake.

Burian hadn't realised it yet, but despite the industrialised surroundings he was slowly being drawn into a mysterious situation that was completely new to him. Being a murderous bully, he had never before been out on his own, let alone in search of an elusive quarry in a strange environment. His stationary targets had always been helpless women and children in their homes, as the men had already been killed or captured by the first wave of the German front line troops. Sat in his armoured vehicle, Burian had never had to face anyone with a weapon more threatening than a broom in that hell on earth that was wartime Ukraine. Now, still in sight of the control tower, he was feeling less and less sure of himself.

Allen saw the dogs move back towards the perimeter fence and hedge, close to where he had stashed his cards, and along which Burian had been lumbering in an uncoordinated waddle. While he was still worrying about the situation, he caught sight of another fast-moving black shape from across the other side of the runways. It looked big, but he realised that could be a case of what his old friend, the painter Leonardo, had called 'fog loom', an illusion caused by mist and fog, which by making objects look further away while not diminishing their size made objects look bigger than they were.

Allen sensed he would need all the defences he could muster against the gathering threats. He knew ash wood was more directly associated with weapons – from the traditional ashen spear to the wooden Mosquito bombers in the war – but sensing the threat was not entirely physical he cut a hazel stick for its special powers against evil.

Allen remembered Lizzie stirring her boiling jam with a hazel stick so it wouldn't be stolen by fairies; the jam rather than the stick, he supposed, or perhaps the stick too if it had a lot of jam on it. Apparently fairies also liked sugar. The neighbours had been duly mystified when Lizzie had stuck a jam-tipped hazel stick in the ground near the door and it had sprouted brambles, adding to the rumours of Lizzie's strange powers. It was also well known that a hazel breast band would revive a horse if it happened to be found tired and travel-stained with hag-stirrup knots in its tangled mane from being hag-ridden that night.

Allen couldn't believe he was even contemplating this folklore, but the situation he was in correlated with the circumstances in which the folklore had first been formulated, and in this regard his brain worked no differently from any other, including those from past millennia. The stubbornly persistent illusion of past, present and future was yielding under the pressure.

He sharpened one end of his hazel stick and looked around for some deadly poisonous plants – collectively known as 'thung' – to apply to the point. But he had only heard Lizzie talk of these. He didn't know what they looked like, when and where they grew, or how to extract their poisons. Perhaps she had not given him this information for fear of him making a deadly mistake. He made do with some poisonous berries familiar to him that had survived the winter in the hedge, mashing them up on a stone with the sharpened end of his hazel stick.

He would also have liked some foetid-smelling black horehound, also known as 'stinking roger', much to the annoyance of a villager called Roger. It was used to treat the bites of mad dogs, which is all Allen could think the large black shape on the horizon might be. But he couldn't distinguish it from catmint, which he thought would make a mad dog even madder, so it was just as well he didn't find any. Instead, he gathered some hedge woundwort and selfheal in case he was wounded.

He would have liked to have drawn a circle around himself with his hazel stick, which Lizzie said would protect him from evil. She had also shown him how to make a rosary of hazelnuts for protection against evil, but he was on the move and now was not the time for handicrafts. *He was as ready as he could be.* Thung didn't require faith, although it worked to various degrees according to differing susceptibilities. Allen hoped his crushed berries would be enough.

He didn't bother with herbs for stamina and speed, as he had seen his opponents in the annual races test them out to little or no effect, and curiously for him he was confident that he had enough of both to deal with all known protagonists in the coming confrontation.

As for his appearance, Allen now closely resembled the Green Man, a Celtic symbol of fertility, which was most inappropriate for him. More appropriately, however, the Green Man was also the Celtic symbol of woodland and was sometimes portrayed as a grotesque being with misshapen teeth, squinting eyes and a horrible lopsided leer. Allen always averted his eyes from the carvings of the Green Man in the parish church and the illustrations in his old books. Being so parochial, the people across the main road assumed the legend of the Green Man was unique to Hadleyrow and were convinced it was based on the poor, benighted inhabitants of the Rookery; Allen in particular.

As he stood stock still and invisible watching the dogs and Burian drawing closer, Allen's mind drifted back to the Maroons, who he thought would have been impressed by his camouflage and his skill.

IV

Finally picking up his trail, the dogs turned in Allen's direction. Dogs posed special problems for Allen, as they had for the Maroons. He had noticed that the West Indians at the airport were particularly wary of the local legend of the black hound. Briscoe had told him that Jamaicans had more proverbs about dogs than any other subject, and the ones he had heard contained much less sentimental nonsense than the British equivalents about 'man's best friend'. Like subjugated people everywhere, the native tribes of the Caribbean islands and the slaves had been terrorised by large ferocious dogs brought in by their enslavers, so the islanders continued to have an uncertain relationship with them.

The dogs were following Allen's scent on the air, like a

coloured ribbon. Eventually they would pick up the trail of his unique ground scent from dead skin cells, disturbed soil and crushed vegetation. Ground scent trails could take days to fade, depending on the conditions, and dogs could follow them, like fluorescent footprints on the ground, day and night. They didn't have to see him, which, not being gazehounds, they hardly could. The sense of sight was about as important to a dog as the sense of smell was to a human. Dogs lived in a duller, blue-yellow world, than humans. A blind dog was like a man without a sense of smell; and a dog without a sense of smell was like a blind man.

Allen hadn't bothered to walk along the wet ditch as he searched for his thung, as he knew dogs could smell objects even when they were deep underwater. The dogs' sense of smell could only be confused by swamping it with more overpowering odours.

Fortunately for Allen, the low banks along the remaining hedgerows and ditches were peppered with old rabbit warrens, badger setts and fox dens, so he wouldn't have to obscure his scent trail with foetid-smelling herbs. This was a rich enough mixture to distract even the keenest hunting dog, let alone this motley pack of strays. Allen slithered low on the ground along the hedge bank, searching for an occupied fox den, which would further distract the dogs.

He pushed through an elder thicket. Although the locals believed elder would ward off evil, let alone witches and lightning, they had waited in vain for a spirit known as the Elder Mother to take her revenge when huge amounts of elder had been destroyed with the hedges.

An old story still circulated about a villager who, when he cut a stick from an elder bush, saw blood run from the wound on the tree. Later, meeting an old woman who was

They Couldn't Have Known

suspected of being a witch, who had her arm bound up, he put two and two together and reported her to the authorities. With such clear-cut evidence she was summarily sentenced to being ducked in the village pond. No doubt she was told that she was lucky, as she could have been burnt instead of being nearly drowned. The fire wouldn't have been of elder wood, though, as everybody in Hadleyrow knew: 'Elder be ye Lady's tree, burn it not or cursed ye'll be.'

It was typical of all these vengeful spirits, however, that they never stopped destructive forces, but only bullied the meek and fearful, exactly like Allen's feared intrusive thoughts.

Dwarf elder caused trouble without recourse to the supernatural as its berries caused diarrhoea, also known as 'the danes'. During the Viking invasions this had caused confusion when somebody shouted: 'Watch out, the Danes are coming.' The herb danewort was thought to grow where the blood of Vikings had been shed, although Lizzie thought it was where something else had been shed. She held a similar opinion about the local Danes Stream, from which she would never drink.

Allen soon found the entrance to a fox den excavated among the roots of another old, gnarled hedge oak, which he could see from the telltale signs, was still occupied. He was back home in his beloved countryside and things were going his way. He took a running leap into the tree, grabbed a branch and clambered up into the middle, where the ivy still reached.

He settled down and stared at a slime mould on the bark, wondering whether he could actually see that it was moving, as Lizzie claimed. He nibbled the tender edge of a chicken-of-the-woods bracket fungus growing on a nearby branch. He knew from Lizzie that it posed no risk, but the only fungus that everybody in the village dared to eat was the well-known field mushroom, as only Lizzie knew which other fungi were truly safe to eat. The villagers likened their treatment by the airport authorities to the cultivation of field mushrooms in the dark forcing sheds, claiming: 'We be dropped in the muck and kept in the dark.'

A sudden loud trill from a wren burst from the undergrowth like a warning for him to concentrate. He slowed his breathing and remained perfectly still, looking like just another gnarl of the ancient trunk.

Allen's contrary mind actually brought him some relief instead of the normal torture, when, as real danger was escalating, he was swept along by remembrances of the unspoilt, natural ways of his childhood. One spring, Lizzie and Allen had counted thirty-four pairs of nesting birds of nineteen different species, most of them residents, in half a mile of hedgerow like the one he was sitting in.

A kestrel, quivering over a field with its wings flickering and tail fanned, slipped to the side and jigged through the trees of a small coppice. A flock of linnets swept silently over the fields. He spotted an old bee skep Lizzie had placed in a hollow on the south-facing bank of the hedgerow to keep the colony warm and dry like the traditional 'bee boles' found in the south-facing walls of old gardens. It was festooned with nettles to deter frogs and human marauders, but unfortunately not enough to deter a hungry badger.

V

Allen shook himself out of his reverie. The dogs came on fast as they detected Allen's scent getting stronger on the air, despite his precautions.

They Couldn't Have Known

Allen readied his thung-tipped hazel spear and steeled himself for their attack.

At that moment, to his utter astonishment, Piotr pushed through the hedge right in front of him on one of his surveying forays.

Confused by the sudden appearance of Piotr between them and their original quarry, the dogs started barking as they closed in. The leader, a powerful dog with its head low, ears flattened and teeth bared, lunged at a terrified Piotr. Breaking cover, Allen thrust his hazel spear into the dog's side, which, to Allen's complete amazement, dropped dead at his feet. As it was too quick to be due to the thung, Allen realised he must have pierced its heart.

In their confusion, the rest of the pack milled around their dead leader. During the ensuing mayhem, Allen shoved a dazed Piotr, who had remained rooted to the spot, back through the hedge.

Burian finally lumbered up to the scene, sweating and smelling like a pig from the *salo* – the raw pig fat with black bread and salt – he had eaten all his life, and, more recently, the stolen bacon and pork from the factory. The arrival of this pig who was determined to beat them off their dead leader was too much for the dogs. They ignored Allen and bounded away.

In the chaos, Burian was unaware of Allen, who had slipped back into the hedge. Despite Allen's strong suspicion of Burian's intentions, it did not occur to him to drive his thung-covered hazel stick into Burian. He just didn't think like that.

Allen was now at the rear of the hunt. Having missed Allen, the dogs appeared to have picked up Lizzie's trail once again. He couldn't think of anything else that would have drawn them off towards the Pits. Burian, increasingly demoralised and frightened, lumbered along at some distance behind the dogs. He had been reduced to a fearful shadow of his former arrogant self by nothing more, so far, than the effort of walking a short distance from the modern world of the airport. Burian's ineptitude in this natural environment was undermining him by the moment, reinforcing Allen and Lizzie's positions in direct proportion. The balance of nature was being asserted.

But there was still the other black shape Allen had seen fleetingly on the horizon to worry about. He didn't know what it was or where it was, but he needed to know with increasing urgency.

The unlikely procession began to be drawn into the maze of narrow paths among the dense mesh of overgrown vegetation near the Pits, where hazel, brambles, blackthorn and privet formed impenetrable thickets of 'whitethroat scrub' in complete contrast to the open landscape they were leaving. The beauty of the place overwhelmed Allen, its paths carpeted with red, orange and golden leaves and mosses in every shade of green. Although not colour blind, Burian was totally oblivious to the riot of colour.

Allen wished the appreciation of beauty was always denied to the cruel and mean-spirited, but he knew that it wasn't and that beauty had no moral value. Mother Nature was pitiless, yet produced unsurpassed beauty. It had occurred to Allen that human consciousness was the universe's means of appreciating itself. But if so, Allen didn't think it was worth the price of the suffering of a single conscious being.

But there was something terribly wrong with the power of beauty in human relations. *Would he still love Gill if she were deformed like him, despite the perfection of her inner organs? Of course* not. Had any man loved Lizzie for her inner beauty? What were the chances of love at first sight for the facially disfigured or the blind?

With the shortened perspectives along the twisting and overgrown tracks, there was a great danger that the antagonists would criss-cross each other's paths. This was only avoided by Lizzie knowing exactly where she was going and by Allen resting up and listening to the sounds of the chase, which were muffled by the wind through the leaves.

Despite the imminent dangers, Allen couldn't stop himself trying to identify the trees and shrubs by the sound their leaves made in the wind. Lizzie could do so even in the dark and had been trying to teach him, but all he could identify with certainty was the aspen, the 'whispering' or 'shiver' tree, from the rustling of its long-stalked leaves.

Allen's contrary mind also recalled an old villager who believed the wind was caused by trees and bushes waving their branches about. Ever since, Allen had typically been unable to stop thinking of ways to prove that it wasn't. He continued to do so even as danger grew near.

He heard the sharp sound of Burian blundering into a thicket of crack willow in the distance. Allen knew it must be Burian, as Lizzie would never have made such a mistake. To his surprise, he also heard the dogs moving back towards the airport.

It was a huge relief to know that they were out of the equation. Tactically, he was in a strong position now that the dogs had gone and it wasn't known that he was at the back of the line. But the unknown danger of that black shape, which he assumed was coming up fast behind, remained.

Burian's state could now be considered pitiable, not that he deserved any pity. He was covered in mud and barely capable of standing. He had trodden in the pile of dog muck and vomit that the lead hound had released when mortally injured. His clothes were torn and he was bleeding from the thorns of wild rose and blackberry that overhung the long-disused paths. To his utter horror, a large, orange-yellow blob of witches' butter fungus wobbling perilously on a dead branch had stuck in his hair and smeared his face. And he had lost his dogs.

Like Burian, the dogs were at their best and most confident when, in large numbers, they bore down on defenceless prey that was capable only of trying to run away. They were fearless as they tore whatever they caught to pieces. However, as they had become separated by the dense vegetation and narrow pathways and were thrown increasingly on their individual resources, they had become nervous like Burian. In addition to this, and the fact that Burian stank like a pig, a powerful unknown scent carried on the wind had persuaded the dogs to head back to the safety of the open fields and the runways of the airport.

Following along behind, Allen was totally mystified to see scraps of his most secret notes in the dog muck and vomit Burian had trodden in and deposited further along the path. Confused, he concluded that, as a result of all the tension, he was imagining them, along with the message he could make out on one:

To make an end is to make a beginning.
The end is where we start from.

He took it to be a subconscious confirmation that this period of his life was over and that he must start anew.

He couldn't have known that at the beginning of the hunt the lead dog had sniffed out his cache of cards in the chicken-scented greaseproof paper and wolfed it down like a tasty morsel.

A startled redshank, with its probing beak and long red legs, gave a piercing whistle of alarm as it took off. Nearby, a plant with the same name because of its reddish stalks added to the sense of alarm with its black blotches of the devil's pinch on its leaves. A mixed flock of waders flew in perfect unison, looking for comfort and security together despite the striking differences in their origins, appearances and ways of life; just like those at the airport less than a few miles away.

As they got closer to the mysterious waters of the Pits, the wind dropped and an eerie peace descended on the beautiful but ominous scene. The pig-like squeal of the cry of a water rail seemed to mock Burian in his stinking, pig-like sweat. Allen knew that wasn't right at this time of year. These secretive, enigmatic birds, with their red stabbing beaks, were the prime skulkers of dense wetlands and never drew attention to themselves outside their summer breeding season.

VI

The Pits were a vast, mysterious labyrinth of deep, dark water. Clear and black in winter, they were cloudy and green in summer, with algal blooms triggered by the run-off of fertilisers from the surrounding fields. Scoured out by mechanical diggers, most of the banks fell away steeply into deep water. Narrow causeways with shelving beaches of yellow sand and gravel, washed over by waves in windy weather, ran between pits of various shapes and sizes and of unknown depth, which were thick with entangling weeds. Quicksands added to the danger. The area had been excavated for its sand and gravel in such a haphazard way and over such a long period that there were no accurate maps. For once, progress had engendered a mysterious landscape, albeit from the ruins of the old.

Allen saw a streak of red and blue as a kingfisher dived, returning to a branch with glittering silver in its beak. A heron stood motionless and ghostly in the reeds, its slate-blue plumage a mixture of grey dawn and smoky dusk:

A shadder o' the night
A reflection o' the day.

He saw the flash of fish as they communicated by flickering their silvery undersides; a red-throated male stickleback postured angrily at its own reflection in the silver-mirrored side of a dace; and scales from chub floated up from the depths, sparkling like gold leaf.

Along the causeways, alder and every type of willow grew, spreading into dense thickets on the myriad small islands they linked. Great, dense reed beds colonised the shallower waters, their march halted only by the depths. The villagers searched them for lost treasure. The reeds' green blades and the greyer-green of the sedges pushed through the pale gold and brown of their winter litter. When swept by the lightest breeze, the reed beds rustled and whispered softly in contrast to the harsh, metallic calls of the resident herons and the reed warblers as they announced their arrival from sunnier climes.

Alder, with its deep roots, reduced the erosion of the causeways and islands. Shoots sprouted from the base, forming impenetrable tangled clumps, which gave a further layer of mystery to the Pits. This was alder country.

The justifiably ominous reputation of the Pits had been reinforced by several tragic drownings. A young woman had drowned in recent memory, much to the shock of her young charges at the local primary school. She had had a dainty, slender figure and long, flowing, fair hair. It was thought that a willow bough that grew aslant a pit, to which she had clung, had broken as she reached out for some calming purple loosestrife or orchids growing in the marshy edges. She was found with the corn marigolds she had collected floating around her like a wreath.

Drownings of intrepid swimmers were accompanied by dark observations of getting trapped in the weeds and talk of a giant pike lurking in the waters. It had been seen taking ducklings, dabchicks and the candy-striped chicks of great-crested grebes when they left the safety of their parents' backs, and even the adults themselves. One heartbroken dog owner claimed she had seen the swipe of a huge tail just after her pet had disappeared below the waters. Even if it only gashed a leg, that could be enough to cause a dog or a swimmer to drown.

Suicides were not uncommon and some hinted darkly of at least one case of murder. People who dared to cross the Pits in the dark or had been caught there in bad weather claimed to have seen the flickering dances of will-o'-the-wisps and things of which they wouldn't tell. Allen, in contrast, loved their wildness and desolation. As with the duppies, he had no room left in his crowded mind for the terror of the Pits.

VII

Suddenly Allen became aware of something coming up very fast behind him. He instinctively dropped to the ground and rolled off the track into a thick reed bed at the edge of the pit. Beyond the reeds, the broad floating leaves and white flowers of water crowfoot assured Allen that the water there would only come up to his waist.

He couldn't see the track clearly through the reeds from his perspective. He just caught a glimpse of a large black shape as it sped by in a blur. Sure that it was evil, he threw his thung-coated stick at it like a spear, but it showed no reaction and sped on. *Perhaps he had missed.* Allen hoped whatever it was would get Burian in the back first, giving Lizzie some warning.

Allen scrambled back out onto the path, only to see the black shape move straight past a terrified, gibbering Burian towards a hare poised on the path, which was ready to take flight. The presence of a hare on that path was unexpected, even though they had been forced into the area by the loss of their open fields. In an instant, Allen recalled the old painting in the Hare and Hound and the tale of a hare being hunted by a black hound without a single white hair, which was as fast as its quarry. He also recalled the Maroon's Nanny and to his astonishment found himself shouting: 'Run, Granny, run! Run, Nanny, run!' despite the implications.

The hare took off. It was still a fair distance ahead of the pursuing black shape, which Allen could now see was a hound. He knew that traits of the extinct British wolf survived in local dogs, but this creature did not look wolf-like.

Catatonic by now, Burian had dropped down onto his knees as the hound had brushed past him, not even attempting to fire his gun. Allen was shaken when what seemed to be a bizarre association sprung to his mind with the Maroon's phrase: 'When you see ole lady run, no aks what the matter, run too.'

Allen looked on with horror as the hound seemed to bear down on the hare, which, for some unknown reason, he had called Nanny. But just as the seemingly inevitable was about to occur, a smaller black-and-white blur appeared out of the reeds and took the black hound sideways into the still, deep, black waters of the pit.

Talbot, chasing rabbits off the runways, had picked up Allen's scent and had broken away to find him. As he had drawn close to the Pits he had temporarily lost Allen's scent in the riddle of activities and had been pulled irresistibly to the water. Picking up Lizzie's scent, but puzzled at not finding her there, he had been alarmed by the stink of a sweating pig and didn't notice the hare sitting on the path. Like all dogs, he didn't like pigs, so he decided to lay low. On hearing Allen's cry, Talbot had broken cover and, to his complete astonishment, had run into the side of a huge, powerful black hound.

Coming in as he did, low and from the side, and with the black hound possibly weakened by Allen's thung-coated spear, the impact had been enough to knock the black hound off balance and into the deep water. Talbot's momentum carried him through into the water after the black hound.

To Talbot's surprise, the black hound seemed to dissolve in the water, losing all of its power and menace as it floundered about among the long, waving weeds that rose from the black depths. Talbot, to an equal and opposite extent, flourished. In his element, refreshed and empowered, he easily made it to the bank. Turning, he saw the swipe of a huge tail fin break the surface near the black hound and the water turn crimson. The black hound floundered further out and slowly sank beneath the surface. The patch of crimson diffused and the ripples dispersed, leaving no trace of the drama that had disturbed the waters.

Allen, who had been observing these events, slowly came to his senses. That big black hound had been no legendary monster. Legendary monsters did not get hit by earthly things, nor did they bleed. They might melt in the water, but they wouldn't drown. He finally realised that it was the big, aggressive, notorious black dog from across the main road that had somehow avoided the traffic and reached the airport.

He had seen it before, from a distance, when the owners had brought it across to join the deputy commander's hunting parties, not that the deputy commander had ever allowed them to let it off its leash. It was big, possibly a bull mastiff; the sort of dog that would have been expedited in the old days to prevent it bringing deer down, but these days was allowed to wander around the area without its owners in sight. When Allen had seen it in the distance the fog loom had indeed increased it to unearthly proportions.

As with most dogs, its behaviour reflected that of its owners, who were self-centred, ill-mannered, insecure and arrogant in their ignorance of the impact of their dog's actions on those around them. The only compensation of the increasing noise from the airport was that it drowned out the dog's incessant barking.

Like reed warblers and their gigantic cuckoo chicks in the reed beds, the owners thought the dog was their baby, despite its huge size and aggressive behaviour, and the dog had naturally adopted its owners' characteristics as they were the only point of reference in its pack animal mind. So the miserable trio had turned in on itself more by the day.

After a joyful reunion with Talbot, Allen pressed on after Burian. Although the odds were now definitely tilted in their favour, the chase wasn't over yet and Burian was still armed.

Burian was so exhausted that having fallen to the ground when the hound had brushed past him, he could only crawl forwards on all fours, the gravel hard and sharp against his hands and knees. He had survived the horrors of the war in Europe, but now, within a couple of miles of a modern airport, armed with a gun and on the hunt with a pack of dogs for a little old woman, he was lost and terrified.

The Pits stirred Burian's memories of the old superstitions and fears of the supernatural he had absorbed as a boy. Perhaps Lizzie was a witch after all. He remembered watching her cottage and seeing her sensuous shifted-shape stirring the cauldron before disappearing with remarkable speed over the fields in the dark. He also remembered the owl sweeping from the eaves on silent wings. Owls were bad omens.

As if on cue, a brown owl hooted. Then, hearing a rustling in a thicket, Burian looked up and was transfixed by a final terror from which he would never recover.

There in the branches.

Right in front of him.

Grinning.

Sat a hobgoblin!

There could be no doubt.

There were no moon-cast shadows to play tricks on his imagination this time.

A hobgoblin!

So it was true, they did exist. They had to, of course, otherwise why did everybody and every culture still believe in them? Burian stared in horror with his mouth wide open. He didn't even think about his gun, which, now he was on all fours, stuck out behind him like a rigid tail.

Nearby, a patch of Herb Robert, linked to goblins and magic, scrambled among the long, dank grass with a reddish glow.

The hobgoblin was about two feet in length and brown-grey in colour, with a tail and a hairless pink face that transfixed Burian with its bared teeth and gums. It silently held Burian's gaze for what seemed to him like an eternity before its expression changed to a fearful grimace and it emitted a piercing scream as it slowly turned, raising its tail to expose a florid red rump.

In his terror, it didn't occur to Burian to question whether hobgoblins would have rumps, let alone florid red ones; nor to empty his gun up this one. He couldn't have known either that, being on all fours with what looked like a rigid tail, he had elicited submissive behaviour from a rhesus monkey that had recently escaped during the unloading of a Monkey Special at the airport.

This hobgoblin had been trying to appease him, but had inadvertently tipped Burian's mind beyond the point of no return.

VIII

Allen was now in the position in which he wanted to be: close up behind Burian but unobserved. Beyond Burian, Allen could now see Lizzie on a small beach at the far end of a narrow causeway that ran right across the pit, along which Burian was crawling towards her. It was the first time he had had a clear view of her since the start of the hunt. He didn't know where she had been when he had witnessed the hare and hound incident and Talbot's timely intervention.

Allen was surprised Lizzie didn't appear to be making the best use of the terrain that was so familiar to them both, as she appeared to be waving to Burian to attract his attention. It seemed as though, after crossing the causeway, she had sacrificed her opportunity of an easy escape to stand on the beach and taunt Burian now that he had been reduced to crawling on all fours. But Allen knew that wasn't part of Lizzie's nature, not even when confronted by somebody with murderous intent.

When Allen reached the start of the causeway, he noticed broken vegetation around the entrance to a path on the right-hand side running along the main bank. He also saw some deep footprints in the mud. Allen realised Lizzie must have made these, but he also knew she would never have been so clumsy unless she was deliberately laying a false trail. On closer examination he could see that she had backtracked along this false trail, walking backwards to return to cross by the gravel causeway, on which she had left no footprints. She must have wanted Burian to take the path to the right and not to cross the causeway, but in the confusion and in his sorry state he had missed these blatant clues and blundered on.

Allen's mind raced as he frantically tried to work out what Lizzie was up to.

The hollow sound of a bittern boomed from the reeds some miles away. The rasping call of a corncrake raked the air. A pheasant 'gocked' in alarm. Gulls wheeled on their narrow wings, bright white against the dark water, their plaintiff cries thinner than those at sea. A barn owl shrieked. *It was all wrong.*

Allen looked up. A wispy veil of high cirrus clouds was edging in, presaging a change in the weather. A huge solar halo encircled the low, pale sun with two bright multicoloured spots – sun dogs – on either side. High above, in the wispy cirrus clouds of ice crystals, he could see an upside-down, rainbow-like arc between two columns of clouds – a fire-rainbow or 'smile-in-the sky' – but more like a menacing grin, adding an air of mystery and dread to the already apocalyptic scene.

Something scuttled through the dead leaves in the

undergrowth. A mob of raucous, chattering magpies settled in a nearby hedgerow, but Allen couldn't see to count them to ascertain their message. Time stood still.

IX

Those in the control tower saw the flash an instant before they heard the explosion. The windows caved in and they were blown off their feet. There was no time to count the interval between the two. The control room was covered in sand, gravel and vegetation, and a newt crawled across the radar screen. Most of the temporary buildings around the foot of the tower were damaged to the point of collapse and the tents were blown down. A local homing pigeon that had won a citation for carrying messages to and from France during the war was blown out of the air, fatally wounded. Pond skaters fifty miles away quivered with the shock waves.

The last of the large farmhouses dating from the sixteenth century, recently vacated by Gill's parents, collapsed as if in surrender. The old ship's timbers stood proud of the ruins, like the masts of a ship that had been badly damaged in battle.

Across the main road, bricks shook loose from the Tudor tower of the Norman church and the timbers of the magnificent tithe barn groaned a little, scattering a cloud of white doves as if in exclamation, but without sustaining the slightest damage.

Coincidently, the earth also moved for Piotr and Gill, oblivious to the contribution of the external tremors.

After Allen had shoved Piotr back through the hedge, Piotr had staggered about dazed until an airport worker returning from inspecting the runways had picked him up in his van and given him a lift for the short distance home. He was still confused and slightly panic-stricken when he arrived home. He woke Gill as he slipped back into bed.

'What are you doing back, darling? I thought you were at work.'

'I'm not too sure,' mumbled Piotr.

All Piotr could remember when recounting the tale to Gill was that for some reason the lead dog had dropped dead just as it was about to attack him. The pack had lost interest in him when it lost its leader and somehow he had stumbled back through the hedge and made his getaway. When Gill asked him whether he had seen anybody out there other than the van driver, he had said no, and she had given him a quizzical look.

Driving to the airport in the brand new Austin A40 Devon saloon he had bought after striking a deal with Spot, Denzil saw the flash, but thought it was distant lightning. He counted to fifteen before giving up and counting the cars he overtook instead, many of them on the inside. He could barely contain his excitement. After an increasingly ugly turf war with Spot, it had been agreed that Spot would stick to gambling and protection, leaving Denzil free to exploit drugs and prostitution; an arrangement that normalised a situation that was already evolving by a type of unnatural selection.

Up until then there had only been one or two clubs of any standing catering for West Indians in London: the inappropriately named Colonial Club, the more appropriately named Jamaican Club and one that was unofficially called The Monks' Club in Cable Street run by Franciscan Brothers, which provided the hostile locals with an opportunity to rename it in a way they could not resist. Denzil now had full pockets and was planning to return to the Caribbean to set up supply chains for what he was sure would be a burgeoning empire of his own.

A thud and shower of feathers interrupted his reverie. A big black crow had been slow in its take-off as it scavenged carrion in the road and Denzil had clipped its nearside wing with the offside wing of his car. He watched in his rear-view mirror as the ragbag of bones and black feathers spun over the roof into the road behind him. At the sight of it, he shouted out a traditional mocking call: 'John Crow tink im dandy man but im only so-so feathers!' This was the same phrase, that, to his horror, had been shouted out to him following his arrival in England by an alcoholic West Indian immigrant sat on a park bench.

John Crow, a vulture, was the most significant bird in Caribbean culture: the embodiment of ugliness, blackness, evil and disgrace. If one appeared in a dream, it was believed to portend a tragedy in the dreamer's family, thus guaranteeing its appearance in their dreams. During abusive arguments, islanders would call each other: 'Dutty John Crow', 'Black John Crow' and 'Heng-man John Crow'.

When he looked ahead again, Denzil was shocked by the gruesome sight of the crow's head, stuck on the radiator cap like a mascot with an angry expression on its face, wobbling about with the movements of the car. He tried to discard the thought that it was an omen, as it was a different bird in England. However, in denying its significance, he afforded it some credence, so the thought left its mark even on somebody like Denzil.

Briscoe was shaken from the sleep of the righteous. Seeing the broken windows and crockery scattered across the floor and the curtains still billowing in the turbulence, he couldn't make any sense of it, but he immediately thought his strange friend Allen must be involved somehow.

Everywhere im turn macca juke im, he thought.

There was never a dull moment with Allen. He was a strange outcast, admittedly, but one who shared Briscoe's sensibilities, broad but untutored education, an interest in all around him and an unquenchable thirst for knowledge.

Once the air had cleared and they had checked that nobody had been seriously injured, panic broke out in the control tower.

'Bloody hell! That madman Burian has blown up the Rookery. Where the bloody hell did he get that amount of explosives?' asked the deputy commander.

'It was your idea,' someone said.

'No it bloody well wasn't! We're all in this together. Get on to Whitehall straight away and start the cover-up. If this gets out we're done for.'

'It's bound to get out,' said another.

'Bigger things than this have been covered up.'

'Yes, but that was during the war.'

'We can say one of those Monkey Specials crashed. Nobody will care about that and they won't go looking for bodies. Get somebody to scatter the dead ones from the last Monkey Special over there.'

They looked out at the dark, black cloud from the explosion as it gently drifted away into the distance. They knew things could never be the same after this, no matter how successful the cover-up.

X

Stunned by the impact, Allen lay face down in an eroded gully, spitting out not only sandy soil and vegetation, but also the taste of the red mist in the air. He felt as though he would never stop spitting. He had been blown off his feet and several yards back by the crumping crash of the huge explosion. As he lay there, sand, gravel and broken vegetation showered over him.

As he lifted his head he heard a ringing in his ears, which, though fading, set his heart pounding anew. *Was he hearing the bluebells ring, a sound that summons the fairies and bodes ill for human ears?*

He might as well have done, as the dreaded smell swept over him. He gagged, buried his head in a mossy mound and held his breath, desperate not to breathe in any more of the fine red mist that enveloped him, lest it became incorporated into every fibre of his body.

Nature was quick to reassert itself. The reeds had been blown flat, but not a single one was broken and they were already regaining their upright habit. Allen lifted his head and could just see the long, velvety, dark brown seed heads of bulrushes – reed maces – standing clear of the reeds like guardsmen, swaying but still on parade.

Sand martins returned to quarter the pits while midge-coursing. A column of gnats performed their spiralling pillar dance above his head but wouldn't bite him, nor, with the returning smell of the sweet gale bog myrtle, would the female mosquitoes.

Perched on the branches of a willow tree, a mistle thrush staked its claim to a territory with its rich, strident song. A song thrush mimicked a curlew. Perhaps, like Allen, it had no friends of its own kind. Snatches of songs from wrens and robins, along with the piping of the hedge sparrows, added to the air of returning peace and tranquillity. A beautiful olive green wheatear, fresh from Africa, perched on an alder bush.

Despite his shock, Allen had worked out what must have

happened, which was why he had been so desperate not to breathe in any of the red mist. He realised Lizzie must have known there was an unexploded bomb, dangerously exposed by wind and rain since the war, in the gravel on the causeway. She would have laid that false trail to the right to deflect Burian from taking the direct route across the causeway before taking the shortcut herself, knowing full well where the unexploded bomb lay.

But once across the causeway, she must have seen that Burian, in his demented state, had missed her diversionary clues and was crawling straight across the causeway, which was why Allen had seen Lizzie waving at Burian from the beach in an attempt to warn him.

Allen picked himself up. He didn't know whether Lizzie or Talbot had survived the explosion. Remembering his reaction to the car accident, he fearfully picked his way past the rapidly filling crater, which swirled with pink and yellow water.

Looking out over an expanse of short grass, Allen thought he was standing in a shimmering pool of blood, as the silvery surface of billions of dew-laden spiderwebs reflected the red sun across the sward to his feet.

Allen's friend Goldsmith echoed in his mind again:

And, as a hare, whom hounds and horns pursue,
Pants to the place from where at first he flew,
I still had hopes, my long vexations past,
Here to return – and die at home at last.

Allen himself had been pursued as a hare by hounds and had panted to the place from where he first flew, but had returned to a different place. Neither were his long vexations past. He didn't know the fate of Lizzie and Talbot, nor whether he would renew his friendship with Briscoe and Radish.

Lizzie had told him as a fire once spread across a hayfield she had seen hares leap through the flames to the safety beyond, rather than fleeing before them. He felt he had leapt through the flames and desperately hoped he would reach the safety beyond.

Turning his back to the sun, instead of the blood red sward, Allen saw an elliptical rainbow on the dew-laden spiderwebs framing his shadow. It was like a spectre, which he took as an omen; of what he didn't know.

Printed in Great Britain
by Amazon.co.uk, Ltd.,
Marston Gate.